FOLLOW
THE LEADER

ALSO BY MEL SHERRATT

Taunting the Dead
Watching over You
Somewhere to Hide
Behind a Closed Door
Fighting for Survival
Secrets on the Estate

Mel Sherratt
FOLLOW THE LEADER

f THOMAS & MERCER

This is a work of fiction. Names, characters, organizations, places, events, and incidents are either products of the author's imagination or are used fictitiously.

Text copyright © 2015 Mel Sherratt

All rights reserved.

No part of this book may be reproduced, or stored in a retrieval system, or transmitted in any form or by any means, electronic, mechanical, photocopying, recording, or otherwise, without express written permission of the publisher.

Published by Thomas & Mercer, Seattle

www.apub.com

Amazon, the Amazon logo, and Thomas & Mercer are trademarks of Amazon.com, Inc., or its affiliates.

ISBN-13: 978-1477821855
ISBN-10: 1477821856

Cover design by bürosüd° München, www.buerosued.de

Library of Congress Control Number: 2014915178

Printed in the United States of America

To Alison, for making this journey extra special.

This old man, he played one,
He played knick-knack on his thumb.
With a knick-knack, paddy-whack,
Give the dog a bone.
This old man came rolling home.

1983

Patrick sat alone. Across the playground he could see the other children playing and talking to their friends. Screams and squeals erupted every few seconds. He kept his head down.

Out of the corner of his eye he saw a girl coming towards him. He clutched his bag to his chest and looked everywhere but at her. She stopped in front of him, a gangly specimen of a ten-year-old who hadn't yet grown into her body. Long legs and arms, thin torso, oval face. Pigtails in her blonde hair, braces on her teeth, yet the makings of something special in the years to come.

His overgrown fringe resting on his National Health glasses, Patrick stared at her. It was Sandra Seymour. She was in his class but normally she'd ignore him completely in the classroom or push right through him in the corridor, as if he weren't there. He often wished that he wasn't. But then again, it's not as if he wanted to be at home either.

'You done your English homework essay?' she asked, nudging his foot with hers.

Patrick didn't move, thinking she was talking to someone who had snuck up behind him. They often did that, the kids in his year – made him think they wanted to talk to him, pick him out for their sports team or maths quiz team. But most of the time, they would be talking to someone behind him who would push him aside to step forward. Make a fool of him. Make him feel like they wanted him around when they didn't.

'I said, have you done your homework essay?' she repeated, her tone a little exasperated.

Patrick nodded.

'Can I look? I saw what you wrote about Arnold Bennett last week – it was so cool.'

Patrick puffed out his chest. Arnold Bennett had been easy to write about. He'd had a bit of trouble trying to grasp the language reading the books, but learning about the Potteries in the early twentieth century had kept him enthralled for many an hour. Bennett was the finest writer the Potteries had ever produced, and it wasn't as if they'd had to read all his gazillions of books; Anna of the Five Towns. Clayhanger. The Old Wives' Tale. *He'd got into so much trouble, though, when his dad ripped up his school library book after he'd come home from the pub.*

'So I wanted to see what you've written this week.' Sandra held out a hand. 'You're so clever.'

Patrick shook his head.

'Come on,' she encouraged.

Still he said nothing. The seconds ticked by.

Sandra sighed loudly. 'Well, I'll just have to pinch it then, won't I?' She made a grab for his bag.

Patrick held on tight to the strap as she pulled it off his shoulder but he wasn't a match for her peevish strength. Neither was the bag, a cheap supermarket one some neighbour had left on the doorstep. There'd been a pile of hand-me-down clothes inside it. *He'd come home the next day to find his dad burning them all in the yard, cursing loudly, saying they didn't want anyone's fucking charity.*

He let go before the contents ended up in the muddy puddles that covered the tarmac surface.

Pulling the bag out of his grip, Sandra stepped back, wiping her hair out of her face. 'It would have been easier just to hand it to me,' she pouted.

'Give it back.' Patrick's voice came out croaky: he hadn't spoken in a while. He held out his hand.

Sandra pulled out an exercise book, dropping the bag to the floor, and leafed through the pages until she found what she was looking for. 'Here it is,' she said.

'Give it back!'

He reached for it but she moved from his grip. Then she took hold of the page, ripped it out and screwed it up.

'Don't do that!' Patrick stepped forward.

With a sweet smile, Sandra held the book out to him. But before Patrick could take it from her, she was off, streaking across the playground. Her pigtails bobbed up and down as she weaved in and out among the other kids.

And then Patrick was chasing her. Faster, faster his legs went, his arms pumping away quickly as he tried to gain ground.

Sandra looked back at him over her shoulder. 'You can't catch me!' she laughed as she ran, kicking the boys' football as it got in her way, pushing the girls huddled around a magazine to one side. At the far end of the playground, she reached a row of sheds where the outdoor games equipment was kept. She disappeared out of sight behind them.

Patrick smirked. Silly cow. There was no way out at the far end; he had her trapped. He raced around the corner . . .

An arm grabbed him around his neck, pulling him backwards. He felt himself being turned. His shoulders hit the shed wall with a thud. A forearm across his chest and he was pinned there by the weight of a body.

He looked into the eyes of one of his bullies: Mickey.

'Gerroffme!' Patrick struggled even though he knew it was useless.

Follow the Leader

'Shut your mouth, Shorty, or I'll thump you in it,' Mickey hissed in his ear.

Even if he wanted to shout out again, the lump in his throat stopped him. Behind Mickey stood three more boys, all from his class too: Gray, Johnno and Whitty.

Johnno repeatedly punched a fist into his outstretched open palm as he stared at Patrick. 'We're going to mash you up good and proper,' he said. 'You're nothing but a pervert, Shorty.'

'I haven't done anything!' Patrick cried.

'Sandra is Johnno's girl,' Mickey told him, 'and you were trying to kiss her.'

'I wasn't!' Patrick looked over at Sandra, expecting her to back him up, but she stayed silent.

'You were – and you're going to pay for it.'

Mickey's fist slammed into his mouth, then into his stomach. Patrick groaned, trying to breathe through the pain. He gasped for air: you'd think he'd be used to pain by now.

Shoved to the ground, he heard laughter above him. A kick to the back. Another. One in the leg. He curled up into a ball. Through it all, he could see Sandra standing in front of him, arms folded, a snide smile crossing her face this time.

'Let this be a lesson to you, my boy.' Mickey stood over him, using a grown-up voice and pointing his finger at him. 'Don't mess with the best.'

There was time for one more kick before they left him alone. Lying still, he watched as they walked away, saw Sandra grab for Johnno's hand and look up at him adoringly when he placed his arm around her shoulders.

Bleeding and tearful, Patrick pulled himself to sitting and waited for the bell to ring, for everyone to go back inside for the next lesson. Drops of blood had made a mess of his shirt; his trousers were stained where he'd landed on the grass. He tried not to cry at *the thought of going home, knowing he would get a beating from his father. And it wouldn't be because his clothes were dirty. It would be because he had lost another fight. An unfair fight, but his father wouldn't listen. 'You should learn to stick up for yourself,' he'd say. 'Take it like a man, and learn to fight back like a man,' he'd say.*

What did he know? It was easy for him to say that.

Patrick coughed, wiped the blood from his lip and got to his feet cautiously. One day, when he was big and strong, and able to stand up for himself, they would all get their comeuppance. He'd make sure of that.

Chapter One

Allie Shenton awoke in darkness, the beats of *A Town Called Malice* bursting into the quiet of the bedroom as the alarm went off at six a.m.

'No, no, no!' Her husband, Mark, yawned as he turned over and spooned into her back, his hand across her waist. 'It can't be time to get up already. And can't you change that flipping song?'

'I happen to like The Jam.'

'So do I. Just not at this time of the morning.'

'What would you prefer me to use?'

'"Wake the fuck up – it's time to go to work," done in your best Homer Simpson voice, would be better than that.'

Allie reached over to her mobile phone and tapped Snooze, giving them another ten minutes before they started their day. Already, she could feel the contrast of the chill in the bedroom against the warmth radiating from underneath the duvet.

It was Monday morning – but not just any Monday morning, which in itself would be a ball-ache: today was the first day back after the Christmas and New Year break. Both Mark and Allie had managed to snag time off from Christmas Eve onward, and now it was all over. January fifth 2015. Mark would go back to the bank where he oversaw the commercial section, and she would go back to her job as detective sergeant at Hanley Police Station.

'Do we have to get up?' Mark nuzzled into her neck.

Allie squirmed. 'I suppose we do.'

'We could pretend that you forgot to set your alarm. That would give us a couple more hours.'

'You know I have to keep my phone on.'

'I could say I dropped it down the loo or something.'

Allie reached behind and slapped his thigh. 'Nice try, but some of us actually enjoy going to work.'

'You're just sadistic.'

'I know.'

'We could say you left it in the car.' His hand crept up her pyjama top, caressing her stomach and moving up over her breast. She let out a gentle moan and turned over to face him.

'But that would be a lie.' She bit gently on his bottom lip. 'A good one, nonetheless.'

Mark kissed the tip of her nose. 'Might as well get up, then.' He gave her bottom a squeeze before getting out of bed and heading into the en-suite. 'Jesus Christ – it's cold.'

Allie snuggled down into the bed again, her thoughts turning to the beginning of another year. This Christmas had been hard – they all were. Instead of spending time with her family, Allie was reminded (as if it wasn't with her every day) that there was no one left. Seventeen years ago, her sister Karen had been raped, beaten badly and left for dead. She'd suffered damage to her brain, leaving her severely handicapped and mentally incapable of looking after herself. Their parents hadn't survived the grief much longer. And though Allie knew she'd never rest until the rapist was found, it had been a real shock when, three years ago on New Year's Eve, she'd received a note allegedly from Karen's attacker. Allie had tried often to push it away but the words came back to haunt her every time she visited Karen at her residential home.

'*Karen, until we meet again, my fallen angel.*

One day you will be all mine.

*And you, little sister, Allie.
Don't you ever stop looking for me.'*

Allie despised herself for feeling vulnerable whenever she entered the residential home, yet she couldn't help it. This man, this animal, was possibly watching her. And it had made the accountability that she hadn't been there for her sister even more unacceptable. She would never forgive herself for being fifteen minutes late to pick Karen up on the night in question. Fifteen life-changing minutes, not just for Karen, but for the whole family until both their parents had died.

She had always blamed herself – it *had* been her fault. If she hadn't stayed that extra few minutes with Mark, if she had behaved as a proper sister to Karen, she would have been there on time.

But nothing more had come of the note. And at this time of the year, it always made her wonder again – had the words been an empty threat? Something else that she would never know. And that was more disturbing than the guilt she felt about keeping it away from Mark. Had she been right not telling him about the note, and the decaying rose that had been delivered along with it? She squeezed her eyes tightly shut as tears formed and threatened to spill at the injustice of it all.

After a moment's calm, she scolded herself. She could either start the week with deep regret that would drag her down or she could do something that she knew would leave a smile on her face.

In a flash, she got up quickly and tiptoed through to the en-suite. The water was still running. She slipped off her pyjamas, stepped around the shower door. Her heart melted as she saw the grin flash across Mark's face.

'Need a hand washing yourself down, sir?' she asked coyly, reaching for the soap.

Mickey Taylor walked along the canal path with hunched shoulders, hands deep in the pockets of his jeans to ward off the biting cold, a scowl on his handsome face. His daily walk with his dog hadn't managed to cheer him up. Since when had his life become ruled by so many women? Everything he'd done over the years was for his family and how did his wife repay him? Nag, nag, nag. What with Kath *and* Molly, his seventeen-year-old daughter, still at home, he had it in duplicate. Walking by the canal with Harry was the only place he was guaranteed a bit of peace and quiet. His elder daughter, Rebecca, had left home three years ago but had come back recently. Luckily, she had just gone again – although now she was living near the Wirral with another bloke who had no brains and even less money. Mickey wondered how long it would be before she was back again, to the bank of Mum and Dad.

Harry, his Spaniel, ran to him, dropping the ball a few feet in front. Before Mickey could pick it up, he'd raced up the path away from him again. As he threw the ball, Mickey's footsteps trod heavily along the narrow tarmac pathway. How many times he'd wished his life was as simple as his dog's. Harry was fed, watered, fussed over and loved – *and* he had no responsibilities. Mickey was dictated to by the mood swings of three women. He threw the ball again, watching it rise into the air and arc down to the ground. He wished he could bounce away with it and go to wherever it landed. Trapped. That's how he felt now.

Harry came scooting back to him, dropping the ball at his feet.

'You're such a lucky bastard, Harry,' he said, picking the ball up again and lobbing it along the path.

'Hey, Mickey! Wait up!'

Mickey turned to see a man coming towards him. 'You after me, youth?' he asked, his brow furrowing.

'Yeah, I thought it was you when I saw you back there.' The man threw a thumb over his shoulder in the direction he'd just come from. 'We used to know each other. Remember me?'

Mickey stared a while longer before recognition lit up his face. 'Of course!' He gave a faint smile. 'Vaguely, yeah. Christ, man, that was years ago now. I haven't seen you –'

The man ran forward and punched him in the stomach.

'Christ, what's wrong with you?' Mickey stepped backwards. 'You knocked the wind out of me.' He clutched his middle, pulled away a hand, his face etched with disbelief when it came away covered in blood.

The man lunged at him again, the knife that was now visible going in and out twice before the attacker stepped deftly back out of his reach. Colour drained from Mickey's face as he saw his own blood dripping from the edge of the blade.

Mickey staggered another step backwards. 'What the fuck . . .' He dropped to his knees, blood oozing through his fingers as he tried to cover the wounds.

The man drew back his foot. With a sickening sound, he caught Mickey on his chin. Pain seared through him as he felt his lower teeth smash into the top set. He fell over onto his back, blood pouring from his mouth.

The man straddled him quickly. Another stab – deeper this time. Again, the blade was removed.

'Help me!' Mickey croaked.

The man stood a few feet away from him as he gasped his last breath. His hand reached up and fell heavily.

The last thing Mickey saw as his head fell to the side was Harry on the path in the distance, the ball at his feet.

Chapter Two

'I'm going to be late now, because of you.' Mark came into the kitchen thirty minutes later, just as Allie was making toast.

'I didn't hear you complaining much at the time.' She raised her eyebrows.

But Mark didn't smile back. He ran a hand through his hair, his eyes flitting around the tidy room.

'What can't you find?' she said with a sigh.

'My work ID pass.' Mark scrambled around inside the kitchen drawer, scattering receipts and takeaway leaflets all over the kitchen floor. 'I've only been off for ten bloody days.' He scratched his head. 'Have you seen it anywhere?'

Allie bent down to pick up the leaflets, put them back into the drawer and closed it. Then she reached into the cupboard above Mark's head, where he kept his spare change on a saucer. By its side was a box that had contained a watch she'd bought him for their tenth wedding anniversary. She opened it and produced the card, waving it in front of his face.

'It's where you always put it and where you always forget you've put it,' she told him with a shake of her head.

'I didn't put it there! You must have moved it.'

'No, you put it there.'

'Well, I can't remember –'

'It was you!' Allie snapped. 'I'm not one of those women who go through their partner's pockets.'

'Always time for that yet.'

'Why, you cheeky git. I'll have you know –'

Allie's phone went off. This time the sound of The Kaiser Chiefs' *I Predict a Riot*. Her heart skipped a beat as she knew its importance. It was the ringtone for the police station contacting her.

'DS Shenton,' she answered.

'Change those bloody ringtones, will you!' Mark's parting words as he went out the door. Allie stuck two fingers up to his disappearing form, and leaned her back against the worktop as she listened to the caller. Within seconds, she was alert and running upstairs to get dressed.

A body had been found near to Caldon Canal.

Allie crossed the bridge over the canal and caught sight of a uniformed officer. A member of the public stood by his side, one hand on a post, the other clutching his chest. An older man, late sixties at a glance. From the look on the man's face Allie surmised he was the person who had found the body, and wondered if his stomach was doing a loop-the-loop as much as hers was.

It was a strange feeling to be excited about being called out to the scene of a death. Would it be suspicious? Would it be a suicide? Maybe just a prank gone horrifically wrong? An act of violence gone too far? Or even murder with intent? She wondered what she would find today. Couldn't help feeling adrenaline building up inside her at the thought of a case to get her teeth into. Getting justice for a crime committed was why she had joined the police force, and until she didn't get this buzz any longer she was staying with it.

She stepped over a low wall, climbed down the bank, treading carefully and then steadying herself as momentum made her jog the final few steps onto the level. As she walked, she swept her long dark hair away from her face and secured it into a ponytail with a band, so that it wouldn't get in her way whilst she looked around. Then she pulled on a woollen beanie hat to keep her ears warm. Her breath formed clouds of mist in front of her. Ahead, she noticed PC Andy Rathbone standing guard. Although he'd been an officer for a few years, he was new to their station. He seemed adept at his job, a strong man to have on side.

'Morning, Andy.' She gave a faint but friendly smile. 'Not a good start to the year.'

'Morning, Sarge. No, it's a bit of a bloody one, I'm afraid.'

Andy marked down her time of arrival before she slipped on shoe covers, gloves and a white suit. Then she lifted the flap and stepped into the tent.

The victim was on his back a few feet away from the tarmacked path. Fully dressed, a swollen, bloodied face with puffed eyes, clipped auburn hair, a silver stud earring in his left ear. By his side, a pool of blood had formed; a limp hand had fallen into the middle of it. Allie recoiled momentarily as flashbacks of the last murder she'd dealt with on her patch came rushing into her mind. A local woman, Steph Ryder, had been murdered in early December 2011. The back of her head had been bashed to a pulp with a force more vicious than the act of taking her life needed. It had been a nasty case. She took a few deep breaths.

Stooped over the body was forensic officer Dave Barnett. Detective Inspector Nick Carter was on the other side but stood to his full height, towering over Allie as she moved to his side. His short blonde hair neat and tidy, he looked tanned and relaxed after a recent holiday.

'I was heading to do a crime prevention talk in Burslem,' he said, looking down at her. 'I was a couple of minutes away when I got the shout.'

'What do we have?'

'Male, forty-two. Michael Taylor. Driving licence has an address half a mile away. Four stabs to the abdomen, one of them fatal by itself, it seems. He was kicked about the face too. Bit his tongue.' Nick handed her a black leather wallet, wrapped up inside an exhibit bag. 'This was found in the inside pocket of his jacket.'

'Mickey Taylor?' Allie moved to the side of the body and went down on her haunches, feeling her heels pressing into the wet icy ground. She peered closer. Christ, she hadn't seen Mickey Taylor since her late teens, when she and her sister used to go out on the town. He'd been part of a gang of older kids she knew vaguely because they hung around with Karen. If she remembered rightly, Karen had had a huge crush on him during her last year at school but it had never been reciprocated.

'Do you know him?' Nick asked, bending down again to take a closer look.

'Vaguely,' she replied.

'Does he have a record?'

'I'm not sure – he used to go to my school. That's where I remember him from.'

It was the scar that did it. Underneath his right eye: 1988. She'd been there the day that fifteen-year-old Samuel Williams had pushed Mickey off the flat roof of the gym. He'd landed face first on the upper-school playground. By the end of that day, the rumour mill had him with a mouthful of smashed teeth and a broken nose and leg, when in reality he'd ended up with three stitches to a cut, a black eye and grazed skin on his cheek.

'He's the same age as my sister. I think he left just after I started in my second year,' she added as she stood up again. 'I wonder why he ended up like this.'

'Probably some random attack.' Dave stood up too, stretching his tall, thin frame as he did so. He pushed his glasses up his nose. 'He's hardly cold. Out walking his dog this morning and then gone, just like that, poor bastard. Seems he was in the wrong place at the wrong time.'

Allie doubted it would be that cut and dried. But then again, she knew that Dave probably didn't think that either. Between them, they had worked on seven murders in Stoke-on-Trent during the sixteen years she'd been in the police force.

'The victim was wearing a thick coat,' said Dave, 'but it was open so the knife didn't need to go through it. Just his thin jumper over his shirt.'

'Any watch?' Nick asked.

Dave shook his head.

'A mugging gone too far?' Allie questioned, moving slightly so that the police photographer could take another shot. 'Any money in that wallet?'

'Sixty pounds – two twenties, two tens.' Nick glanced at her as a flash of light went off above them. 'So his name doesn't register with you apart from school days?'

Allie shook her head. 'But it might with Perry. He went to my school too. They're the same age so he might remember more about him. I'll check once I get back to the station. Shall I head there now?'

'Yes. Start setting things up for me too.'

'Will do, boss.'

Allie exited the tent, breathing in fresh air as she snapped off the sterile gloves, desperate to put her leather ones back on.

Already there were a handful of onlookers on the bridge: a man in a fluorescent orange beanie hat; an elderly couple with a dog sitting at their feet; a child of about twelve in uniform late for school.

Walking back to the car, Allie let her eyes flick around. In days gone by, the canal system would have been widely used to transport pottery ware to other cities. Now the pathways were mostly worn out by walkers, cyclists and runners; the odd holiday barge came past every now and then. They were about a mile from Hanley, the centre of Stoke-on-Trent, and not far from Etruria Industrial Museum, the last steam-powered potters' mill in Britain. The area in front of the mill was clean and tidy – easily pleasant if the weather was good and the pollen count low. The surrounding streets, however, left a lot to be desired – mostly boarded-up and overcrowded run-down terraced housing, abandoned cars and dumped rubbish.

As she stepped up onto the grass verge that would take her back to the road, she thought for a minute about where the body had been found. If it was a straightforward mugging with no intention to kill, surely the suspect would have panicked and rolled Mickey Taylor into the water so that it looked like he'd drowned? Made it look like he'd possibly had one drink too many, stumbled on the way home, hit his head and fallen in? The body might have resurfaced if it had gone under, but evidence might have been washed away too – which led Allie to thinking that the murder could have been premeditated. But then if someone *had* intended to do away with Mickey, again why would they leave the body on the towpath?

Two options and the man was hardly cold. Murder or robbery gone wrong? You decide: phone a friend or let the audience pick.

'Allie!'

She turned on her heel to see Nick jogging to catch up with her, his hand curling around another exhibit bag. He'd taken up running recently and, for the first time, Allie noticed he seemed to be winning the battle against middle-aged spread. She jogged back a little and closed the distance between them.

'We've just rolled him onto his side. We found this in the back pocket of his jeans.' Nick held up the bag as he drew level with her. 'I'm not sure if it's significant or if it's just something he's picked up if he has small children.'

Inside was a green plastic letter – the magnetic kind used by children to spell words on fridges.

It was a capital E.

Chapter Three

Allie's base was opposite Hanley Crown Court. They shared the street with the city's main library, the Potteries Art Gallery and Museum, home to the recently discovered Staffordshire Hoard, and Sentinel House, the city's local newspaper. She drove into the car park by the side of the station and squeezed her car into the tiniest of spaces.

It was quiet downstairs considering it was the first Monday back at work. Behind one of two desks protected by a glass screen, the duty sergeant smiled at her as she moved through the tiny reception area. To her right, in a row of bolted-down orange plastic seats, sat an elderly man with a tartan shopper at his feet. Close to him sat a young couple, their toddler child racing a toy car over the carpeting. The girl blew unsightly bubbles with her gum – pop, pop. The youth next to her, legs out in front, arms crossed, stared at Allie as she walked past. Allie wasn't fazed by his cockiness. He'd soon move his foot out of her way if she caught it with her heel.

She swiped her card to gain access to the main building, turned to her left past the lift and jogged up two flights of stairs. There was already a buzz of activity in the open-plan office: several officers on phones, a whiteboard at the far end of the room set up for details as they came in. Allie's small part of the larger team were seated in the far right corner. She walked down a narrow walkway created by four banks of desks on either side. The room was so crowded that Nick didn't have an office. His desk was set on its own in the opposite corner.

When Allie got to her desk, a flash of blonde hair bobbed up and down opposite her. Sam Markham was nodding as she took a phone call, her hand writing down details. Sam had been working with Allie for eight years now. Small and fragile-looking but with a kick-ass attitude that would push her forward in any situation, she was an asset to the team due to her meticulous analytical skills. Sam took pleasure in getting her teeth into the tasks that some officers might despair of – checking records, watching CCTV recordings, spotting irregularities. More than once it had been her determination and eye for detail that had allowed the team to make a conviction.

At the desks to her right were a detective constable and an empty seat. Perry Wright, four years her senior, had his eyes glued to his computer screen. The other member of her team, Matt Radcliffe, was on long-term sick leave due to a car chase the previous year. Through no fault of his own, it had ended with him crashing his car, resulting in a crushed ankle, a dodgy back and an injury to his shoulder.

'Bit of a shocker this one, boss,' said Perry. 'Someone I knew.'

'Yes, I thought so.' Allie sat down and switched on her computer. 'Did you know him well?'

'I hadn't seen that much of him since we left school.'

'I saw him around town every now and then when I used to go out with Karen.' Allie frowned. 'Can you remember what he was like before then?'

'He was a laugh if you got on with him but a bullyboy if not. A tough bastard, but I don't think he's been in any kind of trouble since he married and settled down. All the lay-dees loved him before that though, apparently. Can't you remember?'

'No, I was a bit young for that! I was twelve when you left – I'm four years younger than you, don't forget,' Allie reminded him. 'But then again, I remember you said you were a heartthrob too and I can't say I recall that either. Especially if you had the same spiked blonde hair and fake tan glow that you have now.'

A few feet away, Sam laughed before rolling her eyes as the desk phone she'd just replaced the receiver down on started to ring again.

'If you weren't my superior . . .' Perry chided her. 'Anyway, it seems Mickey Taylor did have the last laugh. I've just been checking out his business online – Taylor Made Pottery Factory. You know, the one that's won awards for design and engineering. He's done pretty well for himself.'

'I wonder if there's anyone jealous of that success.' Allie raised her eyebrows. 'Can you do a bit more digging around – maybe call Simon, see if he has anything on him?' Simon was the crime reporter for *The Sentinel*. 'I'm heading over to Mickey's house shortly to talk to his next of kin. I'm meeting Nick there when he's finished at the crime scene. And then you and I can go to his factory afterwards – check out the staff, their whereabouts, take a look around his premises.'

'Sounds like a plan.' Perry nodded.

'There's probably going to be family members working there too, so we'll need to make sure that everyone has heard what's happened to Mickey. I know it will be on the news but let's not assume.'

'It's a small world' was a phrase often heard in Stoke-on-Trent. Most people Allie knew, or had known, had lived in Stoke and stayed in Stoke and gone on to do other things without making a name for themselves, just a living. It was easy to become embroiled in day-to-day life, year after year. The majority of its residents worked there; hardly anyone travelled far. Daily commutes were worsened only by the occasional accident on the M6 or A500, blocking roads and causing chaos to rush hour traffic. Snow brought the city to a halt just as quickly. Other than that, most journeys from work to home for the majority of the workforce took less than an hour.

Yet Allie loved her birthplace. For all its faults, pointed out by this government survey or that departmental chart of figures, it was a city with a heart. It had a population just short of a quarter of a million, was no worse than the larger cities of Birmingham and Manchester in terms of its crime figures per number of residents and its people were helpful and friendly. Well, mostly.

A call came in from Nick to let her know he was on his way over to talk to Mickey Taylor's family, who had already been informed of his death. Once she'd checked through a few urgent messages and set a few things in motion, Allie set off to join him. As she made her way back down the stairs, her shoulders sagged at the job awaiting her. Visiting the family was always the hardest part.

Patrick Morgan walked quickly but steadily, body hunched as if to keep out the cold. With his feather-light physique, he was used to feeling invisible when he went out in public. The knife he'd used earlier was tucked away in the inside pocket of his coat, inconspicuous, out of sight. Not that it would matter if he were to walk down the street with the knife held out in his hand. No one would notice him even if he'd dyed what little hair he had left bright green, let alone wielded a bloodied knife. But it was imperative that he walk back along a main road, stick to his normal routine. Even in his own neighbourhood, he wasn't taking any chances.

He'd gone over the plan in his head hundreds of times. He'd have to be quick. Someone might stumble upon them if he didn't do the job in a minute or two. Obviously it wouldn't stop him but he didn't want to chance getting caught at the beginning of the game.

He knew Mickey Taylor was a creature of habit. He had worked out where best to strike along the stretch of canal where he walked his dog every morning and evening, had determined that he always came alone. Last month's final task had been to check out the timing, figure out when the bridge wasn't in use as much and see if it was all possible. Being fairly small, Patrick was able to keep himself well hidden in the hedge while he counted the minutes when people went across it and when it went quiet again. Timing was going to be everything – certainly it would mean the difference between getting caught and getting away.

After the attack, Patrick had gone on to the next bridge, cut through a small hole in the fencing and walked quickly across a large field. About half a mile away by then, he'd crawled into a thick hedgerow out of sight.

He'd done it.

He hadn't been sure that he would; he thought that he'd either bottle out before he'd faced Mickey or that, once he'd spoken to him, he would then lose his nerve and make a complete idiot of himself. Everyone had looked up to Mickey; girls *and* boys followed him around the corridors like sheep. He was one of a gang who had bullied Patrick at school. One of several who had made his life hell and walked off without a backward glance once the final bell had rung on the last day.

Before he'd gone to the canal, Patrick had tried to put out of his mind the fear of Mickey getting the better of him, remembering who he was and laughing at him, punching him when he showed any aggression. But no: Patrick had taken the knife and rammed it into his stomach. And it had felt so good.

He'd wanted to do it over and over – but he'd had to rein himself in at four blows, though. Four was sure to finish Mickey off, plus there was less chance of getting blood on himself. When he wasn't out running, he'd worn dark-coloured clothes for a few months too – so if anyone did spot him out on his travels, he'd blend in even more. The black jumper, jacket and jeans he had on today hid any blood that might have soaked into them.

He'd sat there for four freezing hours until it was time for him to be seen. Every weekday morning, he went out at eleven to fetch what groceries he needed from Morrison's supermarket on Festival Park. He always cut through Portland Street, turning right into Century Street and continuing on until he came out on Cobridge Road. He too was a creature of habit; everyone knew that, and everyone would think he was going about his business as usual, nothing out of the ordinary.

He'd gone prepared, taking with him a few baby wipes to clean away the blood from his hands, rub over his face just in case there was any splatter he couldn't see. It wouldn't do to plan all this only to have a smear of blood give him away. He'd remembered not to discard the wipes – he wasn't entirely sure that the police would check the bins that far out but, well, you never knew, did you? And he'd removed his jacket, taken off his top jumper to reveal another underneath. He'd pulled out the Morrison's carrier bag he'd brought with him and shoved the jumper inside. For all intents and purposes, it seemed as if he'd gone to the supermarket as he did most mornings and was now carrying his shopping back to his house.

He turned right into Century Street, where there were parked cars on either side of a row of terraced houses, and headed on towards Portland Street. Once there, he began to walk just that little bit faster. Even at eleven a.m., it was quiet; the day was cold but at least it was still dry. In the distance, two men from the city council were picking up litter, white plastic bags flapping about in the wind. He hadn't spoken to either one of them in the years he had lived there but he knew them both by sight. It was good that they would get to see him this morning, hopefully recalling him doing exactly the same as he did every day if they were ever questioned.

At Waterloo Road, he turned right and crossed over, continuing down the bank until he reached the grassed area that he could cut across to get to his house. Finally, a few minutes later, he was in Ranger Street.

Only when the front door of number twenty-seven closed behind him did he let his shoulders drop. He closed his eyes, standing for a moment in the silence of the house. Holding out his hands in front of him, he watched them shake uncontrollably. He took off his gloves, rubbed some warmth into his fingers. There was blood under his nails, soaked through the woollen material. He needed to wash it all away. And his clothes – he needed to wash those too.

He went through to the kitchen. Stripping where he stood, he bundled his clothes into the machine and put on a cycle. Then he mopped the already clean floor. Around him, the worktops were spotless, not a teaspoon left out of a drawer after a quick cup of tea this morning. Plain beech-wood units stood in a line along one wall. Off-white tiles above those had a shine on them that would make any car manufacturer jealous. So too had the one full-length long window at the far end of the room, overlooking a small, tidy yard at the back of the house.

A faint smell of lilac intermingled with a whiff of lemon Jif clung in the air. Patrick associated the smell with a multitude of secrets kept well hidden over the years. He'd been twenty-five when he'd taken the worst beating ever from his father, coming close to losing the sight in his right eye. Luckily, exhaustion from the ferocity of the attack had left Ray unable to continue with his assault. Another kick or two would probably have finished Patrick off.

More often, he wished he hadn't survived the attack at all.

Before heading upstairs to take a shower, he went into the living room. Naked, he didn't feel at all vulnerable as he stared at the map, seeing where the next murder would take place. On the sideboard to his right, a small bundle of letters bearing the logo of HM Prison had been shoved behind a photograph of a woman and two small children. Patrick picked up the first letter, redelivered three weeks ago. He pulled out the note inside, read the only words he was interested in. The writing was sprawling, similar to that of a child learning to join up the letters for the first time.

10.53 a.m., Friday 16 January.

The words were few but carried huge meaning for Patrick. Life was about to become a whole lot worse come next Friday if he didn't carry out his plan. And he couldn't – wouldn't – allow that to happen. He'd waited such a long time for that day to arrive.

For every memory that he had lived with for years, all the resentment it had caused, he'd stored it up for that day.

For every time Ray had come home drunk and taken his anger out on him, told him how useless he was as he'd struck him, he'd waited for that day.

For every time that Ray had filled his life with fear, his head with negativity, his thoughts with abandonment, he'd waited for that day.

He wasn't about to let that cruel bastard back into his life. Ray would have to learn the hard way just exactly what his son had turned into while he'd been inside doing time for murder. Patrick was a fighter now. No, more than that: he was a *killer* now. As well as mentally preparing himself for this for years, he had been physically preparing himself for it too. He'd been running thirty miles each week, often in the dead of the night when his shift at work had finished, building up his stamina. He'd been lifting weights too, combinations that he hadn't thought possible, getting stronger month by month. He might have a puny frame but it was perfect to hide behind.

Ray wouldn't know what hit him.

Chapter Four

Holly Lane didn't live up to the picturesque promise of its name. Roughly half a mile from where Mickey Taylor had been found, it was in a built-up area of the city, the properties dating back to just before the war. But the lane was wide, with several holly bushes dotted around the pavements.

Allie parked behind Nick's car on the road and they walked up the spacious drive together to the Taylors' residence.

'Never get used to this, do you?' Nick muttered as he rang the doorbell.

'No.' Allie glanced at the doorway as she waited, in awe of Mickey ending up with something as grand as this. Her feeling wasn't disbelief, exactly, but more admiration that he had made something of himself. Mickey Taylor might have been the school heartthrob but now that she'd had a little more time to think about it, she'd remembered that he was in one of the classes where all the troublemakers, slow developers and general nuisances were put. Now she was older she understood why they had been segregated, but it still annoyed her. Putting people in boxes made for troubled lives. Children were often labelled before they'd left school – but people changed, none more so than teenagers. Allie would always prefer to form opinions of her own.

The door was answered by Mrs Clamortie, Mrs Taylor's mum, and before being shown into the living room, Allie and Nick learned that her husband had gone to fetch Mickey's youngest daughter from college. The interior of the house matched the outside in age. Dark woods, floorboards and panels, blood-red Chesterfield settees. Noting some of the antique figurines and ornate frames dotted around, Allie assumed that either Mickey or his wife had a good eye for business.

Mrs Taylor sat on the sofa clutching a handkerchief. Tears poured down her face as she spotted them. Mrs Clamortie moved to sit down next to her daughter and they clutched each other's hands.

Allie realised as soon as she saw her that she had indeed known Mickey's wife at school. Kath Clamortie had been two years above her if she remembered rightly. Looks-wise, she'd hardly changed. Like Allie, Kath had kept herself trim and had razor-sharp one-length brown hair and a thick fringe. Unlike Allie, she wore the best of designer wear, and heels that Allie would kill for – she was wearing a pair of Jimmy Choos Allie had been coveting for ages. When Nick introduced her, Allie could almost hear Kath working out where she'd seen her before too.

'We're so sorry for your loss, Mrs Taylor,' Nick said. 'May we sit down?'

A slight nod of a head followed. Then she looked up.

'You used to be Allie Baxter?' she asked Allie.

'I did,' Allie replied.

'Karen Baxter's sister. I knew her before . . . She was a lovely person.'

Allie smiled briefly, not willing to let Karen enter her thoughts when the job in hand was so tough.

A phone rang from another room and Kath looked at her mother desperately. 'Would you get that?' she asked.

'Of course,' she said. 'I'll try not to be too long.'

'It's hardly stopped ringing,' Kath explained. 'People can't believe it so they're ringing to check, I suppose. They mean well but *I* don't believe it yet.' She cleared her throat, pulled another tissue from the box beside her and dabbed at her eyes. 'I don't want to.'

Allie's heart went out to her. She knew she'd be the same if anything happened to Mark.

'Are you able to answer a few questions?' Nick asked.

'I – yes,' said Kath.

Allie pulled her notebook from her coat pocket.

'Can you tell me when you last saw Mickey, Mrs Taylor?'

'It was about six thirty this morning. Mickey took Harry out for his usual walk. That's our dog, Harry. He's a spaniel.'

'Did Mickey always go along that particular part of the canal towpath?'

'Yes.'

'And always at the same times?'

'More or less. I was in the shower when he left the house today.' Kath's eyes brimmed with tears again. 'We'd been bickering. I never got to say goodbye.'

'Bickering?' said Nick.

'I wanted to redecorate the hall again and he wasn't having it. That kind of bickering.'

'What time did you come downstairs?'

'It was less than half an hour later. I heard the seven o'clock news on the radio as I came into the kitchen. I saw Harry appear at the patio doors about fifteen minutes later. I let him in and assumed Mickey was messing about in the garage. It was only later that I looked and he wasn't there.'

'So the dog came home alone? No one brought him back?'

'As far as I know. I just saw him and assumed that Mickey had come home too.'

'Can you remember how much time had lapsed between you seeing Harry and checking on Mickey?'

'Twenty minutes at the most.' Kath looked up at them both in turn. 'I made coffee, you see, and took one out to him. But he wasn't in the garage when I got there. I tried his phone but there was no answer. That's when I began to panic.' Kath wiped away more tears. 'We were going away this afternoon. Manchester for the night – Mickey has a meeting there in the morning. I was going to do a bit of shopping while I waited for him. We were supposed to be staying at the MalMaison. I . . . I need to let them know that we won't be coming.'

'I can do that for you, duck.' Mrs Clamortie came back in and sat down again. 'That was your Aunty Judith. She sends her condolences.'

'Once you'd tried him on his mobile phone,' Nick continued, 'and there was no answer, what did you do then?'

'I called a few people to see if they had seen him. That was when I saw the police car pull into our driveway. I ran to the door, but he wasn't . . .' Kath sobbed, '. . . he wasn't with them.'

Allie was glad when Nick let her take a moment of comfort in her mother's embrace before continuing. She sensed they were almost done anyway.

'I'm sorry, Mrs Taylor, just a couple more questions,' Nick started again. 'How long have you known Mickey?'

'We've been together since high school.'

'What was he like back then?'

'Mickey was gorgeous.' Kath smiled a little at the memory. 'Mind, he thought he was God's gift with his Goth-punk look. He told me years later that somehow he'd managed to throw it together and it came out good by accident. Luckily the girls seemed to like it.'

'So he was popular then?'

'Yes, he was. Back then he could have had his pick of any girl at Reginald High.'

'Do you know if he'd been in any kind of trouble lately? Fallen out with anyone?'

Kath shook her head. 'He nearly ended up in prison just after we married. He was only young then. Scared the hell out of him so he gradually cut all ties with his friends, started his own company and hasn't looked back since.'

Allie wondered if there was anything to be found in Mickey's abandoned friends, making a mental note to look into it.

'Do you have any grandchildren, Mrs Taylor?' she asked.

'Yes, two boys. Three and two. My elder daughter's – we had her when we were quite young.'

'Has Mickey been playing games with them lately that involved spelling out words? You know, with the colourful magnetic letters that can be attached to a whiteboard?'

'I don't think so.' Kath sniffed, her eyes filling with fresh tears. She looked at her mother. 'Mickey wasn't the best when it came to spelling. Why do you ask that?'

'Does the letter E mean anything to you?'

Kath and her mother glanced at each other again before both shaking their heads.

'There was a plastic letter in the back pocket of Mickey's jeans. We need to figure out if it was placed there by whoever did this to your husband or if it was there before Mickey went out.'

'But, what . . . I . . . I – I don't know.' Kath burst into tears again. 'I don't *know*.'

After a nod from Nick, Allie stood up, smoothing down her skirt. 'There'll be a family liaison officer with you shortly,' she told them both, 'to keep you informed as to where we are within the investigation. Once again, we're so sorry for your loss.'

'Whoever did this needs to rot in a cell,' Mrs Clamortie said as she held on to her daughter again. 'They shouldn't be allowed to get away –'

'Mum!' The door opened and a teenage girl with a shock of red hair and wearing school uniform burst into the room. 'Mum,' she sobbed.

Mrs Clamortie stood up quickly. 'Molly.'

Molly pushed past her to her mum. 'Tell me it's not true.' Molly turned to Allie then. 'Tell me!'

With Mrs Taylor stumbling over her words, Allie took over. Years of experience in similar situations still never prepared her for the anguished cry of grief when it came.

Leaving the house with Nick shortly after, Allie held in her own tears as they walked away.

'Sometimes I hate my job,' she told him. 'That poor girl. So young to lose a father, and in such tragic circumstances.'

'This is why we do this job.' Nick shoved his hands into his coat pockets. 'So we can get bastards who tear families apart.'

'I hope we can clear this up quickly, even just to give them peace.'

'Let's concentrate on getting back whatever information we can ASAP. Someone must have seen something down there on the canal side. And we need a press release sorted while house-to-house is being carried out.'

As they got into separate cars to make their way back to the station, Allie looked at the house one more time. Getting justice – that's why she did her job. Justice for a wife, a daughter, a sister. And she would do her best to see that happened.

'So what was he really like?' Allie asked as she and Perry drove along Potteries Way towards Burslem later that afternoon.

'Huh?' Perry glanced at her with a frown before indicating to change lanes.

'Mickey Taylor. Did you know him well? Were you one of his crowd? What did you get up to? Did the lay-dees like him too?'

Perry sniggered. 'You have such a nose for gossip.'

'It's my job!'

'No, it isn't. Besides, there's nothing to tell. I knew him until I left school – haven't seen him much at all since. I know his wife if it's the same Kath that he was knocking off at school. He got her pregnant just before we left. And I know of his factory now I've Googled it, and that's all really.'

'Some detective you are,' Allie tutted. She leaned forward to switch up the heater. 'Well, this factory – legit, is it?'

'It seems so. The website says he's been in business for twenty years – won loads of awards. He's done okay for himself considering.'

'Considering?'

'To be honest, I thought he'd be locked up by now. His wife must have had some hold on him. I can just about remember her. She was good-looking but nothing special.'

Perry drove towards the centre of Burslem and, a few minutes later, turned off Moorland Road and on to a small industrial site. There were seventeen units on the map by the entrance; they were after number five. Taylor Made Pottery Factory was the middle unit of a block of nine.

Perry squeezed his car into a space opposite the frontage. They approached the door to the reception area with caution over slippery tarmac. As they drew nearer, a woman rushed towards them from inside the building. Allie pressed her warrant card up against the glass and they were let in.

'I couldn't believe it when Derek told us what had happened,' the woman said, shaking a head of blonde-grey curls.

'Did you know him well, Mrs . . . ?' asked Allie.

'Campbell – Doris Campbell. Yes, I've been here since the business started. Mickey was like a son to me, his brother too. Martin is in a terrible state.' She burst into tears.

Once she'd composed herself, they followed her through the office and down a narrow corridor. Allie glanced at the certificates on the wall – Outstanding Business Award 2008, The Sentinel Business Awards runner-up for small businesses, certificates of training courses taken. An award for pottery design of the year 2013.

'He was well liked, then?'

Doris turned to them slightly, a fond smile on her face. 'Yes, he had such a warm personality, and always the joker. Never unkindly, mind. He's going to be missed by so many people.'

The door at the end of the corridor led them into a large warehouse, its silence immediate. Allie tried to imagine how it would be normally: machinery whirring, kilns firing, bells on machines ringing, drowning out any chances of hearing a radio piped through in the background.

Today a group of people with heavy hearts sat around. Four women and three men huddled around a coffee machine. Two men stood over by a window deep in conversation. A larger group were sitting around three settees laid out at the far end of the room, next to a row of kitchen units and a drinks machine.

'We stopped production as soon as we heard,' a voice behind them said.

They turned to see a man with the aging features of Mickey Taylor, the same shock of auburn hair. His cheeks were red, eyes swollen. A younger man stood behind him: Allie assumed that this was Mickey's brother, of whom Doris had spoken so fondly.

'Derek Taylor, Mickey's father,' he told them. 'This is my son, Martin.'

'We're so sorry for your loss,' Perry told him.

'It's just a job to you.'

'I know it's hard to deal with, but –'

'I'm sick of waiting around here while his killer is on the loose. You should be chasing him down, not questioning the people he worked with.'

'Martin.' Doris laid a hand on Martin's arm, but he shrugged it off.

'You've every right to feel angry, we get that,' Allie spoke firmly. 'But,' she looked at him for a moment, needing to gain his trust, 'please, any tiny detail you may remember could help us find the person responsible.'

'I need some fresh air.' Martin walked off.

Perry stopped Doris from going after him. 'Give him some space,' he said. 'He'll talk when he's ready.'

'Sorry about that.' Derek flinched as a door slammed. 'I lost his mother only last year and now, well,' he paused, looking away for a moment, 'I can't believe this has happened too. Mickey was a great support to us both.'

'How was business, Mr Taylor?' she asked, changing the subject in the hope of distracting the obviously upset man.

'It was good. Mickey's life couldn't have been better. Well, perhaps a little less stress once in a while, but with orders piling in, having to recruit extra staff brought along more headaches. Still, Mickey had the last laugh.' Derek smiled faintly. 'His teachers at Reginald High School had been certain he'd make nothing of himself but he'd proved them all wrong. Taylor Made Pottery Factory has been going strong for twenty years now.' Then his demeanour changed. 'Why would anyone kill my boy?' His voice broke and he held back a sob before he spoke again. 'He didn't do anyone any harm. He was kind and gentle and a – a gentle giant.'

'We often called him that,' Doris confirmed. 'Come and sit in the office for a moment, Derek. I'm sure the police will come back before they leave.'

'Let's get this over with,' Allie said quietly as she and Perry were left alone. 'We can interview the family at the end.'

Chapter Five

Just after half past ten that evening, Perry let himself into his house, closing the front door as quietly as possible. It had been a long, busy day and he was exhausted. Finding the living room empty, he went upstairs and opened the bedroom door to see his wife asleep with the light on, her Kindle on his pillow. He gazed at her, half-expecting her to be wide awake and fooling around, to break down in giggles if he stayed watching much longer. But after a few seconds, she still didn't move.

Not wanting to wake her straightaway, he switched the light off and showered in the main bathroom. But after a quick bite to eat and a hot drink, he climbed into bed beside her, the warmth of her body instantly comforting. Normality, he sighed, that's what he wanted. Mundane, day-to-day normality.

Lisa snuffled in her sleep and he pulled her close. Half-sitting, half-lying, he waited for his mind to rest after the events of the day. Mickey Taylor – he'd been glad he hadn't had to go and tell his wife what had happened. Allie had told him about the daughter, too, how hard it had been for her to watch her fall apart.

Lisa wrapped an arm around his chest and pressed her body along the side of his. 'Hey,' she said sleepily.

'Hey yourself. You're to bed early.'

'Yes, felt knackered when I came in from work – again. How about you? Was it a bad one?'

'Nothing for you to worry about.'
'Did he have a family?'
'Yes.'
'Oh, that's so sad. Did you have to visit his wife?'
'No, Allie went with Nick. Then we went to his factory. There were lots of staff who thought highly of the guy. Took us a while to get through them all. They were all upset too – not a one unaffected by it. We have to go back in the morning to question the early shift. I doubt anything will come of it, but you never know.'

Lisa lifted her head and gazed at him, trying to focus in the dim light through half-closed eyes. 'Ouch.'

He ran a hand over her hair. 'I'm a big boy, Lees. I can cope with it.'

'I still worry for you. Was it tough?'

'I wouldn't be human if I said it wasn't.' Perry thought back to the moment when Mickey Taylor's father had finally been unable to contain his grief. 'Or good at my job. I want to nail the bastard who did this though. I . . . I knew him.'

Lisa propped herself up on her elbow. 'Oh. Are you okay?'

Perry nodded to reassure her, knowing he needed to hide his distress. But even though he had dealt with a few murders over the years he'd been in the force, nothing could have prepared him for it being someone he knew. Even though he hadn't seen Mickey Taylor in years, it had come as quite a shock.

'Mickey was a piss-taker, one of the jokers,' he explained. 'I had some good times growing up with him, having a laugh. If I'm not asked to attend the funeral, I might go anyway. Show my respect.'

Seeing Lisa stifle a yawn, he realised it wasn't fair to keep them both awake. He pulled her further into his arms, enjoying the feel of her skin against his. It made him realise that he was alive, able to face another day. Not like Mickey Taylor. He wondered how his wife and daughters were doing. Would they be coping? Sleeping? Crying? Unable to go to bed because they didn't want to wake up in the morning and realise their nightmare wasn't a nightmare but was in fact a reality, that they had lost a husband, a father and a friend because some heartless idiot had taken him away from them?

Maybe the team would get a break tomorrow, realise that it was just some random act of violence – a druggie after a quick hit or something. Something simple yet, if so, bloody tragic.

He reached across and turned out the light. Exhausted and emotional, Perry hoped sleep would wear him down soon.

Allie parked her car in the driveway of her home and killed the engine. She let herself in, hoping to remove the heaviness of the day along with her coat as she left it in the hallway. In the living room, she found Mark sprawled along the length of the settee.

'Hey.' Allie ruffled his hair. 'How was your first day back?'

'It seemed to go on forever. But not as long as yours.' Mark yawned and stretched his arms in the air. 'You got anything concrete?'

'Not yet.' Allie perched beside him and relayed the details that she could.

'I can't believe this is someone else you know,' Mark said afterwards. 'I hope this isn't going to become a habit.'

'I knew him vaguely!' Allie nudged his shoulder, thankful that he was joking. But she did pause for a moment, recalling her last murder investigation. Both she and Mark had met Steph Ryder, although neither of them could claim to have known her all that well. It was a good thing, really, Allie deduced, considering the circumstances leading up to the arrest of her killer.

'Mickey Taylor.' Allie shook her head slowly. 'I still can't believe it. Perry knew both him and his wife. He reckons he was a right lad at school.'

'We were all right lads at school. Most of us grew up, though, when we walked out of the gates for the final time and joined the real world.'

'I suppose. Most of the time I can distance myself from my work, but it was really sad. Gorgeous house, one of the large detached ones on Holly Lane. And, do you know, apart from the obvious signs of grief, Kath's really looked after herself. Makes a refreshing change.'

'You mean she still looks good for our age group?'

'*Your* age group, old man,' Allie mocked. 'I'm younger than you.'

'And, boy, will you never let me forget it.'

'No, I never will.' She bent down to kiss his forehead, so grateful that they still got on so well after fifteen years of marriage. She watched him for a moment longer, letting his familiarity stabilise her. It made her feel peaceful, lucky to have him to come home to.

She went through to the kitchen. Despite the lateness of the hour, she was hungry after grabbing what she could throughout the day. The first hours of any murder enquiry were manic, with hardly a moment to breathe. There were no properties near to the scene of this one, but house-to-house enquiries had started around the surrounding streets, which meant setting up the enquiry, rounding up extra bodies, appealing for witnesses and dealing with them – although there hadn't been any so far – scouring CCTV to see if it had panned over the area at the right time and caught anything, waiting for forensics coming in, getting the Financial Forensic Unit to check Mickey's position, obtaining the family's phone records. If it weren't for the fact that everyone they wished to speak to, or anyone who could give them information, would be asleep now, most of the team would still be at their desks.

Mark padded into the room, barefoot, dressed in navy pyjama bottoms and a white T-shirt. Allie's stomach flipped over at the sight. She felt blessed that he could still do that to her, that he still warmed her heart, still made her insides tingle. She reached up as he drew near, running a hand over his late-in-the-day stubble.

'You hungry?' she asked as he pulled her towards him, squeezing her tightly around the waist.

'For you?' He kissed her. 'Not at all. But I'll have whatever you're having food-wise.'

She pushed him away playfully.

'How was Karen?' she asked. Mark had said he'd visit when she'd rung him earlier, knowing that she'd be late home. Despite Karen's brain condition, she was aware of happy and sad. If Allie didn't visit for more than three days in a row, she would sulk. It made Allie feel even guiltier.

'She was good.' Mark yawned. 'I said you'd be by tomorrow. You will be able to sneak a few minutes with her?'

'You know I'll do my best.'

'Yeah, I do know that.'

'Meaning?' she frowned.

'You know what I mean. Family first and all that.'

Before she could defend herself, Mark left the room. Allie groaned quietly. Despite his protestations, sometimes it would be good to come home without the worry of being chastised for working long hours. She knew only too well that she needed to keep work and play separate, and there was a fine line to tread.

But he was wrong when he said she didn't think of her family. It was at times like these that she did nothing but. That's why she often needed to distance herself from Karen, to stop the raw pain from seeping in again. Of course, it had deadened somewhat over the years since the attack. But often in cases such as Mickey Taylor's, when she had to spend time with victims' families, it brought her own feelings to the forefront again. She couldn't help that.

But it was what made her do her job well, and she didn't want to change that at all.

Chapter Six

Rhian Jamieson let out an impatient sigh as she waited her turn in the queue at the Co-op. The woman standing in front of her packed her shopping slowly while her toddler wrecked the display of cheese and onion crisps at her side. Rhian clocked her cheap jeans and sweater underneath a denim jacket that must have been fashionable at some time or other. Lank hair, several strands coming loose from a ponytail, was scraped severely away from her face. Dark circles under her eyes and a spotty chin, face devoid of any make-up.

Rhian twirled a strand of her own freshly washed hair around a finger, unable to understand how someone could let herself go that much. The woman seemed barely older than her, yet at twenty-six, Rhian probably looked better now than she ever had in her life. Slim waist, blonde hair, glamour model figure and pouting lips, designer coat, leather-look skinny trousers and stiletto ankle boots – she knew she looked amazing.

'That's eighteen pounds forty-seven pence, please,' said the checkout assistant as she waited for the customer to finish. There were several people in the queue behind Rhian now, some starting to roll their eyes and check their watches. Rhian gnawed at her bottom lip to stop herself from screaming out as the woman thrust a note into the cashier's hand. Why couldn't she hurry up!

Fifteen minutes later, Rhian was out of the shop and rushing to her car. It was her own fault, really – she hadn't planned on being out so late the night before but she'd bumped into friends while out shopping. Her confession that her fella was working away for the night had led to an impromptu evening doing manicures for several women. It had been lucrative at least – and pleasing that her new business venture was taking off. She'd forgotten all about getting some food in so would have to tell Joe she'd been to M&S – she was sure he'd never know.

A few minutes into her journey, she had to slow for a red light. While she was stationary, she glanced into the black people-carrier stopped at her side. The woman driving it pushed neat blonde hair behind her ear and checked her eyes in the rear-view mirror, rubbing a finger under each one before she was satisfied with her reflection. Behind her, a young child was sleeping in a car seat. Rhian's heart melted at the sight of a pink hat and matching coat. Recently, she'd begun to feel a maternal tug towards babies, which shocked her completely. She'd always thought she'd never have children so it was a strange feeling – although she wondered if she would cope with a small being relying on her twenty-four-seven.

As the lights changed to green and they both drove off in opposite directions, Rhian imagined what it would be like to pull into the drive at home and pick up a baby rather than a bag of ready-made food from the back seat. But then again, an afternoon lounging in a luxurious bath with a glass of something chilled before Joe was due back was pretty tempting too.

She turned into a small estate of newly built houses off Victoria Road. A minute later, she was in Smallwood Avenue and parking her car in the drive of number four only to find that Joe was home before her. Frowning, she wondered what had brought him back so early.

Rhian had been living with Joe for the past two years. Joe owned the property, a four-bedroom house in a row of almost identical ones. It was tidy, although lacking charisma, but Rhian loved living there. It still gave her a buzz to let herself in, walk the length of the long hall. Off it was a living room equivalent to the size of the downstairs of her parents' home, and after that was the kitchen with its conservatory that opened out onto a garden with a hot tub that she made the most of whenever the weather was fit.

'Only me, babe,' she said as she opened the front door and pulled her key from the lock. She hung up her coat and went through into the kitchen.

Joe was sitting forward in a chair, watching Sky News. All hunched up, looking intense – it didn't do anything for him. Rhian's friends often teased her, knowing she was only after a sugar daddy, always asking what it was like to wake up next to someone sixteen years older. But she did enjoy the status of dating an older guy, and the perks that came with being with this one. Was it worth it just for the money he gave to her? Hell, yes. But even though everyone assumed he was rolling in money because of his ex-wife, Rhian knew differently. Joe had money of his own stashed away too. He'd told her he'd never go short, having come away from a bad marriage with a good pay-out. It was one of the reasons she was still with him. That, and his broody look and sex appeal. Even at forty-two, he was certainly eye candy.

'You're home earlier than planned.' She went to sit in his lap but he pushed her aside, intent on watching the screen. 'What's up?'

'Job finished early,' he said. 'There was a bloke murdered yesterday.'

'What – you mean here in Stoke?' Rhian gasped.

'Yes, haven't you heard? It's been all over the news.'

'No, I must have missed the bulletins.' Rhian omitted to tell him she hadn't heard a thing because she'd been gossiping with friends. She turned to focus on the screen a little better, watching a clip of a white tent over the side of a canal bank. She leaned a bit closer. 'Ooh, that's Etruria, isn't it?'

'Yeah, poor bastard was attacked while he walked the dog. I know him, too. We went to school together.'

Rhian turned back to him sharply. 'Please don't tell me the dog is dead too.'

Joe shook his head. 'No, it made its own way home.'

'Oh, the poor thing.'

'We're talking about a bloke who's been murdered.' Joe's pitch was one of exasperation. 'Out for a walk with his dog, stabbed and left for dead. I can't believe it's Mickey.'

'When did you last see him?'

'We didn't keep in touch after school, but –'

'Well, you hardly know him then.'

'Doesn't make it any better.'

'I suppose.' Rhian paused. 'Anyway, what do you fancy to eat for lunch? I got a piece of gammon at half-price – needs to be eaten today, really. Or a couple of ready-meals.'

'I'm not hungry, and I have to go out again soon. That's why I'm back a little earlier.'

'Do you have to?' Rhian pouted. 'I thought we could have some afternoon delight, so to speak.' She waggled her eyebrows comically, waiting for him to acknowledge her, but he said nothing, just kept his eyes on the screen.

A few moments later, knowing she wasn't going to get his attention, Rhian moved away with another sigh. He was good at that – ignoring her, making her feel invisible when he had more pressing things on his mind. Still, taking the rough with the smooth was something she was used to. With Joe, the rough was bad but the smooth was always worth waiting for.

Day two of the enquiry had been frustrating for Allie. So far there were no leads. No witnesses, no ID from forensics that could put anyone else on the scene. Any CCTV cameras that would have been on the area didn't reach down and underneath the bridge to show what had happened on the towpath. Finally, she'd tasked Sam with trawling through the ones that panned around the city to see if there was a chance they had been in range, but again, there had been nothing. Despite media coverage on the local radio stations and front-page coverage of the story in *The Sentinel*, no witnesses had come forward with any further details. They were at a loss at the moment until more forensics came back.

As her hands flew over her keyboard, her mind went back to the letter E that had been found in Mickey Taylor's pocket. It wasn't even the beginning of Mickey's name: the worst scenario they had been going over in that evening's briefing was that it might be the beginning of a word. If so, it could be a sign of more to come – which was a horrible thought in itself. Everyone was certainly stumped as to why it was there. Without the magnetic letter, no one would have been any the wiser – the murder would have been taken for a random attack, a robbery gone wrong. But the letter changed everything.

She finally left the station just before nine that evening. Before heading home, she popped over to Riverdale Residential Home on the off chance that her sister might still be awake. At the main doors, she pressed her key fob to the monitor to allow her access. Walking through the now-darkened reception area and along the brightly lit corridor to Karen's room always reminded Allie of how long she had been coming there, how seventeen years of her sister's life had been taken away from them both. Still, it was pleasant, and the staff and the facilities were second to none, and it was only a mile from where she and Mark lived in Werrington. Her sister had the best they could offer her.

Follow the Leader 47

Karen was propped up in bed when she walked into her room. Her dark hair was washed, her fringe held back with a purple clip. Her face seemed a little more puffy than usual but that was because Doctor Merchant had tried a different cream on her psoriasis and it had caused a slight reaction. She noted that the patches looked better than the last time she'd visited, though.

Allie wiped a bit of dribble from Karen's chin and bent to kiss her forehead. 'Hey, Sis. How are you doing?'

Karen groaned, an angry response, her eyes firmly set on the small television screen behind her.

'Not sulking, are you?' Allie's shoulders drooped. 'I'm sorry; I've been busy with a case.'

Karen groaned, louder this time. Allie breathed a sigh of relief: it was a frustrated groan, not one of annoyance. She turned to look at the television, catching Bradley Walsh walking across it in a crumpled flasher-mac–type coat. She stepped to one side with a smile, realising that she was blocking her sister's view.

'Well, well, now,' she teased. 'I can't have you missing *Law & Order UK*.'

She drew up a chair and sat down beside the bed, concentrating on her own murder case as Detective Sergeant Ronnie Brooks tried to solve his. Allie hoped Mickey Taylor's murder wouldn't be one that remained unsolved – a random attack that hadn't been witnessed by anyone, with no camera evidence to follow up, a silhouette of a person perhaps disappearing into the distance. This was always the frustrating time on any investigation: either waiting for someone to confess because they couldn't sleep with their guilt or eventually realising that someone was going to their grave never telling a soul of the wrong deed they'd done. But she and her team wouldn't give up until all angles were covered. It was early days yet.

She sighed, got out her phone and sent a message to Mark. She wouldn't be long but she wanted him to know that she had left work. He'd probably be expecting her to be at the station all evening.

'I can't believe the Christmas break is over already, Kaz,' she said, sitting forward to rest a hand on her sister's arm. 'It was good to just catch up with Mark – and do normal things, you know. Watch TV, do a bit of shopping in the sales, go for a pub lunch or two. I swear we must have eaten our weight in chocolate, though.' She patted her stomach with her other hand. 'I need to get back to the gym.'

She stretched her aching neck from side to side, her eyes catching a group of framed photos on the opposite wall. They'd found most of them when clearing out Karen's flat after the attack. They were of family and friends, happier times. Allie wondered if Mickey Taylor would be in any of these photos. There was one with a group of teens; she got up and moved closer to check it out, looking for the flash of red hair. Yes, over on the left side: three boys. The middle one looked like Mickey. Over on the right stood three girls, arms round each other's shoulders – one of them was Karen. Allie ran a finger over her image. She'd recognise that smile anywhere, even though she hadn't seen it in such a long time.

She peered closer. Was one of the girls Kath Clamortie? Removing the frame from the wall, she took out the photo. Written on the back in blue ink were the date and the school name: Reginald High School – 1989. Under that was a list of names: Me, Sandy, Mickey, Gray, Kath and Nath. She looked at the boys again. One of the others looked familiar too, but she couldn't place him.

Allie put the photo back on the wall and sat down, giving Karen's hand a squeeze. She'd give anything to have one last chat with her sister, even if only to make sure everything was okay for her. It was such a sad existence to be in the home all day, every day, for the rest of her life.

'I miss talking to you so much, Sis,' she said quietly.

Follow the Leader

Noticing that Karen's eyes were closing, Allie watched her for a moment before pushing herself forcefully to her feet. Sometimes, seeing her lying there, unable to respond, felt just as bad as if she had been taken away altogether. Just like someone had taken Mickey Taylor from his family.

Allie would stop at nothing until they had justice for him too. Because she never gave up thinking that one day her sister's attacker would be caught. One day, he would get exactly what he deserved.

And she hoped, more than anything, that she would be there to see it.

This old man, he played two.
He played knick-knack on his shoe.
With a knick-knack, paddy-whack
 Give the dog a bone.
 This old man came rolling home.

1989

'What do you think, girls?' Sandra Seymour pouted and looked at the group before her. 'Don't you think I'm the best looking out of all of you?'

'You're so full of yourself!' Johnno laughed at her.

'I was joking,' she retorted.

'Yeah, right.'

'You weren't supposed to be listening.' Sandra prodded him in the chest. 'But if you must know, we were having a competition to see who had been out with the most boys. Surely that proves who is the best looking, then?'

'More like who is the biggest tart.'

'Why, you cheeky bugger!'

Johnno grinned. 'That can't be right anyway, because you haven't been out with me – and I only go out with the best.'

'Ha, as if. Who'd want to go out with you?'

'Yeah,' Karen Baxter shouted over. 'Who would want to go out with you?'

'Well, you, for starters, Kaz.'

'In your dreams.' Karen huffed and folded her arms. 'You're so full of yourself, Johnno. I'd rather shoot myself in the head.'

'You'd go out with *me*, though, wouldn't you?' Mickey took Karen's hand.

Karen pulled it away quickly, blushing furiously. 'No, I wouldn't.'

'Ooh – ooh.' A chorus rang up from the boys.

A few feet away from them but hidden safely indoors, Patrick listened through an open window of the corridor. The gang were in the upper school playground, congregated around the doors to the main building, the low-walled flower borders a perfect place to sit. It was where the cool kids hung around – and where anyone who wasn't cool kept out of their way.

He heard everything – all their flirty comments, all their put-downs with the double-entendres. He glared at them. If they ever spoke to him, they meant every one of the spiteful things they said to him. There weren't any jokes, just nasty comments that held true meaning.

He'd stayed behind after the last lesson to chat with the teacher. History – he couldn't get enough of it and they were learning all about the Industrial Revolution. But now he was late to get to the playground, and he'd have to walk right through the people he hated the most. He was safer in here, although he was pushing his luck to be inside during a break.

A minute later, his luck ran out when Mrs Turner, the arts teacher, came round the corner.

'Come on, Patrick,' she said, beckoning him over to the door.

'Don't feel very well, miss,' he fibbed. 'Feel a bit sick.'

Mrs Turner nodded. 'Get some fresh air. It'll make you feel much better.'

Dragging his feet, Patrick went outside and found himself in the middle of the group. They all turned to see – Johnno sporting the biggest grin as he caught his eye. He grabbed Sandra's hand and pulled her near.

'Can you settle a problem for me, Shorty?'

Patrick wouldn't look at them, kept on walking down the steps.

'You reckon I should go out with Karen or Sandra?' Johnno said loudly. 'I thought I'd ask you, seeing as you're the one that every girl in the school wants to go out with.'

'I don't want to go out with him!' Sandra pointed rudely at Patrick. 'I have a reputation to keep up. It's not going to get wasted on some smelly, creepy swot that daren't say boo to a goose. I want a man, not a mouse.'

'But you've just been going on about how many boys fancy you.' Johnno swung Sandra round by her hand until she was in front of Patrick. 'I reckon you should kiss him.'

Sandra baulked. 'You have to be joking!'

'I'm not. Kiss him.'

'No way!'

Patrick tried to get past but Johnno pulled him back. By this time, the group had crowded behind him. Johnno pushed Sandra towards Patrick but she tried to squirm out of his reach.

She screwed up her face. 'No!'

'Leave me alone.' Patrick tried to push through them again but this time was stopped by Mickey.

'Where do you think you're going?' he said.

With Johnno holding on to Sandra, and Mickey blocking Patrick's way, the two were pushed together as the chants around them deepened.

'Kiss him. Kiss him. Kiss him!'

Soon Patrick had someone holding on to each of his arms. As Sandra was pushed towards him, she squealed in dismay. Johnno, still behind her, held her wrists tightly down at her sides. Screwing up her face, she turned it to the side. Patrick did the same as he saw her getting nearer. He pulled back his head but they were pushed together all the more. Behind the group, he could see more kids laughing, more coming to see what was going on.

'Shorty has a crush on you, everyone knows that,' said Johnno, snidely. 'Kiss him.'

Follow the Leader   55

'No!'

When she was an inch from his face, Sandra drew back her foot and kneed him in the groin.

Patrick dropped to his knees, then onto his side, groaning as he rolled around the playground. He felt a kick in the back, at the base of his spine, that made him groan even more. He couldn't see who it was. Another two kicks and then a shout.

'Mr Stewart's coming over!'

The crowd dispersed as quickly as it had formed. Patrick gasped as he tried to ignore the pain between his legs. She'd done a proper job, had Sandra Seymour.

'Right, you lot.' Mr Stewart clapped his hands. 'Nothing to see now. Come on, move along!'

From the ground, Patrick watched Johnno run to catch up with Sandra, who had marched off in a huff. Watched as he whispered something in her ear, heard her laughing. She glanced back at him for a moment before pushing Johnno playfully. Then Johnno slung his arm around her shoulders and they continued to walk away.

No one else gave a backward glance.

Chapter Seven

Suzi Porter opened the front door, entering the house with the same foul mood that she'd left it with that morning. She'd had to get up at the crack of dawn to make sure she was ready and in the studio in Manchester for eight o'clock. She'd been planning on going out to dinner in the white shirt she'd been wearing: damn the clumsy make-up artist for squirting foundation all down the front of it. Suzi was sure she'd done it deliberately after she'd caused a fuss about not wanting to cover her clothes with a robe. And damn the incompetent stylist for bringing her the wrong size clothing so she'd had to resort to wearing her own top in the first place – she was a size twelve, everyone knew that, not a ten. Bigger sizes could always be pinned to suit. Not that it mattered too much, for minutes later it would be whipped off for more revealing photographs. It was all just bloody politics.

It was just before six p.m. on Wednesday afternoon when her driver dropped her off. The journey back via the motorway had been horrendous. An accident had blocked two lanes, causing two miles of tailbacks. Now her head was pounding with the stress of sitting around doing nothing.

Seeing her husband's car parked in the drive, she shouted to him as she went through to the kitchen.

'Kelvin?'

'Up here!'

Suzi flipped off her heels, left them where they dropped in the middle of the floor and tiptoed over marble tiles to the fridge. Reaching inside for a half-empty bottle of wine, she poured herself a large glass, gulped it back greedily and poured another. Even the taste of it did nothing to alleviate her mood. She could feel a migraine coming; her arms were aching after the photographer had insisted she have them up in the air while she draped herself around a pole, and her right eye was beginning to puff after the wrong sort of cream had been used to remove all the paraphernalia needed to make her look half-decent. Shit, what she put herself through to earn a decent crust.

She lit a cigarette and took a deep drag, moving to stand at the back door before Kelvin caught her smoking in the house. She let go of the smoke with a sigh; the cool air blasting in did nothing to invigorate her. God, she was knackered, and she had another shoot tomorrow. At least she didn't have to worry about picking up the kids. Ollie and Jayden were staying over with Kelvin's mum and dad that evening. She sighed again as she blew more smoke out. That was, if Kelvin wasn't still sulking after their argument last night.

When Kelvin came into the kitchen minutes later, she was sitting at the table, wine glass in her hand.

'Don't knock too much of that back if you're coming over to me later,' he said.

'It's only my first!' Suzi lied.

'You'd better make it your last. It's at least a double measure.'

'Stop nagging. You don't have to start on me the minute I get in.'

'You don't have to grab a drink the minute you get in.'

Suzi prickled. 'Look, I've had a shit day so I'm in a mood already. Don't make things worse.'

Kelvin scoffed. 'When are you ever *not* in a mood?'

'Is this still about last night?' Suzi pinched the bridge of her nose. 'I said I'd make amends by going out with you this evening, didn't I?'

Kelvin had wanted to take her out last night but she'd fallen asleep as soon as she'd come home. When he'd finally rung from the club to see what time she would be there, thinking she was already on her way to him, it had been too late to take the boys to their gran's. He'd come home fuming, hence the row.

'You make it sound like a chore,' he cried. 'Is it too much to ask that you spend some time with me?' Kelvin leaned on the table as he stared at her. 'Honestly, I don't know why I bother.'

Suzi noted the change of clothing and the smell of fresh aftershave, a clean white shirt. Kelvin always looked handsome in a rough and rugged way – round face, bald head, deep-set eyes and a boxer's nose. But right now, she was too irritated to care.

'Do you want me to come over to the club later or not?' she asked, eyebrows raised.

'As long as you don't start an argument. We can do that here for free.'

'Here we go,' she sighed. 'Making excuses up because you don't want to spend any money. You're such a cheapskate.'

Kelvin's face contorted. 'Don't ever call me a cheapskate.'

'But you are. Most men whose wives earn a lot of money would just enjoy the fact, but you,' she leaned closer and pointed at him, stopping very close to his eye, 'you just wallow in your own self-pity.'

'No, I don't.'

'Yes, you do.'

Kelvin glared at her for a moment longer and then reached for his car keys. 'I'm going back to work, before I say something I'll regret. I'm not staying to listen to your garbage.'

Suddenly realising he was about to leave, Suzi relented. 'Don't go, Kelvin.' She grabbed his arm as he walked past. 'I'm sorry. I was only having a laugh.'

Kelvin shrugged her hand away. 'Too late. I'm gone.'

'Kelvin!' She followed him quickly to the front door. 'Wait!'

Follow the Leader 59

'I'll be back around ten. Entertain yourself until then because I certainly don't want to.'

Before she could stop him, he was gone.

'Well, fuck you,' she muttered under her breath. She went back into the kitchen and poured another drink, whiskey this time. Now that tasted much better.

The doorbell went a few minutes later. Suzi knocked back the drink, stormed to the door and yanked it open. 'If you think you can –' She stopped when she saw it wasn't Kelvin. 'Yes? What do you want?' she added, half expecting the man standing there to thrust some handheld electronic contraption at her so that she could sign for a parcel.

'Hi!'

Suzi didn't reply.

'You don't remember me?' The man feigned hurt.

'Should I?' She peered at him.

'It's me, Matt – Matthew Thompson.' He raised a hand in greeting. 'We went to the same high school, were in the same class, actually.'

Suzi paused. There had been a Matthew Thompson in her class at school but she would have remembered if it was him, wouldn't she? He'd been one of the nicer-looking boys at Reginald High. Or would she remember him? Look at how different she looked nowadays with her fake breasts, lifted eyes and Botoxed forehead and lips. Images change through the years, as well as people.

As he stood there expectantly, she decided to play along rather than look stupid.

'Matt!' She smiled, beckoning him in. 'Come on through. How the hell are you?'

'I'm good, thanks.'

'I didn't recognise you at first.' Suzi looked embarrassed.

'Well, I suppose it has been a while. *You* don't look any different, though. Still as gorgeous as ever.'

She laughed coyly. 'Still the joker, I see!'

Suzi closed the front door, and led him into the living room. As she watched Matt taking in the expensive décor and furniture, she couldn't help but get a warm feeling. Not many of the gang from school had made anything of themselves and, despite earning her money glamour modelling, she had used her assets wisely – even if they had been enhanced to double D cups.

She stood in front of the fire, leaning on the marble surround to steady herself. Christ, that wine had gone straight to her head; she could almost hear a tune beating inside it. She checked the time: six thirty. If she didn't offer Matt a drink, she could get rid of him quickly. Then she could get ready to go out that evening. If Kelvin was at the club, then she wasn't going to wait around for him. She'd call Tom: he would always have time for her. She gave Matt a faint smile: she'd give him twenty minutes, half an hour at the most.

'So . . . ?' she raised upturned palms.

Matt pulled out a framed photograph from a plastic supermarket carrier bag. The photo was of three rows of children in school uniform – the back row standing, the middle one sitting on a bench and the children at the front sitting cross-legged on the floor.

Suzi stared at the photo. 'Ohmigod,' she shrieked, 'is that us?'

Matt nodded, his eyes crinkling up. 'Ugly-looking bunch, weren't we?'

She studied the rows of faces, boys and girls she'd grown up with but hardly ever saw now. Suddenly, she brought the picture frame closer, eyes widening as she recognised herself.

'That's me, there, with the pigtails!' she laughed, pointing at a girl in the back row.

'Yes, that's you.'

'How old were we – about twelve?'

'Yes.' He moved closer. 'Can you tell which one I am?'

Follow the Leader

Suzi stared again, sliding her index finger along the row of faces. She *could* remember Matt from school, although, glancing at him now, nothing about him seemed that familiar. He seemed a little shorter, his eyes were dark, miserable-looking even, and he was very lean, almost puny. Mind, after the surgery she'd had, who was she to question appearances? Everyone changed with age and once men lost hair, like Matt had, it was hard to tell one from the other, especially after so many years.

She pointed to a boy on the photograph. 'Is that you?'

He shook his head. Smiling, he pointed to another boy. 'That's me.'

'Really?' Suzi looked again, then let out a gasp. 'Is that Mickey Taylor?'

'Yeah, terrible news about him, wasn't it?'

'I couldn't believe it, still can't. I mean, what's the chance that you'll know someone who was murdered? It gave me quite a shock, I can tell you.'

'Yeah, me too. I hope the police catch the bastard who did it. They don't seem to have many leads though.'

Suddenly having found a common ground, Suzi didn't feel threatened by Matt anymore. Since leaving school and becoming famous, she often had people contact her, mostly through social media as it had become more popular over the years. Maybe he'd liked her Facebook page and was a fan of hers but didn't want to say.

'Do you fancy a glass of wine?' she offered, the thought warming her. 'You're not in a hurry, are you?'

'That'd be great, ta. I'll sit myself down, then, shall I?'

Minutes later, Suzi came back into the room with two glasses of wine, handed one to Matt and then sat down in the armchair opposite him. She curled her feet up to her side.

'Can you remember much about him?' she asked, taking a sip.

'About who?'

'Mickey Taylor.'

He shook his head. 'He wasn't around much when I was there.'

Suzi grinned. 'Yeah, that's right. He was always getting into trouble for skiving off. I can't believe he was so successful. I always thought he was a bit of a thicko.'

'You shouldn't always judge a book by its cover.'

'I suppose not.' Suzi paused. 'I used to go out with him, you know.'

'Did you?'

Suzi nodded. 'Well, I had a few dates with him, until that bitch Kath Clamortie got knocked up by him. Imagine if she hadn't. Me and Mickey, we could have earned a fortune together. We'd have been like Posh and Becks round here then, both having done well for ourselves. The golden couple!'

'Maybe, but he did okay without you anyway.'

'But imagine how much *more* successful he would have been with me behind him too! I must admit, he never gave the impression that he had it in him to run something as good as Taylor Made Pottery Factory. I had no idea it belonged to him until I heard it on the news. It's a huge place. Fair credit to him – he did well for himself clearly.'

'You sound a bit annoyed.'

'Do I?' Suzi sighed. 'It's been a long day.'

'I bumped into Patrick Morgan a couple of weeks ago – can you remember him?'

Suzi frowned while she searched her memory. 'Patrick Morgan. Patrick Morgan. Oh, wait! Yes, I remember him now. He was the class punch bag.'

'What?'

She giggled. 'You know – the one that got punched from every direction. Everyone made his life hell, poor bloke. Us kids could be so cruel. How was he?'

Follow the Leader 63

'Hmm?'

'Patrick. How was he when you saw him?'

'Oh, doing well. Married, three kids, big house. He has his own company now too. Loved telling me how rich he was.'

'Well, I never would have thought.'

'Why? He was clever too.' He cleared his throat. 'From what I can remember.'

'But not clever enough to give Johnno what he wanted.' Suzi shook her head. 'The times he took advantage of him, stealing his homework and either spoiling it so Patrick had to redo it, or copying it off as his own. The English teacher – God, what was her name? – kept fobbing him off as clumsy with all the excuses he came up with.'

'He showed us up, though, didn't he?'

'What do you mean?'

'Not many of us went on to make anything of ourselves when we left school. But Patrick did okay for himself.'

'I did okay for myself too,' Suzi snapped.

'By stripping and showing everyone your tits?'

Suzi gasped.

'I'd hardly call that setting the world on fire with your intellect and skills.'

She stood up unsteadily, putting her glass down on the coffee table with a bang. 'I think it's time you left,' she retorted. 'My husband will be back soon.'

He stood up too. Suzi didn't have time to move before she felt the sting of his hand across her face. Her head reeled to the right. Cold eyes stared at her, almost hypnotising her. She couldn't stop the fist that crashed upwards into her nose, then into the side of her mouth. Disorientated, she staggered backwards, flailing as she fell onto the floor, crashing into the coffee table. In a second, the room disappeared into blackness.

Chapter Eight

Patrick took both of Suzi's hands and dragged her through to the kitchen at the back of the house. Removing the binding he'd brought with him from his pocket, he pulled a fancy chair out from under the table and hoisted her on to it. As her head flopped forward, he tied her arms behind the chair back and one foot to each leg at the front. When satisfied she was secure, he slapped her around the face.

'Wakey, wakey!'

Suzi lifted her chin slowly, then, seeing him in front of her, she tried to stand up. She wriggled her hands and feet. Then she screamed.

Patrick swiped his hand across her face again. 'Please be quiet,' he told her. 'You don't want to alert your neighbours, now, do you?'

'What do you want?' she whispered.

Patrick placed his hands on her knees, smiling when she whimpered. 'You really don't remember me, do you?' Then he frowned, slowly shaking his head from side to side. 'That's a shame.'

'Please!' Suzi thrashed about some more. 'My husband will be home soon.'

'No, he won't be back until around ten. Isn't that what he said as he was leaving?'

'Wh – what?'

'You know he'd much rather be at work than here with you, don't you? He doesn't want to come home to your nagging and your self-absorbed ways. He doesn't want to be left looking after your kids while you swan off here, there and every fucking where. Does he know about your extra fun at the gym?'

'How do you –?' Suzi began to cry. 'Have you been following me?'

'Don't flatter yourself.' Patrick stepped back. 'I was only doing it to suss out your routine. I needed to learn your moves so I could figure out the best time to do this.'

'Do what?'

'Whatever I want, really. Such fun!'

'Please, let me go. I'll do anything, give you anything. I can –'

'My name – it isn't Matthew Thompson,' he interrupted. 'You really don't remember me, do you?'

Suzi shook her head manically.

'The years of torment you and your gang of friends put me through. You'll never know the anguish of being the odd one out, will you? What did you just call me back then, when you were going out with Mickey Taylor or whoever else you were slagging it about with? The class punch bag – of course I remembered. I know because I've retained every fucking WORD! And you're going to pay for what you did to me. You and Whitty and Johnno and all the gang – you're all going to pay for it.'

Suzi began to thrash around in the chair. 'Please, let me –'

'We're playing a game, you see. You started it way back in the playground when we were ten. Follow the Leader – you remember? You ran off with my homework and I chased after you, behind the sheds where I couldn't see who was waiting for me. But you knew who was there, didn't you? And you knew that no one could see what they'd do to me. No one would be able to stop them, unless it was too late.'

'We were just kids! We weren't aware of how it would affect you.'
'Liar.'
'I do remember. We were always on to you.' Suzi was crying hysterically now. 'It must have hurt you so much. I'm truly sorry!'
'LIAR!'
'It was just games!' She sobbed. 'Stupid, childish games.'
Patrick clenched his fists. 'You think I was playing games when I rammed a knife in Mickey Taylor's stomach two days ago?'
Tears fell from her eyes again.
'I made sure Mickey knew who I was before I killed him too.'
'What . . . It was . . .' She screamed again.
Patrick moved forward and straddled her. He grabbed her chin. 'Shut the fuck up or I will make things much, much worse.' From his pocket, he pulled out his knife and flicked it open. As she whimpered again, he pressed the blade across her throat, barely touching her skin but enough to make her understand that the threat was real.
Suzi sobbed uncontrollably, struggling to catch her breath.
It was then he felt her body give in. He glanced down, saw a puddle forming and laughed.
'You've pissed yourself, just like I used to do when I was scared. Tut tut – such a naughty girl. You'll have to be punished for that.'
'What do you want with me?' she sobbed.
'I want . . .' He placed the knife down on the floor. Then he moved his free hand slowly down her neck, over her chest, lingering to squeeze her breast before ripping open her blouse.
'No, please,' she whispered, squeezing her eyes shut for a moment.
'Open your eyes.'
'No! Please, I'll do anything.' She began to wriggle again. 'Anything you want. Please, not that.'

Follow the Leader

'Look at me!'

She opened her eyes. He smiled: finally, he had her full attention. She wasn't going to scream; she wasn't going to struggle. She was going to let him do whatever he wanted because she thought that he would leave and she could then get on with her life.

Oh dear. She was in for a surprise.

He picked up the knife again, ran the blade down her chest and held the tip against her stomach.

'I don't want you,' he told her. 'I just wanted you to know that I could have you.'

He plunged the knife deep into Suzi's stomach. Patrick heard her gasp, watched her face contort with the shock and the pain. Before it completely took her breath away, he stabbed her again. Ah, the power he felt. It was almost orgasmic as he thrust the knife in again and again.

Suzi coughed as blood filled her mouth, but now she couldn't look at him.

Pretty soon, she had no strength to cry out. Her head dropped.

Patrick sat still while his breathing returned to normal, the sound of his heart beating in the still of the room the only thing he was aware of. He grabbed a handful of Suzi's hair and pulled her head up. She was almost ugly close up, smoker's lines around her mouth and dark circles under each eye, yellowing teeth, signs of her hair thinning from too much product. He bet her skin had suffered from all the crap she must have had to wear on it. It was a vicious circle – add more to look good but make the skin suffer so it reacted badly. And although her eyes were devoid of anything now, the light in them had probably gone out a long time ago. He wondered when she'd last had fun in her life, a real belly laugh with friends, when she wasn't swanning around like a diva. He didn't feel any sympathy for her.

He let her head drop again and wiped the blade of the knife clean on her bra, red smears on virginal white. She'd broken a fingernail too, he noticed; boy, she wouldn't like that, little Miss Perfect.

When she was Sandra Seymour, she had been such a bitch to him at school. Always trying to get him alone and then lure him to where the other boys would be able to get him. Unseen, they'd kicked him, punched and tormented him. They didn't care what they did as long as they weren't caught. And then when he went home with bruises, he got more from his old man for not sticking up for himself.

But Sandra Seymour, or Suzi Porter, whatever the press would call her, was a pawn in his game, useless to him now. Already he'd started to think about his next target, move on to the next stage of his plan.

Patrick closed his eyes for a moment and remembered the first thrust of the knife. He couldn't believe how good it had felt, how much pain had been released with every stab – his pain, her pain, their pain. There was blood all over his clothes, but he couldn't do much about that. He'd worn black again in readiness. But he needed to wash his hands: it would take him minutes at the most.

Checking his watch, he jumped from Suzi's lap and went over to the sink. Two down: five to go. He wouldn't be here long now. All he needed to do afterwards was slip out the back. Of course his fingerprints would be everywhere, but no one would catch him because he wasn't in the system.

They just wouldn't know that yet.

Chapter Nine

Rhian checked her watch for the umpteenth time before turning her attention back to the television. She listened carefully to the evening's news as it kept everyone up to date with the ongoing investigation of the man who had been murdered over on the canal towpath two days ago. Rhian hadn't known of Mickey Taylor until Joe had told her about him, but she certainly knew lots about him now. Reports of his murder had been on national news bulletins since Monday and were sprawled across the front page of *The Sentinel* again that night.

The TV reporter panned around with his hand, saying that it was a popular spot for people to be found dead, but that most of the time it was usually the canal itself that caused the death as people drowned. No one had been murdered there until yesterday. A new low for Stoke-on-Trent, Rhian surmised, although she wanted to pull the reporter up on his stupid choice of words. A spot where people went to die should never be referred to as being popular, surely?

The time on the screen said it was ten past eight. She sighed. Where the hell was Joe? He'd told her this morning that he hadn't planned on being home late so she'd made an effort and prepared him a shepherd's pie from scratch. She'd followed a Jamie Oliver recipe, quite proud of her effort she was too, but the last time she had looked at it, it had started to burn at the edges as the juices inside bubbled over. She was starving: she'd give him ten more minutes and then she was diving into it regardless of whether he was home or not.

Moving in with Joe had not been in Rhian's life plan but it had been an added bonus. They'd met during a night out in Hanley. Some young bloke had been taking great pleasure feeling her up on the dance floor. Joe had marched over and stopped him with a swift punch to the ribs that had gone unnoticed by the bouncers. He'd bought her a drink and, although he was sixteen years older than her, they'd become an item more or less immediately. Within a month, Rhian had persuaded Joe to let her stay there. The relationship wasn't everything she had hoped but it was better than living at home with her parents. Plus, after conveniently losing her crappy bar job through poor attendance, because she didn't have to fork out board or rent every month, she had started to put her qualification as a nail technician to good use and set up a mobile service for her friends. Pretty soon, she had a few regular clients and more than enough of an emergency fund put by, if she wasn't too stupid with it.

She flicked over the channels to catch up on *Coronation Street*. But a few minutes into the program, her mind began to wander again. Just lately, Joe had been staying at work quite a lot more than he normally did. She looked back – she reckoned for the past two months there had been a lot of late nights, weekend meetings and phone calls he didn't want her to listen in to. Not for the first time, she wondered if he had another woman. Fuck, she'd rip her eyes out if he had and she caught them together.

Relieved when she heard his car pull into the drive, she went out to greet him. 'Where have you been?' she whined as she stood shivering on the doorstep. 'I've something delicious in the oven and the smell of it is driving me mad.'

Follow the Leader

'There was a problem at work.' Joe kissed her briefly on the cheek.

She closed the door behind them, only to turn to see he'd removed his coat and was heading up the stairs.

Rhian grabbed his arm to stop him. 'Where are you going now?'

'I need to shower.'

'But I'm starving. Can't we eat first?'

'I won't be more than a few minutes.'

'But . . . oh, what's that? Is it blood?' She pointed to a red stain on his T-shirt. 'Are you okay?'

Joe looked down. 'Oh, it's fine, it's not mine,' he explained. 'One of the blokes at work cut himself this morning, the dozy bastard, and I had to administer first aid and take him to A&E. There was blood everywhere.'

He thundered up the stairs.

Rhian pouted. 'Shall I dish the food out? I'm so hungry I could eat a horse.'

'Yeah, you do that.'

The bathroom door slamming made her jump. She glared at her reflection in the hall mirror. Damn that man! He hadn't even said she looked nice. She'd made an effort with her appearance too, wearing a simple yet flattering woollen dress that stopped slightly above her knee and showed just enough cleavage not to seem slutty. She'd put up her hair, a few loose strands sexily dropping onto her shoulders. Underneath the dress, she wore nothing but a black lacy thong she was hoping he would remove later with his teeth.

He's home, you stupid mare; stop whinging, she chastised herself. Determined not to antagonise him by moaning, she raced through to the kitchen to open a bottle of wine.

Joe's hair was still wet when he came into the kitchen ten minutes later. From the bags under his eyes and the way his shoulders drooped, Rhian realised she'd be pushing it for the marathon sex session she'd envisaged. But, she laughed inwardly, it was more than perfect for an early night. They could curl up together afterwards and have some quality time together for a change.

'Come and sit.' She beckoned him over to the table. 'It's only shepherd's pie. It's a bit well done now though.'

Joe headed over to the fridge and pulled out a bottle of beer. 'I'm knackered, duck. I'll take mine on a tray. I want to catch up with the news. Anything new on Mickey Taylor?'

Rhian counted to ten as she placed the plates on trays, remembering not to slam the cutlery down. In silence, they went through to the conservatory. They spent most of their time in there since it had recently been redecorated, since Rhian had insisted on putting her mark on something. Only when Joe's son, Jayden, came to visit was it occupied by anyone else. Ten-year-old Jayden loved the large plasma TV to play games on, and the squishy leather settees to throw himself around on when he was doing anything more energetic. Dressed in pale creams and caramels with the odd shock of bright orange, the room was warm and tranquil. But Rhian didn't feel relaxed as she sat down next to Joe. The television was on again, she sighed – bloody conversation stopper.

'So what was so important that you were late again this evening?' Rhian asked.

'Nothing more than usual. I was at the office until I came home. I had some paperwork to finish off.'

When no more words were forthcoming, Rhian decided to change tack. 'Please be careful, babe. You know that man, that Mickey Taylor, was murdered. I'm worried the police haven't caught his killer yet and –'

'Don't worry about that. It'll be some chancer, out to rob him of his money.'

'*The Sentinel* said that it didn't look like robbery was the motive. I reckon –'

'Well, I reckon you shouldn't believe everything you read in the papers.'

They finished their meal in another silence. Afterwards, Joe stayed riveted to the news as Rhian took out the trays and left them on the worktop in the kitchen. She'd clean them tomorrow. Impatient to get back to him, she took him another beer.

'Were you really at work this evening?' she asked him again.

'I told you, I was finishing something off.'

'*Something?*'

'Something that pays well, that's all you need to know.' Joe reached a wad of notes from his pocket and handed them to her. 'Here, treat yourself.'

Rhian grinned and sat down next to him again. How she loved being fobbed off. She could get those jeans she'd seen in Top Shop. And maybe there would be enough left over for another night out with the girls.

'Thanks, gorgeous.' She leaned over to plant a kiss on his lips. 'I might go out with Laila and Shelley next week for a drink. Do you fancy coming with us?'

'Not my style, you know that.'

'Maybe not, but I'm fed up with staying in on my own most evenings.' Rhian stopped counting at one hundred pounds. 'It's not because you're seeing another woman, is it? Because if you are, then I'm –'

Before she could finish her sentence, Joe turned towards her, his hand on her knee. She watched it rise slowly up her thigh, inside her dress, to the side of her thong. She moaned as he slipped his fingers inside; her breathing took on a life of its own.

'Rhian, Rhian,' he spoke slowly. 'What do I have to do to make you shut up?'

She threw the money to the floor and pulled him closer, running her hand through his hair as he kissed her. She knew his game, the scheming bastard. But she could play it too. Knowing just what he wanted, she reached for the buckle on his belt.

Afterwards, as Rhian lay beside him, Joe tried to control his temper. Fuck, she might be sexy and give great head but sometimes he could just lean over and punch her. He hated keeping her sweet at times. In the past, she'd been an alibi for him on several occasions but that had all been work related – nothing serious. In his line of work, you just never knew when things might need a little tweaking of the truth. Rhian would say anything for him, for the right price. She knew the score, enjoyed it too. It was what she did for him. But her constant snipes and moans about him being up to something dodgy really pissed him off at times. He wasn't stupid, knew she was only interested in him for his money. Plus a man of his age still needed sex, so her younger, willing body was a bonus. Of course, some of the blokes that he worked with paid for it, but he would never do that. He could take his pick of women if he wanted. He had when he'd been married – until his ex-wife had found out and put a stop to it with a boot up his ass.

Rhian was like his ex-wife in some ways but in others she was completely different. Yet, even though she was sixteen years younger than him, for someone so young she knew her own head when it came to kids. She'd told him categorically that she didn't want any – something he was certain of after she'd taken a long time to warm to his son, Jayden, even though it had annoyed him at the time. She was far too selfish to have kids. Perfect, as he didn't want to start a family again at his time of life. Some of his friends were granddads now. Christ, that made him feel old.

And, despite what he put up with – her moods and childish tantrums, her inability to see mess around the house, her failure to cook a half-decent meal – he felt confident that she would cover for him, say anything for him. Giving her money was a way of keeping her sweet. He wouldn't jeopardise his plans – what he *had* actually been doing that evening.

He ran his fingers through his hair, left his hand behind his head as he pushed away thoughts of what would happen to him if he was caught. The job was dodgy but it was going to pay off soon, as long as he could keep it quiet for a little bit longer. Because if his boss got wind of it, he'd be in serious bother. And no one wanted the wrath of Terry Ryder.

Allie jumped from sleep as her mobile phone burst into tune. She glanced around, disorientated for a moment until she realised she was at home. She must have dozed off on the settee. The clock on the wall said ten forty-five. Mark, who'd clearly been asleep on the armchair, groaned.

'*Beat Surrender?*' He scoffed. 'Seriously, you changed your ringtone to that?'

'You were the one moaning about it.' Quickly, she reached for her phone. 'DS Shenton.'

'This is the control room, Sarge. There's been report of a murder. Female – stabbed at home. I've been told to radio you in.'

Allie sighed: not another domestic gone too far.

'One more thing,' the caller continued. 'Forensics have found another letter.'

Chapter Ten

Before he left for his late shift, Patrick switched on some music, hoping to drown out the sound of next door's television. He made coffee and a toasted sandwich – cheese, thinly sliced tomato. Even so, he found it hard to eat anything, a permanent smile on his face. He had never felt so empowered: happy, content, excited even. Everything was slipping into place.

After so long being pushed around, Patrick was leading the game. *Come along now. Everyone take my hand; pick a number; pick a name. I want him on my team. No, he's coming on mine.*

Dressed in his work clothes, he went into the living room. As he passed the sideboard, he paused at the pile of letters again, this time picking up the framed photograph in front of them. If he was in a good mood, he could look at the black and white image of three people, happy and smiling, and remember them fondly. The three of them racing downstairs on a Christmas morning. Playing football with Robert. Helping Louisa to learn her eight times table, teaching her a rhyme to make sure she recalled them all in the right order. Going to the corner shop together and having a twenty-pence mixture, sitting on the grass comparing the colour of tongues after eating Black Jacks. Waiting outside the pub for his dad with a packet of crisps and a bottle of orange pop.

More often than not, when he looked at the photo he'd recall nothing but the hurt and the anger that he felt when they'd left. The photo was of his mum, younger brother, Robert, and sister, Louisa. His memory of the two of them was hazy but he thought that Robert would have been two years younger than him: his sister, Louisa, maybe five. Time had fogged over the years he'd been on his own with his father, Ray. He didn't have a clue why his mother had taken them and left *him* behind to be bullied by the man. He'd certainly lost count of the times that their names had been thrown into his face.

Patrick had been nine when they had left. That was the last time he'd seen them. He didn't even know if they still lived in Stoke-on-Trent or if they had moved to another city altogether. All he could remember was being sent into Hanley to get Ray some belly pork from the meat market and when he'd got home, they had all disappeared. All their clothes had gone too. Worse than that, Patrick had got it in the neck from Ray when he found the note that his mother had left for him.

In the note, his mother had said there was only room to take two children with her so as Patrick was the eldest, she'd left him behind because she knew he could cope. Cope with what? The beatings that she was running away from? All Ray's anger had transferred to Patrick. As a teenager, he would cower in his bed, having been alone all evening until Ray came home from the pub. Ray always wanted to fight. He'd drag Patrick out of bed, pull him down the stairs and beat him. Often Patrick would be covered in blood and bruises but still Ray wouldn't stop. He missed a lot of school but if anyone questioned him, Ray told them Patrick was clumsy.

Ray had broken Patrick's arm one afternoon after he'd had a skinful. He'd come home from the pub and had hurled Patrick across the room so quick and so hard that he hadn't been able to stay on his feet. His wrist had taken the brunt of the fall. The school nurse had insisted on taking him to the clinic, which had transferred him to the hospital for x-rays. Even Patrick's crying out in pain hadn't stopped Ray from having another go at him when he'd been brought home with a plaster cast up to his elbow. Ray had explained that away, too, as Patrick's clumsy fault for slipping. And then he'd taken another beating because Ray was furious that he'd brought unwanted attention to their home life.

It took a while but, in the end, Patrick hadn't blamed his mum for leaving. But what he couldn't understand was why she had taken his brother and sister along but left him behind. He never believed the story that there was only room for two young children where she was going. He knew he would have been an asset to his mother. She would have had to go out to work; he could have looked after Robert and Louisa for her. He was their brother!

What had been so wrong with him that she hadn't wanted to take him too? Instead, she'd left him in the hands of the bully she had run from. He thought back to the times when he had been woken by her screams as Ray had laid into her. He could still remember the sounds of the slaps, the punches, the screams, the bangs. It was all inside his head. He could never escape from it. And, at nine years old, he'd become the punch bag for his drunk of a father. How could she have done that to him?

In the early years after Ray went to prison, he'd tried to trace them but he hadn't been able to find any leads. He wondered if they'd changed their names – he couldn't remember his mother's maiden name and there was nothing in the house to tell him. Eventually, he'd given up.

But it was as he was doing this that he'd thought about his plan. Social media was taking off, with more and more people using Facebook and Twitter. Patrick joined both and found that it was absurdly easy to befriend people online, easy from timelines to work out what people were up to. It was ridiculous, really, he'd often thought, how much information people shared without thinking.

In a year or so, he'd built up a file on most of his victims, followed them and watched them, making sure he knew their routines off by heart. When he had all of those sorted, he went on to the other people he wanted to take down – came across a few surprises, too, and ended up adding a name to the list, someone that he didn't know at all.

When everything had been written down, worked out, planned out, he'd only had to continue to keep an eye out for any changes and then wait for the date. And here it was: January 16.

This time he would be the winner.

Through the dark and quiet streets, Allie drove over to Longton, in the south of the city. From Anchor Road, she turned right onto a residential estate. At the far end of Red Street, a house had already been sealed off with tape. She parked as near as she could get and walked to the one she was after.

Allie doubted any of the neighbours would get to sleep that night. Groups of people had congregated on the driveways of the houses either side. It seemed a tidy area, lots of newish cars and neat gardens, the lights from the emergency vehicles illuminating the street, breaking into the dark.

She announced her presence to the officer at the door, pulled on the necessary protective clothing and stepped into the hall of number twenty-two. She followed the voices but, at the doorway to the kitchen, she hesitated for a moment, the sight in front rendering her immobile. Then she took a deep breath and went inside.

A woman was tied to a chair, head slumped onto her chest, blonde hair hanging down covering her face. Allie's eyes were drawn to multiple stab wounds to her chest and abdomen. It seemed frenzied rather than meticulous. The skirt the victim was wearing was soaked in blood, and a large quantity had settled in a puddle in her lap. The white shirt she had on had been ripped open, buttons pinged off, she assumed. Splatters of blood were dotted here and there, no significant pattern. Her feet and legs were bare, toenails painted almost the same red as the blood.

The DI was already on scene in the room. So too were Dave Barnett, two more forensic officers and a photographer.

'The control room said the call had come in via the victim's husband, Kelvin Porter.' Nick broke into her thoughts as he noticed her hanging back in the doorway. 'He came home from work to find her like this.'

'Poor bastard,' said Dave. 'It's going to give him nightmares for a long time.'

Allie moved closer to see what she could of the woman's face. She didn't look peaceful, her eyes giving away the horror and the pain she had suffered during the last minutes of her life. It was hard to see the woman like that but Allie knew it had to be this way. Nothing could be touched until evidence was gathered.

'Do you think she was sexually assaulted before being dragged to the chair and tied to it?' she asked, looking at the woman's ripped top.

'I can't be certain yet, but from first glance, it's not looking that way,' Dave replied.

Allie looked around the room, saw two wine glasses on a small table with numbered yellow markers next to them – exhibits five and six. 'I didn't see a forced entry,' she continued. 'She knew her attacker?'

'I reckon so.'

'So we need to rule out the husband?'

'Yes, but he was at work. He's the general manager, Trentham Country Club. We need to check but it seems he was there from seven until ten, and then came straight home. Emergency call was logged at 22.21 which fits in with the drive from Trentham to here.'

Allie stood back and let the crime scene officers do their job.

'Did she let her attacker in or did they knock on the door? And, just for now assuming it's a male as her blouse is ripped open, did he force himself into the house the way he might have forced himself into her body? Or was it a random burglary followed by an even more random attack because someone got scared?' She spoke to no one in particular.

'So a definite "he," then?' questioned Nick.

'Don't you think so?' she queried. 'If we can rule the husband out, someone, probably male, came deliberately.'

'Not robbery then?'

'Possibly,' Allie nodded. 'But it's one thing to rob a house, another entirely to tie up the occupant before brutally killing her. It doesn't make sense.'

'It doesn't make sense to me why anyone does this type of thing at all,' said Dave.

Nick came over to her then. 'The letter V this time,' he spoke quietly. 'It was tucked inside her bra.'

'Shit.'

'We need to keep this away from the press for a while. The other thing I need to tell you is that her name is Sandra Seymour but you'll probably know her as Suzi Porter.'

Allie caught a breath. 'As in glamour model, Suzi Porter?'

'The very one.'

'She went to Reginald High School, at the same time as Mickey Taylor. I think they were in the same year. I remember my sister talking about her. She was really jealous when she made the big time – not so when she realised what she was actually doing.'

'Reginald High School was your school too, right?'

'Well, yes, but –'

'So you know both of our victims.'

'I wouldn't say I know her. I've *heard* of her – most people in Stoke have probably heard of Suzi Porter. You knew of her, didn't you?'

Nick nodded. 'She's made quite a name for herself.'

'Perry will know her too, no doubt.'

'Can you make a visit to the school?'

'Not possible. It closed in 1995.'

Reginald High School had been one of several over the city with large catchment areas before it had closed. A long time since, and the education landscape of the city was undergoing a massive transformation. There had been objections when the Building Schools for the Future program had been announced. Now, as well as secondary schools, there were academies, a pupil referral unit and special schools, each one a key part of the regeneration of the Potteries.

Allie blew a breath out through her mouth. Two bodies in three days. Two letters, E and V.

'Why didn't you tell me her name straightaway?' she asked Nick.

'I wanted you to work the room first. I also needed another perspective . . . wanted you to keep an open mind rather than make assumptions based on what she did for a living.'

'Why?'

'You wouldn't treat this differently if you knew she was a glamour model?'

'No, I wouldn't!'

Nick paused. 'Do you see any other connection between the two of them?'

'Well, I suppose it could be a long shot but . . . by all accounts, Mickey Taylor was one of the popular boys. One that every girl wanted to date.'

'Right, and Suzi – Sandra, whatever her name was?'

Follow the Leader 83

'I think I remember Sandra Seymour being one of the most popular girls.'

Rhian was awake early the next morning. Warm and sleepy underneath the duvet as the rain bounced off the windowsill, she turned to face Joe. He was on the other side of the bed with his back to her. She didn't mind – it was how they always woke up – but she stretched out luxuriously, making sure she touched his leg with her toes. Maybe it would wake him and they could have a repeat performance of the night before. But he didn't stir.

After the sex last night, they'd lain together for ages on the settee. It had been good to get time with Joe at last, even though she had nodded off. And – she grinned at the memory – she could take the loneliness when it led to glorious orgasms. The older man certainly won over guys the same age as her when it came to experience at good loving. She moved across and snuggled into his back. But, although he pulled her near, he slept on.

Ten minutes later, she looked at the clock. It was only half past six but, with her mind alert as the rain sleeted noisily across the windowpane now, she decided to get up. Slipping her feet into fluffy slippers, she tiptoed downstairs and into the kitchen. Closing the door behind her, she switched on the kettle and the radio and pulled herself onto a stool at the breakfast bar. If she'd had her way, this old kitchen would have been ripped out by now and replaced. Even though she'd been with Joe for two years, most aspects of the house still had 'bachelor' stamped over them. The kitchen units were dark wood with cheap Formica worktops, and the stainless-steel sink was nasty and scratched. To her mind, it really let the house down.

With coffee made, she reached into a drawer for the kitchen brochure she had ordered online and flicked through the pages.

The designs she was interested in were turned down at the corners – glossy white, aubergine and pale grey.

She hoped Joe would come round to her suggestions soon; so far he'd been reluctant to splash the cash. Why is it that men always thought what they had was good enough until they were shown something else? She wondered again if she dared to go ahead without his consent and order the work to be done anyway. He'd surely be able to cough up funds, with the long hours he was working lately. And that cash he'd thrown at her last night amounted to two hundred quid, so he wasn't short at the moment.

The hourly news bulletin came on. She stopped with her mug halfway to her mouth when she heard the update.

'Police are looking into the death of local glamour model Suzi Porter, who was found murdered in her home in Red Street, Longton, yesterday evening. Ms Porter, known previously as Sandra Seymour, was found with multiple stab wounds. A spokesperson for the Police says that her husband, Kelvin Porter, was brought in for questioning but has now been released pending no charges. They have no further comments at this time and a press conference will be held later this morning.'

Rhian's hand began to shake and she struggled to put her mug down.

She raced to turn the radio up but the news reporter had already moved on to the next story. She stood in the middle of the kitchen, covering her mouth with her hand, wondering if she'd caught the right name. But then she realised how stupid she was being. She had definitely heard the reporter say Suzi Porter. The report had also said Red Street in Longton. Rhian had only ever sat outside number twenty-two in Joe's car but she had been told a lot about it by Joe's son, Jayden.

Red Street was where he lived with his mum.

Suzi Porter was Joe's ex-wife.

Chapter Eleven

'Are you sure it was her?' Joe got out of bed quickly. He grabbed for a shirt from the wardrobe.

'Of course I'm sure!' Rhian stepped back before he knocked her out of the way in his haste. 'It said her name and her address.'

'What else did it say?'

'That she died of multiple stab wounds last night.'

'What time – do you know?'

'It didn't say.'

'Fuck!' Joe ran a hand through his hair. 'Do they think it was Kelvin?'

'No, they questioned him but he's been released.' Rhian paused. 'Joe –'

'This has nothing to do with me!'

'I know that, but . . .' Rhian stepped forward again. 'Well, the police are bound to question you, too.'

'Why would they do that?'

'You're family.'

'I *was* family.' Joe pulled on a pair of jeans. 'She's my ex.'

'You see?' Rhian drove home her point. 'So it would be better if *I* knew where you really were last night.'

'I told you! I was at work.'

'I can tell you're cagey about something – and if I can, so will the police.' She sighed. 'If I need to cover for you, I will, but you have to tell me what you were doing.'

'I wasn't anywhere near Suzi's house. Christ, I need to get over to see Jayden.' Joe paused. 'He'll have to come and stay with us.'

In her haste to tell him the news, Rhian hadn't stopped to think of that. 'I don't think that's a good idea,' she said.

Joe frowned. 'Why not?'

'He's going to be traumatised. Maybe he'd be better staying with Kelvin and Ollie, people he's with all the time.'

'I'm his father, for fuck's sake. I know him better than anyone.'

'You know what I mean.' Rhian went to him and touched his arm. 'Ollie is his brother. You can't split them up when they've both lost their mum.'

Joe gave a dry laugh, its tone nasty. 'Don't worry. I knew he wouldn't be able to stay here. You're hardly mother material, are you?'

'Joe!' Rhian dropped her hand as if she'd been burnt by his touch.

'Well, you're not, are you? You're too full of yourself to care about anyone else.' Joe stopped. 'I need to take a shower.'

'But you've just got dressed! Joe – Joe!'

Joe turned back to her as he got to the en-suite. 'You tell the police nothing, do you hear?'

'I don't have anything to tell them.' Rhian scowled. 'But you're clearly hiding something.'

He grabbed her roughly by the arm and pulled her near, until she was an inch away from his face. 'Nothing! Do you hear?'

'Yes! I hear you.' Rhian tried to shrug away her arm. 'Let go, you're hurting me!'

'Say it!'

Follow the Leader 87

'I won't tell them anything!'

Joe pushed her away before slamming the door in her face. She moved to sit on the edge of the unmade bed. Christ, the morning was going from bad to worse.

There had been no love lost between her and Suzi. Neither of them had liked each other from the moment they had met. Yet, even though they'd been divorced for a long time, any moron could see that Suzi still had feelings for Joe. Rhian cast her mind back – what had she called her when they'd first been introduced? A trophy girlfriend, something young to show off on his arm. Suzi had told Joe that he was having a mid-life crisis. Suzi had told *her*, very unkindly she'd thought, that Joe was on the rebound and needed to be careful of people like her – the cheeky bitch. They'd been separated for seven years by that time – how the hell could Joe be on the rebound?

God, but dead. As shocked as Rhian was, though, she couldn't help but think that Suzi Porter had got what she deserved. She was a bitch – Joe was always telling her that. And it did get her out of the picture for good now – despite the circumstances, Rhian was definitely thankful for that. Perhaps now Joe would be able to concentrate on her more often too. He'd always been sloping off to meet Suzi, saying there was a problem with Jayden that she wanted to discuss with him.

A cold shiver ran through her. Had they really been meeting to discuss Jayden? She frowned as her mind went into overdrive. Something wasn't adding up and she was determined to find out what it was.

Where had Joe really been all those nights he said he'd been working late?

Joe stripped off again quickly, stepped into the shower and turned on the water. As the spray poured over him, he lifted his face, letting his tears mingle for a moment before slapping his palm against the tiled wall. He wanted to scream, but Rhian would hear him. How could Suzi be dead?

But then panic set in. Rhian was right. The police would come sniffing around; he'd be one of the first suspects. It was always the family who were questioned first. This was such bad timing for him. But, more to the point, he couldn't believe the stupid bitch would even *begin* to question him about where he was last night.

Fuck – what if the police started digging around to see what he was really doing? And if Ryder got wind that he was to blame for bringing the law into his offices, then he'd be in trouble anyway. Screwed, no matter which way he turned.

Joe had worked as general manager at Car Wash City for three years, ever since the last manager had disappeared and Terry Ryder had been sent to prison. Before that, he'd worked for Terry doing one odd job or another for over ten years. The car washes were legitimate businesses – they raked in a fair bit of money each week throughout the city. But the police didn't know what Ryder had really been up to. Joe didn't know either; Terry kept that side of his business close to his chest. And if the police did have intelligence, all six offices would have gone when Terry Ryder was no longer there to look over them.

Working for Terry was lucrative and kept Joe in the style he was accustomed to. He knew that was what Rhian liked about him. She thought he was a player when in reality he was only the caretaker. But he made a purpose of keeping himself to himself, not wanting to trust anyone in this game. He'd heard what happened to people who crossed Ryder and he didn't want any part of it. He enjoyed the money he was paid too much for that. Although it was never enough.

So when Ryan Johnson, another of Terry Ryder's acquaintances, had come with news of a lucrative job, who was he to turn down the opportunity to make a few grand on the quiet? No one would be any the wiser – providing the police didn't come snooping around. Even more so, the job was being sewn up soon so, even though it was lousy timing, he needed to go down to London for a few days next week.

He shuddered again, his thoughts momentarily returning to Jayden. Maybe he would be better staying with Kelvin and his half-brother, Ollie, as long as Kelvin was in a fit state to look after them right now. Kelvin would most probably stay with family, or at a hotel. Until the police had completed all the forensics and removed all traces of the murder, Joe supposed he wouldn't be allowed back into the house. That's if he ever wanted to return there. Suzi was bound to have shed some blood.

Pushing aside his guilt, he convinced himself it was the right thing to do. More than likely, Kelvin would want to keep both boys with him anyway – they'd grown up together since Ollie had been born. Yes, he'd persuade Kelvin that they would be grieving for their mum – let them stay together for a while and then once this job was over, they could work out what was best for them.

Nothing could go wrong – an injection of cash was all he needed and he'd be okay for a while.

As investigations continued that morning around the murders of Mickey Taylor and Suzi Porter, Allie left Perry with a team of officers going house-to-house on Red Street and Sam with a list of tasks that Nick had given to her during the morning's briefing. While they cracked on with those, at Nick's instruction she went to see both Suzi Porter's husband and ex-husband.

Kelvin Porter was staying at his parents' house. Allie wondered if he might not ever go back to live in Red Street. She knew she wouldn't be strong enough to live with the memories; she'd already had quite a job compartmentalising the image she had of Suzi Porter slumped on the chair. Every time Kelvin went into their kitchen, he might see her sitting there, dripping blood, tied up for all to see.

Allie had learned that Suzi Porter had two sons. The youngest one, Oliver, was five and from her marriage to Kelvin, and the oldest, ten-year-old Jayden, was from her previous marriage to Joseph Tranter. Both boys had lived with their mother. Allie thanked the Lord for small mercies that neither of them had been home that evening. But she hadn't ruled out the possibility that the killer might have known this – was it convenience or coincidence that he'd struck on that particular night?

Trentham was in the south of the city and a couple of miles from the Porters' home in Longton. Allie walked up a path beside a well-kept garden and knocked on the door of a large semi-detached house. A minute later, she was shown into their living room by Kelvin's mother.

Mr Porter stood up as he spotted her. 'Is there any news?' he asked.

Allie could hear the plea in his voice. 'We're making lots of enquiries at the moment, Mr Porter.' She pointed to the settee. 'May I sit down?'

'Yes, of course.' He sat down again across from her.

'Would you like a cup of tea?' Mrs Porter asked.

'Yes, thanks.' Allie looked up with a smile, instinctively knowing the woman would feel better if she had something to do.

'It's a good job I have her at the moment,' Kelvin sighed as Mrs Porter bustled from the room. 'My father died a few years ago now and she's been like a rock ever since.'

'Did she get on well with Suzi?'

'Not really.' Kelvin's eyes dropped to the floor momentarily. 'I think they tolerated each other, mostly.'

'Oh?'

'Mum never felt good enough. I couldn't tell her otherwise. But Suzi had a way of doing that to people, making them feel small without trying. She always needed to be the centre of attention and, well, you know kids when they visit their nan. She spoils them and Suzi didn't like it.'

'I thought that's what nans were for,' Allie smiled kindly, noting the box of neatly piled toys in the corner of the room. 'I wanted to ask you a few more things about Suzi. About Joseph Tranter, too.'

Allie watched him nod his head in recognition, waited for a reaction. But the mention of Joseph's name didn't stir up any kind of emotion.

'I'm not much for the bloke but I got on quite well with him, despite Suzi's attempts to make me do otherwise.'

Allie nodded. 'Divorces often leave couples unable to communicate without becoming angry.'

Kelvin shook his head at this. 'She tried to twist Jayden against him, too – that's the elder boy, their son.'

'That's a shame.' Allie paused. 'How did she do that?'

'She'd often bad-mouth him, try to stop Joe having access – you know, the usual nonsense. But, like I mentioned, I always found him okay.'

'When was the last time you saw Mr Tranter?'

Kelvin frowned. 'A couple of weeks back. It would have been on a Sunday, when he picked Jay up. He sees him every other weekend; collects him on Sunday morning and drops him off around six the same evening. As far as I can see, he dotes on the boy. I'm sure he would have seen him more if Suzi had let him.'

'And how do you think he felt about your wife?'

'Jay or Joe?'

'Both, really. How was she with them?'

'Jay's a good kid, considering his earlier upbringing.'

'And Mr Tranter?'

'I'm not sure they ever got on that well. Two big egos together – it doesn't work, does it?' Kelvin's shoulders rose up defensively. 'From what Suzi told me, he used to knock her about a bit. I think that's why she's insecure now. It was all an act – I loved her for it but hated it too.'

'She was a little difficult at times?' Allie hoped to sound sympathetic rather than probing.

Kelvin smiled tenderly. 'She often tried my patience.'

'Do you think Joe still had a lot to do with Suzi?'

'Personally I think he was glad he was out of it but he still wanted to see his son. Although he was always badgering Suzi for cash. She was always bailing him out for something or other. We used to argue about it all the time. But she defended him, saying he'd helped her get to where she was today.' Kelvin shrugged. 'I didn't like it, but what could I do?'

'And you, Mr Porter? How did you find Suzi?'

'Sometimes lovely, sometimes crazy, depending on her mood.'

'Did it not bother you what she did for a living?'

'Not really, but she hadn't been getting much work in lately. Said they were always going for younger models now. She'd been doing lingerie ads only for the past couple of years.'

'You mentioned in your statement that you'd been arguing. Was Suzi in a bad mood when you left the house?'

'She'd come home from work feeling sorry for herself. She was going to come to the club and have a meal with me but as soon as she got home, she started drinking. She's not an alcoholic,' he said quickly. 'There was a bottle of wine open. I told her not to have too much as she would be driving over to meet me, and she started arguing. So I left her to it.'

He looked away then, tears welling in his eyes. Allie waited while he composed himself before asking him any more questions.

'Where did you meet?' Before he could reply, she continued, 'Suzi went to Reginald High School. Did you go there too?'

'No, I went to Trentham High, not far from here. I met Suzi at work when she started going to the gym.'

'Do you know any of her school friends?'

'I knew a few on sight but we didn't have anything to do with any of them, apart from Joe, obviously.' Kelvin shook his head. 'Suzi was called Sandra at school. Did you know that?'

Allie nodded, glad when Mrs Porter came in with drinks. She wasn't sure what reason she would have given if he had asked why she wanted to know about the school.

Chapter Twelve

Joseph Tranter's name hadn't been as familiar to Allie as Mickey Taylor's or Suzi Porter's when she had first heard mention of him going to Reginald High School too. She made a mental note to check with Perry once she got back to the station, see if he could remember anything more about him now.

As she was shown into the living room of his home, Allie realised she wouldn't be seeing Joe in his best light anyway. He was a tall and broad man with greying, sharply cut hair, but his dark eyes were bloodshot, and he had the ashen look of shock on his face.

'Mr Tranter?' Allie produced her warrant card again. 'My name is Detective Sergeant Shenton.'

The woman who had shown her into the room moved to stand next to Joe in front of a marble fireplace, eyeing Allie with an expression she couldn't quite fathom yet. She looked mid-twenties at a guess, with blonde wavy hair, far too much make-up for Allie's liking and not enough meat on her frame either. She'd obviously been a smoker in her time, lines already appearing above her top lip, which might explain why she was stick-thin apart from an enormous bust.

Allie sat down at Joe's request, her eyes drawn for an instant to a collection of studio photos of a young boy on the wall, next to several of the couple. A black gym bag was on the floor in front of an armchair with a fleece jacket flung over it. Joe moved them out of the way before sitting down too.

'I assume you know why I'm here,' Allie told them. 'I'm investigating the murder of Suzi Porter.'

'Who happens to be his *ex*-wife.' The young woman spoke matter-of-factly.

'And you are?' Allie stared at her pointedly.

'Rhian Jamieson. I'm Joe's girlfriend – have been for some time now.'

'Two years,' Joe quantified. 'We've been together for two years.'

'And we're totally in love and happy, aren't we, Joe?' Rhian walked over to him and slipped her hand into his, immaculate nails sparkling with a layer of silvery glitter. 'So you can't get him for murdering *her* as he was with me last night.'

'I assume the police are here to eliminate me from their enquiries,' Joe pointed out, looking at his girlfriend with barely concealed impatience. 'Isn't that right?'

'Yes, that's right.' Undeterred by the sudden outburst, Allie opened her notepad and addressed him. 'I believe there was no love lost between you and your ex-wife, Suzi Porter, Mr Tranter?'

'You could say that. The only good thing to come out of the marriage was Jayden, our son.'

'Where did you meet Suzi?'

'We'd known each other since we were at school.'

'Which school was that?'

'Reginald High.' Joe frowned. 'You don't think that has anything to do with this, do you? Except that, well, I knew Mickey Taylor too. We both did – me and Suzi, that is. We used to hang around together in a big group.'

'Were you in the same class?' Allie asked another question instead of answering his.

'No, but we were in the same year. I think there were five forms in each one, if I remember rightly. We did share lots of lessons, though.'

'And did you date at high school?'

'A couple of times. But we started seeing each other seriously once we'd left.'

Allie wrote in her notepad before looking up again. 'Can you tell me where you were last night around seven p.m.?'

'Here,' he replied. 'We were both in at that time.'

'Doing?'

'I'm sorry but that's hardly any business of yours,' Rhian retorted.

'What usually happens here,' Allie's tone was just as sharp, 'is that if you say you were watching television, I would ask you what you were watching – specifically around seven p.m. – and then you would tell me.'

'I can't remember. I bet she had that *One Show* program on, though.' Joe laughed, and then tried to hide behind a cough.

'So you were both at home at seven p.m.?' asked Allie.

'Yes,' said Joe.

Allie looked at Rhian.

'Yes,' she said finally.

If the pregnant pause wasn't enough for Allie to deduce that she was lying, the blush that was spreading up from her chest was.

'Yes,' Rhian repeated before Allie dropped her eyes. 'I remember now. We were watching *The One Show*.'

'Did you get on with Suzi's parents, Mr Tranter?' Allie turned back to him.

'I hadn't seen them in years before we split. I don't think Suzi had either.' He raised his eyebrows and looked at her meaningfully. 'They didn't like what she was doing.'

'Well, would you like it if your daughter got her kit off for every Tom, Dick and Harry?' Rhian scoffed. 'It must have been right under their nose every time they went into a shop!'

Allie ignored her again. 'But it didn't bother you, Mr Tranter?'

He shrugged. 'She brought in the money. That was all I was interested in at the end. And Jay.'

'What do you do now for work?'

'I run a chain of car washes.'

'Car washes?' Allie bristled. There was only one successfully run chain in the city that she knew of, with a base in each of the six towns. 'As in Car Wash City?'

'Yes, I oversee them all from the Longton office. You know of them?'

Momentarily thrown by memories rushing at her, Allie took a moment to compose herself. 'Your boss would have been Terry Ryder?' she said, trying to keep the shake from her voice.

'My boss *is* Terry Ryder,' he corrected.

'That's hardly likely, considering he's in prison.'

'I'm keeping an eye on things until he comes out.'

'Good luck with that,' Allie muttered. It was her turn to blush. She turned to focus on a bemused-looking Rhian.

'When did you last see Mrs Porter?' she asked.

Rhian baulked. 'Don't tell me I'm a suspect too! I hardly know the woman. She never lets me near her precious son.'

'He's my son, too,' said Joe.

'Whatever.' Rhian sat down next to Joe and folded her arms. 'I haven't seen her in months and even then it was from the passenger seat of his car. I was never allowed near her, Miss Bloody Perfect.'

'Did she see you as a threat?'

Rhian smirked. 'Of course she did.' She swept a hand over her figure. 'She was getting on and I was taking her man.'

'For God's sake, Rhian.' Joe shook his head. 'Show a little respect – the woman has been murdered.'

'I know and I'm sorry about that, but I'm not going to be treated like a suspect. I had nothing at all to do with her death. I can't see –'

'Why are you so angry, Miss Jamieson?' Allie interrupted. 'I'm establishing facts: it's my job. It's what I do.'

'It's *her* – Suzi.' Rhian sat down and folded her arms. 'It's *always* about her. Everything we do – everything we want to do. Suzi comes first. She was such a bitch at times. Always demanding – always getting her own way.'

'Sounds like someone else I know,' Joe mumbled.

Rhian glared at him.

'When did you and Suzi split up?' Allie turned to Joe again.

'Ten years ago, just after Jay was born.'

'And how did you get on with her once you'd split? You divorced, I assume?'

Joe nodded. 'She couldn't wait to get rid of me. But she wouldn't let me take Jay. Not sure what will happen with him now. I'm going to see him this afternoon.'

'How did you find things after you'd left? It must have been hard going to collect Jayden and seeing her too?'

'Not really. I picked him up on the corner of the street most of the time. Or Kelvin, her husband, would bring him here. It saved falling out.'

Allie took a moment to write down a few more notes and then looked up at him again. 'Just one more question, Mr Tranter. How did you feel about her . . . career choice?'

Rhian tutted but they both ignored her.

'She started off modelling clothes but when someone suggested she could make more money going topless, she was all for it. If you knew Suzi, if she wanted something she got it, no matter what.

I wouldn't have been able to stop her. She was stubborn, didn't care if it upset anyone. I knew a bloke who'd take a few photos and hooked her up with him. If anyone was going to take those kinds of photos, I wanted to be present.'

Allie closed her notebook.

'What happens now?' Joe asked as they all stood up.

'We'll be in touch if we need to clarify anything,' Allie told him.

Rhian glared at her. 'Christ, you still don't believe us.'

'Everything has to be checked, Miss Jamieson.' Allie threw her a warning look in return. 'This is a murder enquiry.'

In the hallway, before she left, Allie turned back and handed Joe her card. 'If you need to talk about anything – in general or in relation to the conversation we've just had – call in at the station, or ring me. I'm based at Hanley. Ask for DS Shenton.'

'He doesn't know anything,' said Rhian, folding her arms again.

In front of her, Joe's face was screwed up with rage. At least he was trying to keep his thoughts to himself, Allie noted.

Stepping outside, she heard raised voices before she was at the bottom of the drive. She shook her head slightly. What were they lying to cover up? She doubted Joe Tranter had anything to do with the murder of Suzi Porter.

But they were hiding something.

Rhian closed the door after Allie with a bang. When she turned round, Joe had disappeared. She marched into the living room to find it empty, then headed into the kitchen. He stood with his back to her, hands either side on the worktop. As she stepped closer, Rhian noticed they curled into fists but it didn't stop her.

'What's going on?' She prodded him in the shoulder. 'If you were with that . . . trollop last night, then I need to know. I think I have a –'

'The woman is fucking dead.' Joe turned towards her quickly. 'Can't you give it a rest? Of course I wasn't with her.'

'Well, what was all that with the sergeant? You let her walk over you just then, being all nicey-nicey!'

Joe shook his head in exasperation. 'I don't want to give the police any reasons to start snooping around, here or at work. Of *course* I'm going to be nice to her.'

'You really think you can fool the police?'

'I don't fucking have to. I haven't done anything wrong!'

Rhian folded her arms. 'I want to know,' she said. 'Were you screwing Suzi?'

Joe's face twisted in a snarl. He pushed past her and disappeared into the living room.

Rhian followed him quickly. 'You were, weren't you?'

'I'm warning you – leave it!'

'No. If you want me to lie for you, then I want to know –'

Joe came so close to her face that Rhian flinched. She stepped back, her heel catching the settee behind her, and fell backwards onto the cushions.

Joe placed a hand on either side of her and leaned in closer. 'You need to mind your own business.'

Rhian turned away from his menacing eyes, heard him taking deep breaths as she tried to steady her own.

Eventually, Joe spoke. 'I knew I couldn't trust you.'

'Don't say that,' Rhian whispered. 'You can always trust me.'

'I thought I could but now I'm not so sure.'

A lone tear trickled down her face. 'Joe, I –'

He stood up, glared at her for an instant and then stormed out of the room.

'Joe! Wait!'

Joe climbed into his car, sat for a moment, and then banged his hands on the steering wheel. What the hell was that stupid bitch insinuating, coming on so heavy like that? She'd made him feel as if he was hiding something, going over the top with her accusations. What an idiot he was to think he could trust her. He prayed, for both their sakes, that the investigation into Suzi's murder would be over soon, that the police would do their job, catch her killer and life could return to normal. The last thing he needed was the police breathing down his neck. It only took one of the nosy fuckers at work to get word back to Terry and he would be in for it, even without him finding out about the job. Terry wouldn't rest – he'd want to know why the police had been there. It would also lead the police to the cars stored around the back behind the gates.

What a day – and it wasn't even lunchtime. And he had such a busy week planned too. With money in his pocket, he could be a bit choosier about his next job, though, maybe not do anything until later in the year. He just needed to be careful not to get caught. Joe had heard the tales, seen firsthand a few times what Ryder was capable of. And, despite the man being in prison, he knew there were others on the lookout for him outside.

He started the engine and reversed quickly out of the drive. He knew he should go and see that his boy was okay first but his mind wouldn't rest until he'd checked that everything was fine at work. Jayden would have to wait.

As he drove out of Smallwood Avenue, he didn't notice Allie sitting in her car.

Chapter Thirteen

Thursday morning, Allie sat at her desk resting her chin in her hands. It had been twelve hours since they had found the body of Suzi Porter and, apart from a few snatched hours' sleep, work had been non-stop. It was at times like these that she was glad she was a small part in a large team. Yet, even though Nick was constantly asking her to go for inspector, she was happy with her role as sergeant. There was enough paperwork and red tape at her level; she didn't want to move further up and then have to work out strategies and policies and whatnot. She liked the hands-on approach.

Having known both of the victims, plus a lot of the people they would have been at school together with, Allie had given Perry the task of checking out that link.

'There's not enough to piece anything together,' Perry told her as he came back to his desk. 'It does seem that Mickey wasn't ever in trouble again after leaving school.'

'Anyone stand out to you when we spoke to the rest of the staff at the factory on Tuesday?'

'Not really.' Perry got out his notebook and flicked through it. 'No one crossed Mickey because he was fair if you treated him right, you know what I mean?'

'And no other connection between him and Suzi Porter apart from Reginald High School?'

'I've checked with the central library next door. Because our school closed in 1995, they hold exam results but not year registers. Want me to go further afield? It might take a while.'

'Yes, thanks.'

'And, as you know, she was divorced from Joe Tranter, so all three would have known each other. They would have all known me too, for that matter.'

'Yes, I thought so.' Allie nodded. 'Was Tranter in your class or your year?'

'My class,' Perry confirmed.

'He has form, though, doesn't he? Now I remember – he was locked up for theft when I first started in uniform.'

Perry nodded. 'He came in for domestic violence a couple of times when he was married to Suzi. No charges brought against him, though, and nothing since.'

'His story that he was at home when Suzi was murdered doesn't ring true. His girlfriend backs him up but I'm not sure. I might see if I can get her on her own.' Allie thought for a moment. 'He definitely had motive.'

'Although he probably had more to lose in the cash stakes.' Sam passed them each a mug of coffee and sat down, joining in the conversation. 'Records from Financial Forensics Unit show that he got a lump sum when they divorced,' she continued. 'It's all gone now – bank accounts are all but empty and two credit cards maxed out. His salary goes in at the beginning of the month and is spent by the end too.'

'And, according to Kelvin Porter, Suzi was always giving him hand-outs. Said it was for their son, but even he doubted it. I suppose he could just be living beyond his means, like some people do?' Allie said, and then sat quiet for a moment in the noise of the office. 'And then there's this letter business,' she added. 'I wish we could get our heads around it.'

'E. V.' said Perry. 'It's got to be a word being spelt out.'

'Or an anagram?'

'I hope not.' Sam shuddered as she went to pick up a ringing phone. 'That means there will be more killings. Don't like the sound of that. . . . DC Markham.' Her head bobbed down.

Allie glanced across at the photographs of Mickey Taylor and Suzi Porter on the whiteboard in front of them. Several lines written in black marker pen were linking them, but there were lots more with no links at all. Unanswered questions – there were so many of them. She'd feel much better, she assumed they all would, when the evidence had been collated and the pieces began to fit.

'It could be the beginning of lots of words,' said Allie to no one in particular.

Perry swung back and forth on his chair. 'Do you really think it could be something to do with our school?'

'Not ruling anything out yet. After the briefing, let's head over to talk to Kelvin Porter's colleagues. Suzi's a member of the gym there. We should be able to shed some light on their relationship.'

The interest around Suzi Porter's murder was gathering momentum in the press due to her status. So when they arrived at Trentham Country Club, Allie and Perry knew there was bound to be lots of curiosity: staff who wanted to know more, members who wanted to be associated with her, everyone claiming to know more about her than they really did.

The club was set in twelve acres of land on the outskirts of Trentham in the south of the city. The building was fairly new, a modern and minimalistic structure, the mood inside one of calm and optimism.

Allie introduced them both to a young woman sitting at the reception desk.

'I'm Maggie, head receptionist,' she informed them, tapping a manicured nail twice on her name badge. 'We couldn't believe it when we heard.' She didn't give either of them time to reply before continuing. 'Suzi Porter, of all people.'

'Why do you say that, Maggie?' Allie wanted to know.

'Well, everyone knew Suzi. She was a huge celebrity around here. Acted like a right diva, though.' She pushed blonde hair behind her ear. 'Always thought people should be at her beck and call. Always rude, hardly ever friendly. Really up herself, you know.'

'You didn't like her, then,' Perry stated the obvious sarcastically.

'I'm only telling the truth.' Maggie shrugged.

'And it's what we want to hear,' Allie advised. 'We need to build up a picture of Suzi – places she frequented, people she saw, things that she did. Any regular routines and appointments, whom she might see, etcetera. Can you check to see the last time she came in, please?'

'Let me see.' Maggie's fingers tapped on a keyboard. 'She was in on Monday morning. I think that was the last time, yes.' She scrolled the mouse up and down the screen. 'Monday morning. She had a session booked with Tom.' Maggie looked back up at them then. 'Tom is the physiotherapist. He does a great massage.'

'Is he here now?'

'Yes, I saw him come in around nine.'

'Where can we find him?'

'I'll put a call out for you.'

While they waited, Allie stared through the glass wall in front of them into the gym. Rows of pounding feet on treadmills and stationary bikes. A few people dotted here and there on weight machines.

'Ever been here?' she asked Perry.

He pursed his lips. 'Not enough real working out for my liking. I bet the closest that room gets to clients working hard is when someone like Suzi comes in and they're rubbernecking.'

'Not everyone likes pushing heavy weights and growing muscles,' she protested.

'It's all show, if you ask me.' Perry shrugged. 'I like to sweat.'

'I think it's got a good vibe.' Allie saw a young woman lifting a weight that looked twice as heavy as she was. She raised her eyebrows and looked at Perry. 'See, not all show.'

Through the glass they watched as a man walked towards them, the gym logo splashed across his black T-shirt. Allie would put him at mid-thirties. His look gave out a mixed impression – a hint of a bad boy but with the air of someone who cared more about appearance than being able to fight his way out of a situation. The square jaw and close-cut blonde hair might have made him seem menacing, if it weren't for his baby-faced chubby cheeks and cheeky grin.

'Tom Shaw?' Allie held up her warrant card as he walked towards them. 'Might I have a few words?'

'It's about Suzi Porter, isn't it? I can't believe she's been murdered.'

'Yes, can you tell us the last time you saw her?'

'Why?'

'Just routine questions for now.'

Tom looked at them through half-closed eyes. 'I'd have to check in the diary log to be certain – two, maybe three weeks ago.'

'We've already done that.' Allie pointed to the reception where Maggie was trying to look as though she wasn't listening. 'We know she was down to see you on Monday morning.'

'It was a no-show.' He opened the door into the gym. 'She never even rang to say that she wasn't going to make it. I keep my own diary of appointments too.'

'Is she one of your regular clients?' Allie asked as they followed him across the room. She glanced to her side on hearing an almighty growl coming from a man who was lifting weights.

'No, she comes in when she has a spot of backache. She often gets it when she's been standing up all day for a photo shoot.' Purposely, he looked down at Allie's feet, in particular the three-inch narrow heels on her boots. 'Is it any wonder when she wore heels most of the time? You women are martyrs to your beauty.'

Behind Tom, Allie rolled her eyes at Perry. 'Can you see who's around staff-wise and start questioning them too?'

With a nod, Perry disappeared. Allie continued to follow Tom. Up ahead, he unlocked a door and led her through into a small office with a massage couch. As he searched through a filing cabinet, a text beeped in to her. Allie checked it and then put away her phone as Tom turned back, holding a black ring binder.

'Here it is – the last time I saw her was December twenty-second.' Tom showed Allie a spreadsheet for that day's appointment. 'She had an ache in her lower back and I helped to massage it away.'

Seeing him blush the colour of a ripe tomato, Allie decided to wait before continuing.

'I'm not going to admit to anything you can't prove,' he added eventually.

She held up her hand. 'All I want to know is did you see her yesterday?'

'No, I just told you!'

'What time were you here?'

'I was on a late shift. You can check.' He pointed to the file again. 'I was with clients.'

'So were you handing out extras with the massages?'

'I don't follow.'

Allie smiled coyly, dipping her eyes slightly. 'Oh, I think you do.'

Tom coughed. 'They were all men.'

'Ah, not your type.'

'Look, I've already told you that I was here yesterday – two till ten.'

'Yes, you did.' Allie smiled. 'But you could easily have slipped out within those eight hours. I need to rule that out too. So my next question is, did Mrs Porter have any . . . *massages* . . . from anyone else here?'

He shook his head. 'No, I'm the only physiotherapist.'

'Do you know if she was seeing anyone from here?'

'How would I know that?'

'Oh, I'm sure there are lots of rumours that circulate around clubs like these. It's a great place to relax – and I suppose there are bedrooms to hire too?'

'She didn't come to the club that often.' Tom did a fair job of shrugging noncommittally. 'Besides, her husband is the manager here.'

'And was that awkward?'

'Not for me. I have appointments booked for all clients. I just do my job.'

'With the door locked?'

'What?' His brow furrowed.

'Would the door be locked when you were, you know, massaging?' Allie raised her eyebrows.

'Of course the door would be locked. You can't expect people to strip if they think someone might barge in at any time!'

'And that's company policy, is it?'

'Well, no, but –'

'Don't you think that could be open to misinterpretation? What if someone said that you molested them when the door was locked?'

Tom paled. 'She didn't say that, did she?'

'She wasn't in any fit state to speak.' Allie shook her head. 'She was murdered, Mr Shaw. Do any of the other staff know about the extras you provide?'

'Of course they don't!'

'So you didn't see her yesterday at all?' Allie repeated purposely.

Tom looked at her sharply. 'No.'

'Because if you did,' Allie paused for effect, 'and she went home without taking a shower . . . Or if you *did* happen to have sex that very afternoon, well then, once the forensics come back, there may be traces of you on or inside her.'

'I wasn't with her!' Tom raised his hands in surrender. 'And I didn't see her on Monday. She was booked in for nine thirty a.m. I was pretty pissed off about it at the time but I'm actually feeling quite lucky now. At least you can't pin this on me.'

'We don't *pin* things on anyone. This isn't an episode of *Life on Mars*. This is real life.'

'I – I didn't mean that,' he said.

Allie took out her card and handed it to him. 'Let me know if you think of anything that might be of interest.' She pressed it into his hand. 'And I sincerely hope that your story of events is corroborated by what other staff members will tell us, Mr Shaw.'

Allie left the room and went to find Perry.

'Anything?' he asked when he saw her.

'Well, Suzi Porter was into the extras provided by Tom Shaw,' she said quietly.

'Motive?'

'Possibly.' Allie waggled her phone in the air. 'But I've just had a message from Dave. We'll need to check prints, plus see where he was early Monday morning, but unless Tom Shaw killed Mickey Taylor too, he's in the clear. Dave says he's found the same set of fingerprints on both magnetic letters. We have ourselves a double murder investigation.'

Chapter Fourteen

'I can't believe they both had something to do with your school,' said Lisa, snuggling in next to Perry as they got into bed that night.

'Yeah, it's mad.' Perry pulled his pillow down a little. 'It's freaky too.'

'Freaky?' Lisa baulked. 'It's bloody well scary, if you ask me. Are you sure you're not in danger? I mean, how do you know that you won't be next?'

'Because I'm special, Lees. It's not my time yet.'

'It had better not be.'

Perry grinned to lighten the mood. 'You wouldn't be able to cope without me, would you?'

'I wouldn't go that far.'

'You wouldn't!' he teased.

'I might not be able to change a tyre on the car if I had a flat – but, equally, I know a man who can.' Lisa grinned.

'Lost,' he added. 'You'd be lost without me.'

'I think you'll find that's the other way around. I made you into what you are. So I –'

Perry laughed. 'I was fine before I met you.'

'You had terrible dress sense, your hair was a mess and you looked old before your time.'

Perry pulled her on top of him. Lisa squealed, trying to wriggle out of his grip as he began to kiss her. He slipped his hand inside her top and ran his fingers lightly up and down her back. Then he rolled over and on top of her, burying his face in her cleavage for a moment as she squealed again.

'This is where I belong,' he said, turning serious at last. 'This is what I'd miss and this is what no one is taking from me.' He kissed her again, more urgently as she responded.

Sleep after sex always came easy for Perry but he was awake again in the early hours. He checked the clock: quarter past two. Lisa slept soundly beside him. He listened to her breathing, watched her shape in the dark. Although he'd joked about her being lost without him, he knew it would be the opposite way around. They'd met on a boozy holiday in San Antonio, Ibiza eight years ago. He'd been on a lads' holiday and she'd been with her friends on a long hen weekend. He'd seen her a few times in different bars throughout the evening. She was small and thin to his tall and bulky, with long blonde hair and a perfect smile she threw his way. When she smiled a few times more, he'd gone over to chat to her. In the last bar, they'd hooked up.

He couldn't believe it when she said she came from Stoke-on-Trent — but it was the last week in June and, back then, that was the traditional time that the pottery firms would close down for two weeks' annual holiday. Even people who didn't work 'in the pots' often had two weeks off then with partners or friends and, in popular resorts, the bars would be full of Stokies, so much so that it could almost feel like home from home.

He'd spent the next day and night with her before she'd left, and he'd stayed on for a further four days. And as soon as the plane had landed in Manchester and he'd got back home, the first thing he'd done was arrange to meet her again. They'd married three years later.

Did she feel safe with him, he wondered? Protected, even? She always said she did. But could he protect her if he didn't know what they were up against? Despite fooling around with her earlier, the case was playing on his mind, the fact that he knew both victims getting to him more than knowing that they were now linked.

Lisa stirred in her sleep and turned away from him. He snuggled into her back, pulling her body in close. Breathing the scent of her hair, he swallowed. No bastard was going to take this away from him.

The Longton office of Car Wash City was on King Street, half a mile from where Joe and Rhian lived in Smallwood Avenue. Early at his desk the following morning, Joe stretched up his arms and yawned. Fuck, what a night; even he could smell alcohol on his breath despite gargling with breath freshener twice before leaving the house. He was surprised he'd managed to drag himself in at all after the drink he'd consumed last night. After comforting Jayden and chatting with Kelvin, who luckily had agreed it would be better to leave the boys together with him for now, he'd been glad to get out of the oppressive atmosphere. But he'd been unable to stop thinking of Suzi so had headed for the Duke of Wellington pub. Once he'd sat down at the bar, everyone there had wanted to talk about Suzi too. After a few pints, he'd given his keys to the landlord and staggered home just before midnight.

The house had been in darkness. He was hoping Rhian had stayed up so he could apologise and keep her sweet, but the stupid cow had turned off all the lights and gone to bed. Instead of waking her and starting a row, he'd collapsed in the spare room to sleep it off. And, even though he'd had the bed to himself and had slept a heavy drunken sleep, he was aching all over.

He swore loudly, banging his fist on the desk. What an idiot he was telling Rhian that he didn't trust her. Of course he didn't, but spitting it out like that was a sure recipe for disaster.

The door to the office opened and Ryan Johnson came in. Joe's shoulders sagged. Christ, that was all he needed.

'Problem, Ryan?' he asked, glancing up at the bear of a man in a thick black overcoat, a stripy scarf knotted at his neck.

'We need to move on this job, Joe. It's getting out of hand.'

'What do you mean?'

'I'm hearing rumours that we're under surveillance.'

Joe sat forwards. 'What the fuck?'

'How many of the seven do we have?'

'Only five.'

'Can we get another two?'

'For next weekend? Not that quickly.' Joe bit at the skin around his thumbnail. 'And I need to be careful.'

'Why?'

'The old bill are all over me at the moment.'

Ryan folded his arms. 'Jesus Christ, Joe. What the fuck have you been up to?'

'I haven't done anything! Suzi Porter – the woman who was murdered on Wednesday night – she's my ex-wife.'

'Fuck!' Ryan's eyes widened. 'Do the police know who did it yet?'

Joe shook his head. 'They didn't when they questioned me yesterday.'

'They *questioned* you?' Ryan took a step forward.

'I'm family! Well, I was. But I haven't done anything I need to cover up. Not with Suzi, anyway.'

Ryan gnawed at his bottom lip. 'We need to get this job out of the way, this weekend rather than next. Are you good to go on Sunday?'

'I – I don't know. It's going to be difficult.'

'Why?'

'My son needs me. He's only ten.'

'But this job needs to be finished!'

'What if the police need to question me again, start wondering where I am? Or come sniffing around here because I'm not at home? Then we'll be in bother.'

Ryan questioned with a frown. 'You sure you weren't involved?'

'No, I fucking wasn't!'

'Then you have nothing to worry about.' Ryan paused. 'We can be there and back in a couple of days if we push the work through. We'll get paid for what we give him for now. Then when things settle down your end again, we can get the other two. Okay?'

'I suppose. And he'll pay for five?'

'Oh, he'll pay for them one way or another.' Ryan nodded. 'I'll see to that.'

'I don't want any trouble.' Joe held up his hands.

'Then don't give me any grief.' Ryan moved to the door and Joe followed him. 'I'll be here about ten thirty on Sunday morning.'

Joe nodded, watched him leave. Outside, he could see three cars being washed down, several young blokes rushing around earning their pay. The camaraderie was good, but he couldn't see himself ever doing menial jobs like that again to earn his crust. However, he did need his money to keep coming in, no matter how dangerous it was to continue.

Right now, though, it seemed even more imperative to keep Rhian sweet, to make sure the police didn't pick up any scent of what he was up to. He reached for his phone, made a call. After yesterday's fiasco at home, he doubted that she'd be pleased about his latest plans, so it was even more essential that he keep her on side for now.

Rhian held in her anger as she sat drinking coffee in the kitchen. From morning until night yesterday, she'd heard nothing but Suzi Porter's name. If she switched on the radio or the television she was there. A few of her friends rang but all they wanted to talk about was Suzi. Even her mum had been quizzing her every day since on the phone. Suzi seemed to be such news in the city, completely overshadowing the murder of the other bloke; Rhian even found mention of her when she checked her Twitter account on her phone. It was as if she had come back to haunt her.

By her side, a message flashed up on her phone.

'Hey, babe. Give me a call – wondered if you'd heard any more about Suzi yet? Is it true she was gutted like a fish? Euw. Hugs, speak soon. Bx'

Rhian huffed at the friendly attitude of the so-called mate that she hadn't seen in at least a year. All she wanted was the gossip, and she wouldn't give her that, even if she did know something. Beth was just being nosy.

She raked a hand through her hair and switched on the television. But all she was greeted with was *her* again. How had she become so famous? Rhian fumed. Still, she had more important things to think of right now.

She was still bristling from Joe's words the day before. Who did he think he was, saying that he couldn't trust her? It was the worst insult of them all. But what hurt the most was that she couldn't stop thinking of the look that had gone between Joe and that sergeant halfway through the conversation. It was as if they both knew some sort of sordid secret at the mention of Car Wash City. Rhian knew all about Joe's past and that he had been into prison when he was younger – two stretches for theft, a few months each time. Had that woman put him away for one of them? Was there history between them?

To make matters worse, Joe hadn't come home until well after midnight. She hadn't been asleep when he'd closed the front door noisily before bundling himself off to the spare room. Even across the landing she could hear him snoring loudly, the slumber of someone who'd had a skinful.

She'd still been annoyed when she'd heard him sneak in early that morning, rifle through his drawers, open and shut the wardrobe door. It wasn't even light so she'd pretended to sleep, hoping that he'd kiss her awake, chat to her, say he was sorry. But nothing.

She'd stayed in bed until he'd left. And now she was stuck here, not knowing if he'd be out all day or when he'd come home. He hadn't even sent her a text message that she could ignore. Nevertheless, having time to think on her own, she realised it was in her best interests to get on his good side again. Joe was okay in small doses. And she did love him in her own way, even if she didn't intend on staying with him forever. She could play along just as he wanted her to.

She logged on to her laptop and idly began to flick through her favourite clothes websites, looking for a black coat in particular. If there was this much interest in Suzi's murder, there was a possibility that TV crews could cover the funeral. She needed to get herself something special to wear. The thought instantly cheered her up.

She was drinking her second mug of coffee when she heard Joe's car pull into the drive. She raced to the mirror to check her appearance. God, she looked good. She smiled at her reflection, then pouted. Maybe this could be an ideal time to have some make-up sex: she only had a couple of nail appointments today and they were both booked in for late afternoon. She rushed back to the breakfast bar just as he appeared in the doorway.

He took a few steps towards her and pulled a bouquet of red roses from behind his back. 'I'm sorry,' he said.

'For which part?'

'All of it.'

'You said some horrible things to me.' She conjured tears ready to fall.

'I didn't mean any of them.' He held out the flowers for her. Tentatively, she took them from him.

'I panicked when I saw the police,' he explained.

'Did you go to see Jayden?'

'Yeah, I stayed chatting to Kelvin for ages.'

'It's a good job you get on so well with him.'

'I know. It was Suzi who caused the friction.' He paused. 'I'm sorry,' he said again.

'I'm sorry too.' Rhian stepped closer to him and pressed a finger to his lips. 'It's in the past, yeah?'

He pulled her into his arms and she buried her face in his chest, hiding the grin spreading widely across her face. God, he was such a pushover. He might have a temper every now and again, and clearly she had to watch what she was doing, but she could handle him. And what she needed to do right now was keep him sweet until she found out more about what he had really been doing on Wednesday evening.

This old man, he played three,
He played knick-knack on his knee.
With a knick-knack, paddy-whack,
Give the dog a bone.
This old man came rolling home.

1984

Patrick jumped from sleep and sat up in bed, the bass tone of the music reverberating through the floorboards. Elvis Presley began to sing of being lonesome tonight. Rubbing at one eye, he pressed the button at the side of his cheap digital watch to illuminate the time: two thirty-three a.m.

The house was cold and he snuggled back under the covers. He heard voices, low mumbling. Who had Ray brought back with him this time? Sometimes it would be a man to have more drink with. Sometimes it would be a woman and he'd hear them, having sex. It was disgusting. Sometimes there would be a few people and he'd cower in bed, praying that the door wouldn't open.

But then he heard a woman giggle. It was followed by heavy footsteps, taking the stairs in four jumps. The handle on his bedroom door dropped, the door flying wide open with the kick of a boot. It bounced back off the wall, causing Ray to stagger slightly as it knocked him off balance. Patrick sat still as a stone in the dark, watching his father's silhouette against the light from the hallway, and hoped he wouldn't piss himself again

'What are you doing in bed, you idle fucker?' Ray slurred, swaying towards him across the room.

Patrick prayed that Ray had drunk enough booze to collapse when he got to his bed. Maybe he'd sink to the floor in a drunken stupor, like he'd done last week, and he could sneak past him and go to sleep on the rickety settee downstairs.

No such luck tonight. The duvet was yanked away and thrown to the floor like a discarded Durex. Patrick curled up in a ball, skin and bone beneath his pyjamas, bracing himself for the onslaught of punches that was bound to come. Fresh bruises atop of ones that hadn't yet healed from his last attack.

Ray grabbed his arm and dragged him out of bed. 'Come on, downstairs!' he demanded. 'It's party time.'

Eleven years old, undernourished and weak, Patrick wasn't strong enough to protest. From above, he could smell Ray's rotten breath as he kept a firm hand on his arm.

At the living room door, he pushed him forward. 'I have a surprise for you, short-arse.'

The woman sitting on the settee reminded Patrick of his English teacher, Mrs Martin. She always had long hair tied in a ponytail and red lipstick. But she was never dressed in a short skirt, with a fake-fur jacket that looked like its owner, a little worse for its years. And she always smelled nice. This woman smelt like Ray.

'Hellooooo,' she slurred, beckoning him over to the settee. 'Come and sit down next to me.'

Patrick stayed rooted to the spot until Ray put his fist in his back and pushed him forward again. He perched at the other end of the settee as far away as he could get.

'What's your name?' she asked, making a big show of moving towards him.

'Patrick.'

'Patrick!' She burst into raucous laughter.

Patrick didn't think his name was funny.

'So, this is your old man, then?' She held out her hand and Ray came over to them. 'I wonder if he takes after you, Raymond.' She gave Ray's bicep muscle a quick squeeze, laughing again.

'This is Molly,' Ray told Patrick. 'And she wants to have some fun tonight.'

'Yes, with both of you.' She turned to Patrick, running the tip of her tongue across her top lip. She reached over for him and he moved back as far as he could go.

'What's wrong?' She came nearer still, until she was an inch from his face. 'Don't you fancy me? We could have some fun.'

'Stop it!' Patrick grabbed hold of the collar of his pyjama top, pulling it close to his neck.

Molly took hold of his chin. Then she puckered her lips. 'Come on, little fella. Let's see what you've got for me.'

Patrick closed his eyes tightly, hoping the vomit would stay inside his throat.

'Open your eyes,' she told him.

When he refused, she squeezed his chin harder.

'Open them!'

Patrick did as she asked.

She peered at him for a moment, and then burst out laughing again. 'The look on your face, you big numpty,' she cried. 'I don't want a boy, I want a man.' She turned back to Ray, who had his trousers unbuckled in readiness. 'I just wanted someone to watch.'

Patrick shivered. 'I don't want to.'

Ray glared at him. 'I don't give a fuck what you do or don't want to do. You'll do as I say.'

Patrick made a run for the door.

Ray blocked his way. Pushing him down into the armchair, he clouted him across the head. 'Now, son, we can do this the hard way or the easy way. The hard way will be just as much fun for me, so . . .'

Patrick pressed himself into the back of the chair, pulled his legs up and wrapped his arms around his knees. Maybe he could just pretend to watch and then they would both fall asleep.

Ray kissed Molly for a few moments, hands all over her breasts. Then he bent her over the settee, slid his hand inside Molly's skirt and, a few seconds later, entered her roughly from behind. He grabbed a handful of her hair and wrenched back her neck as she laughed again.

'Whore,' he hissed, his breath coming in short bursts. 'Filthy, stinking whore. No one else would have you. No one else would want to fuck you. You're lucky to be with me.' He pushed her head forward again. 'Don't look at me, bitch.'

Patrick covered his ears while they were too busy to notice him. He'd never be rid of the images of Ray pumping her and grunting like a pig.

All at once it was over. Ray thrust hard one last time and they collapsed together on the settee.

Patrick sat there for what seemed like an eternity. He wanted to leave the room, go back to his bed and put his head underneath the covers. Escape from it all. But if he did that, one of them might see him. They might come up to his room; he couldn't allow that. It was his sanctuary – he didn't want that tarnished too.

Fifteen minutes later, when his father's breathing had slowed, he watched as Molly inched her way from beneath him. Slowly, she slid to the floor.

'I need the toilet,' she said to him. 'Where is it?'

He pointed upwards.

She winked at him. 'You can go now, you little squirt.'

Patrick tiptoed out of the room and up the stairs. When he was back in his room, as quietly as he could, he pulled on clothes and trainers and got under the covers. If Ray came to get him again, he would have enough time to leg it out of the front door and come back when he was sober.

Chapter Fifteen

On the outskirts of Hanley, Frank Dwyer stumbled out of The Sneyd Arms pub, pulled his collar in close and tucked his hands in his pockets. Ignoring the police car with its lights on disco alert, the scream of a woman as the man she was with was arrested and held against a wall by two police officers, he continued past. He sniggered to himself: just another happy night out for someone.

The bitter wind caught his breath, stinging his cheeks as he pushed against it along Milton Road. At least the whiskey chaser with his last pint had warmed him up. Close to midnight, he started to sing under his breath. 'Oh, Spanish eyes.'

A few minutes later, he pushed open a rickety gate. Staggering down the path to his house, he caught his foot on the slab the council had yet to fix. Almost falling, he steadied himself. He stretched out an arm and hit the door running, with a bang. He laughed: that'll wake the nosy cow next door, like he gave a shit.

After a lot of cursing, he finally opened the door, pulled the key out of the lock again and slammed it shut with his foot. He threw his keys down onto the tiny table behind the door, pulled off his shoes and threw them down too. Swaying slightly, he waited. But all that greeted him was the silence ringing in his ears.

Frank had lived in Queens Road for over twenty years. As the middle house in a row of town-houses, it wasn't much to look at – it had certainly lost its flair soon after Mario had moved out ten years ago – but it was safe and home, and all he had. Yet, even after all this time, he hated coming home to an empty house. Why he'd had to fall out with the man, accuse him of seeing someone on the side, he would never know. Over the years since, he'd had a few flings but it was hard at sixty-seven to find places to pick up blokes.

Next to come off was his jacket, which he hung over the banister; the same too with his shirt. In trousers and an off-white vest, he shuffled through to the tiny kitchen at the back of the house, where he poured himself a large whiskey and knocked it back quickly. He banged the glass down on the worktop, sat down at the table and poured another.

He spent a lot of time here rather than in the living room, not minding the scum that surrounded him. The wall units would have been white if they had seen a cloth in a while; the small worktop to one side was littered with piles of newspapers, junk mail: catalogues for women, leaflets for guttering, Bargain Booze flyers, cheap food at Farm Fresh. Every day there was something new delivered; every day he just added it to the pile. Sometimes, he'd clear them away, shove them in the bin and wait for the mountain to grow again. Tonight, they were at a moderate height that a gust of wind would have great fun with.

There was a knock at the front door just as he was debating whether to pour another whiskey. Peering up at the clock, he sighed and pinched the bridge of his nose. Why couldn't Danny realise that no meant no: why did he insist on coming round to visit? He hadn't been into young boys for a long time.

Ever since he'd made the mistake of letting him and his friends in one night, Danny had been coming back like a boomerang. It wasn't as if Frank didn't like having him around but evil thoughts had resurfaced – thoughts and feelings he'd tried to keep hidden for years. The first time he'd come alone, Frank had sat and watched television with him before throwing him out as he'd wanted to grab a pint. Danny had said he'd be fine staying there by himself, was annoyed when Frank refused, but he still came back the next evening. He wasn't a bad kid, but Frank didn't want to see him all the time. Danny was sixteen years old. Mud sticks – Frank knew all about that. All that trouble he'd got himself into over that bloody boy at Reginald Junior School – and he'd only touched him the once.

He shuffled back to the front door and slung it open. 'If it's food you're after, I don't have much in,' he said not even moving to look who it was before going inside again. But when no one followed him, he went back towards the door.

A man dressed in black stood in the doorway, a thin cardboard box in his hands.

'Yes?' said Frank.

'Someone ordered a pizza, mate.'

'Not me. You must have the wrong address.'

'Thirty-four Queens Road, right?'

'Yeah, but I . . .' Frank laughed. 'The little twat.'

'Excuse me?'

'Danny. He must have ordered it. Hang on a minute.' He searched out his wallet from his coat. 'How much do I owe you?'

'Who the fuck is Danny, Frank?'

Patrick stepped inside and closed the door quietly. When he noticed Frank's eyes dart into the corner of the hallway, he spotted the cricket bat standing in the corner. From where he stood, he knew he was blocking him from reaching it.

'Who the fuck are you?' said Frank. 'Get out of my house. What the hell do you want?'

'No time for questions, Frank. I think your takeaway is getting cold. You wouldn't want to eat it any other way than piping hot.' Patrick flicked open the box, picked up the pizza and, before he could react, rammed it into Frank's face.

Frank let out a yelp. He took a step backwards, pulling at the dough base and rubbing the hot sauce from his face. The pizza slid to the floor. His words were muffled as he wiped at his mouth.

Patrick kicked him in the groin this time.

Frank dropped to his knees with a grunt. Then a fist smashed into his face. He fell backwards, smacking his head on the floor behind him, the thinning carpet providing no protection.

'What do you want?' He put an arm up to protect his face. 'I don't have any money.'

'I don't want your money.'

'What do you want, then?'

Patrick dragged him back up to his feet, pushed him up against the wall. 'We're going to have some fun,' he said. 'Let's play a game.'

'No! Get the fuck away from me.'

Patrick tutted. 'I think you need to learn some manners, Mr Dwyer. Boys should be seen and not heard, isn't that right, Frank? That's what you told me, all those years ago.'

Frank frowned.

'Yes, that's right. Take your mind back to 1983 – I would have been ten.'

'I don't know what you're talking about.'

'Oh, I think you know *exactly* what I'm talking about. You were my P.E. teacher.'

Frank's shoulders sagged. 'It was a mistake. I paid for it,' he said. 'I lost my job, my livelihood – everything!'

'Not because of me. You touched Charlie too. He told his parents, who told the headmaster, and THEN you lost your job. He was listened to, Frank. Whereas me? I had no one to talk to. No one to tell what you did to me that day, what you forced me to do to you.' He took a little satisfaction as panic began to set in for Frank. 'Do you recognise me now?'

Frank nodded.

'So, who am I?'

'I . . . I . . . I can't remember your name.'

'I'll never forget yours.' Patrick removed the knife from his pocket. 'After what you did to me, you sick FUCK! Have you any idea what you put me through?'

The tip of the blade that now rested on Frank's chin rendered him speechless.

'I've used this knife twice already this week.' Patrick stared at Frank, dark eyes shining with menace. 'Mickey Taylor – you remember him? I stabbed him in the stomach – and then the heart and then, who knows?'

Frank whimpered.

'And Sandra Seymour – Sandra Slagbag I called her when I was at school, even though she had small tits at the time. You should see them now – false but huge!'

'Please, don't hurt me.' Frank pushed his head into the wall behind to get away from the blade. 'I changed – I've never touched any boys since then. I just look at pictures, images, anything to stop the urges coming back.'

Patrick brought his head down, relishing his own pain as it connected with Frank's face.

Frank screamed out as blood erupted from his nose, dripping into his mouth.

'Shush, baby.' Patrick's voice now was calm and soothing.

Frank spat in his face.

Patrick roared and raised the knife in the air, bringing it down swiftly into the side of Frank's neck. He smiled manically as Frank struggled, no match for him now. He pulled the knife out, stood still for a moment.

Frank clutched hold of his neck. He dropped to the floor, blood pumping out of the wound. Finally, he flopped forward.

While he waited for Frank to take his last breath, Patrick pulled out a handkerchief, wrapped the knife in it and pushed it deep into his pocket.

A minute later, his move in the game played out, he stepped over Frank's body and let himself quietly out of the house. At the gate, he turned right and began to run.

Chapter Sixteen

Early Saturday morning, Allie was sitting in the car park of Trentham Country Club, hoping that Rhian Jamieson was a creature of habit and would be on time. During her visit to interview Joe Tranter, she'd noticed the logo that Tom Shaw had splashed across his T-shirt was the same as the one on the bag that she had seen in his living room. She'd checked their register for the gym to find out that Rhian came in most afternoons, but at around nine thirty in the morning at weekends. Allie guessed that she wouldn't let a simple thing like the murder of her partner's ex-wife stop her from working out. Idly, she wondered if she was one of the women who would gossip about Suzi Porter or if it would annoy her because she wouldn't be the centre of attention.

Five minutes later, she spotted the white Focus she'd seen parked in the driveway of the house in Smallwood Close coming into the car park. Allie waited for Rhian to park and get out of the car. Rhian had her head down, checking her mobile phone as she walked.

'Hi, Rhian, might I have a word?'

Startled, Rhian looked up.

Allie pointed to the building in front of them. 'I've just been checking something out and spotted you here. I didn't realise that Suzi Porter was a regular too. Did you see her often?'

Rhian shook her head. 'I told you – I never saw her much. She made sure she went at different times to me.'

'Right. So, how are you?'

'I'm fine.'

'And Mr Tranter . . . how is he doing now?'

'He's fine.'

'That's good to hear. I imagine it must have been quite a shock for him on Thursday morning.'

'As if!' Rhian barked. 'They've hated each other for years. That's why he was with me.'

'I'm sorry, I didn't mean to imply anything.' Allie moved to one side a little as another car came into the car park. 'It's just with them having a son together, I thought –'

'You thought they were still close.'

'Not at all . . . it's just the way you reacted made me wonder.'

Rhian's shoulders rose as she stood taller.

'What do you mean?' The young woman shook her head. 'Absolutely not. They split for a reason. He hardly saw her. I would know,' she added, almost as an afterthought.

'Oh, I didn't mean they were seeing each other in *that* respect.' Allie pretended to be embarrassed, as if she had put her foot into it. 'I just wondered if *you* thought they were.'

Rhian watched the occupants of the car get out and walk past before speaking again.

'No, he wouldn't,' she said quite firmly.

'He was seeing her regularly, though – he must have been because of Jayden.'

'He only picked him up! And Kelvin brought him round mostly because she didn't want to see Joe. So, whatever you're trying to imply, there was nothing going on between the two of them. Okay?'

Allie nodded. 'So you're still saying that Joe was with you at seven p.m. on Wednesday evening?'

Rhian paused for a split second, but it was enough for Allie.

'Yes, I told you so.'

'And there was nothing different about that night?' Allie probed further.

'No . . .' Rhian faltered.

'Remember, anything at all.' Allie placed her hand gently on Rhian's forearm. 'Even the tiniest thing could help us.'

'There's nothing!' Rhian moved from her touch and began to walk away. 'Stop hassling me or I'll report you!'

Allie went back to her car feeling satisfied. She was one step closer to breaking Rhian and finding out exactly what they were hiding.

The third murder came through while Allie was on her way out of the station with Perry. A woman had rung in after seeing her next door neighbour's front door ajar for several hours. She'd knocked twice before pushing the door open a little more, only to find him lying, bloated and bleary-eyed, in a puddle of blood.

Nick had been on his way to an annual general meeting in Liverpool when he'd been informed. He'd turned around and had asked Allie to visit the crime scene and then start house-to-house enquiries until he arrived. DCI Barrow was also heading over. Either Nick had received a bollocking or there had been another letter left behind.

'Wonder if this is another one, Sarge?' Perry laughed, nervously as they went out into the car park.

'I hope it isn't.' Allie threw a bunch of keys at him as she went round to the passenger side of the pool car. 'If this one can be connected to Mickey Taylor or Suzi Porter, it's going to mean having a serial killer in the city. I can't even begin to imagine that.'

A sense of unease settled over them as they drove onto Potteries Way. Sneyd Green was two miles from their station. Once there, they turned off Milton Road and into a small cul-de-sac. A few specialist vehicles were already there blocking their way.

Allie looked up at the skies as she got out of the car, ignoring the black clouds flitting quickly across it. 'CCTV won't cover this far back from the city centre, I'm assuming?'

Perry shook his head. 'I doubt it.'

'I'll get Sam on to it, just in case it caught anything while it panned around. I doubt any of these houses will have CCTV installed but you never know. We'll get the house-to-house uniforms to check it out.'

After they'd been logged in and suited up, they stepped into the hallway. Allie could see an elderly man lying on his side, his face turned to her, dead eyes staring straight ahead. He wore a white vest mottled with flecks of scarlet; there was a pool of blood by his neck.

'Three times in one week?' Dave said as he spotted them standing behind him. 'We must stop meeting like this.'

'Is there –'

Allie held her breath as he handed her an exhibit bag. Inside, it was a red letter this time. E.

'What happened?' she wanted to know.

Dave pointed to the side of the victim's neck and they stepped closer. 'One stab wound this time. Went straight through the jugular and the carotid artery, hence the blood pattern on the wall before he fell. He wouldn't have known much about it.'

'Who is he? Do we know his age?'

'According to his electricity bill in amongst the mess in the kitchen, he's called Frank Dwyer. His passport says he's sixty-seven. Date of birth fourth of September 1947. Lived here for a number of years, so the neighbour who found him informed us before we came in. Kept himself to himself. A regular at The Sneyd Arms pub most evenings.'

Perry nudged Allie and beckoned for her to go outside. She held up a hand indicating he should wait for a moment. 'The front door was open – no signs of forced entry elsewhere?'

'No.'

'Again.'

'Indeed.'

'So he knew his killer, or at least felt comfortable letting this person in.' Allie glanced around, not needing an answer. The hallway was dingy; she would go so far as to say dirty – there was a layer of dust on top of the small table by the door and mirror frame above it. The threadbare cream carpet was covered in pieces of fluff and what looked like crumbs.

'Or he brought someone home for pizza.'

Allie frowned, turning her attention back to Dave. He nodded at the discarded box cordoned off at his feet. 'Not sure why it ended up in his face.'

'Come again?'

'It was smeared all over him.' He pointed at the body. 'That's not all blood you see around his face. It's tomato puree.'

'Weird.'

'Boss?' Perry said again. 'A word.'

Allie followed him outside this time. For relative privacy, they moved to the side of the house. When she looked up at Perry, all colour had drained from his face.

'What is it?'

'He was the P.E. teacher at Reginald Junior School.' Perry leaned a hand on the wall to steady himself.

'You're kidding!' Allie's mouth dropped open.

'I wish I was. And we all hated him. He picked on all the lads who weren't good at sports. Rumour had it that he was always looking at the boys when they were in the changing rooms. There was tittle-tattle about a spy-hole in the walls where he could look straight in.'

'Perry, there were rumours like that when I moved from primary school to Reginald High School,' Allie responded. 'Like if any fifth-years caught any second-years when the teachers weren't looking, they'd shove their heads down the toilet and flush it.'

Perry scoffed. 'And you believed that?'

'Well, not now, obviously. But when I was twelve, of course I did. Children can be really cruel. Do you think it was rumours or was he gay?'

'He used to be known for hanging around the showers too, but if you're asking if he did anything to me, then the answer is no. He might have wanted to touch boys or he might have dreamt about touching them but, as far as I was concerned, he didn't actually do any of that. It was all things made up by the kids. There was one about a spy-hole in the boys' changing rooms to look through into the girls' changing rooms but I'll be damned if I could ever find it.'

Allie raised her eyebrows, although she knew he was trying to make light of the situation.

'Wait a minute.' Perry frowned. 'There *was* an incident. I think Dwyer was supposed to have groped someone – God, what was his name?' He paused for a moment. 'Charlie Lewis. I think that was him.'

Allie paused. 'I suppose he might be looking to pay Dwyer back – even after all these years? Think about it – three murders, three magnetic letters and three people who might be connected? This is looking more like vengeance. Let's call him in and find out if he has a connection to the other two.' She walked back towards the house. 'Start talking to the neighbours, see what else we can find out. And not a word about this as we leave, right? The press will have a field day if they find out about these letters. I – I wonder if he's not spelling out a word but telling us a name.'

Perry nodded. 'You mean EVE?'

'Yes. I'll talk to Nick once he gets here. There'll have to be another press conference, and we'll ask anyone named Eve to come forward.'

Allie put Perry on organising house-to-house enquiries while she went to interview Frank Dwyer's neighbour. She walked up the path to a tidy semi-detached house that adjoined Dwyer's property. In amongst several council-owned properties, this one was privately owned but with no airs and graces to make it stick out too much from the rest. An elderly, brindle-coloured Staffordshire bull terrier came waddling over to greet her as she was ushered into the hall. Allie put out a hand for him to sniff before stroking him, recognising his easy-going nature.

'It's not true what they say about Staffies.' Mrs Green smiled when she saw Allie petting him. 'My Freddie wouldn't hurt a fly.'

Allie followed her into a room with heavily patterned carpeting and a deep pink dralon three-piece suite. A cream shaggy rug lay in front of a coal-effect gas fire; there was a pine-coloured coffee table with a crocheted mat and a bowl of rose potpourri on top. After the dire surroundings next door, Allie felt instant warmth at the homeliness and order here.

'Have you lived in Queens Road for long, Mrs Green?' she asked.

'Yes, just over twenty years now. I was widowed at thirty-five and brought up four boys. I never found anyone to marry after Harold had gone.'

'That's such a shame. I bet you would have stolen someone's heart.'

Mrs Green smiled and patted the silver curls in her hair.

'What about Mr Dwyer? How long had Frank been living there?'

'He came not long after me, I think.'

'Did you get on with him?'

'Mostly.' Mrs Green moved to sit on the armchair in the window. 'I've never had any trouble with him, but he kept himself to himself.' Freddie followed and flopped down at her feet.

'Was he married? Did you ever see any family visiting?'

Mrs Green leaned in closer to Allie, who had sat on the settee near to her. 'I never saw him with a woman.' She nodded knowingly. 'At first, I thought he was a loner. But then he moved a man in with him.'

'And is he still living there now?'

'No, he left.' Mrs Green paused for a moment, eyes flicked to the ceiling. 'It was about ten years ago now. Shame, he was such a lovely man. Used to tend to my garden and hedges for me without any asking.'

'Any idea why they split up?'

Mrs Green's hands went into her lap. 'No, Frank never really spoke much about it. I did try to ask him a few times – you know, say that I hadn't seen Mario for a while – but he wasn't forthcoming. So I stopped. He always looked sad when I mentioned his name, though.'

'And you didn't see him with anyone else, you say?'

She shook her head. 'He very much kept himself to himself.'

Allie took a moment to write everything down in her notebook.

'Do you know any more about how it happened?' Mrs Green asked then.

'We're still making enquiries and looking into things.'

'You could ask that young lad who's been hanging around. See if he knows anything.'

Allie looked up.

'Danny, his name is.' Mrs Green looked pleased that she was telling them something new. 'He seems like a nice lad, from what I've seen of him. But he is that – just a lad.'

'What does he look like?'

'Like any teenager, I suppose.'

'Tall or short? Fat or slim? Black or white? Blonde hair, fair or dark?' Allie offered.

'He's white. I'd say he was tallish – definitely slim, with brown hair.' Mrs Green nodded. 'Short and spiky looking. Always wears one of those hoodie tops. Not with the hood up, though.'

'That's great. Any idea where he lives?'

'I'm sorry, I don't.'

'You've not seen him going into any other houses around here?' Allie questioned, hoping to jog a memory.

'No, and I've only seen him on the scene recently. He hangs around outside the Co-op. You might find him there.'

'On Hanley Road, opposite the Sneyd Arms?'

'Yes, that's the one. Most nights I see him there when I'm walking Freddie. It's a bit disgusting, if you ask me, him being so young.'

'What do you mean?' Allie probed.

But Mrs Green looked awkward. 'Well, who am I to judge what goes on behind closed doors?'

Allie decided to leave it alone for now and stood up.

Mrs Green patted the dog on his back. 'Move out of my way, Freddie.' She nudged him gently with the toe of one foot. Freddie lifted his head and promptly put it back down again.

Allie held up a hand. 'I'll see myself out,' she smiled.

Outside, she went to the next neighbour's house, hoping to shed more light on the boy called Danny. Someone else might have seen him too. But an hour later, she was no further forward.

Follow the Leader

After speaking to a few of the officers who had turned up to help, she left them checking the rest of the surrounding properties. She sighed loudly, running a hand through her hair. Three murders and practically a whole team working on finding the suspect and it seemed like nothing was going to fit.

Frank Dwyer's house was still being processed when Allie noticed Nick's car parked further down the street. She spotted him in the garden, shrugging out of a white suit, and went over to him.

'Suits you, sir,' she grinned.

'Ha ha, very funny,' he smirked. 'Did you get any leads?'

'A young boy named Danny has been hanging around Frank's house. I'm on my way to the Co-op to check out their cameras. Apparently he hangs around there most evenings, as well as here for the past few weeks, according to the next door neighbour who called it in.'

'Did anyone else mention him to you?'

'No. They didn't say much else either.'

Perry came out of a house three doors down and joined them.

'Anything?' Nick asked again.

'Nothing useful.' Perry shook his head.

'This is so bloody frustrating!' She looked at them both in turn. 'What the hell are we missing?'

Chapter Seventeen

Following the murder of Frank Dwyer, everyone was on full alert. Allie had called in at the Co-op to ask the staff about the boy called Danny. They'd identified who he was on their CCTV: Mrs Green had mostly been right in her description of him. As well as leaving her contact details with Mrs Green, Allie had also left her phone number with the staff at the shop, asking them to contact the station when Danny next turned up. Later, when she got to her desk, she began to check through what had come in and waited for the evening's briefing. Another press conference had been set up for straight afterwards.

At six p.m., the incident room was full. People sat on the edges of desks, a group in the corner trying to recall any local cases where there had been more than two victims but so far drawing a blank. Conversation buzzed. Allie was going through a list of witness statements when DCI Trevor Barrow came into the room. This was the first time he'd addressed the briefing since the case had started. It made her feel as if they weren't doing their jobs properly. Three people were dead and they were still putting two and two together, nowhere near making four.

Trevor walked over to Nick's desk, spent a few moments chatting to him. Early fifties with a distinctive head of grey hair, rimless glasses framing blue eyes, he commanded respect: everyone went quiet and gave him their full attention as he turned to address them. He pointed to the whiteboard at his side.

'We now know from forensic evidence that our suspect is male. He's killed three people.' His eyes flitted amongst them. 'Monday, January fifth. Mickey Taylor – forty-two, married with two daughters. Lived in the city all his life. Went to Reginald High School, was a troublemaker by all accounts, but no form since leaving. Married to Kath Clamortie since they left school. Mickey was found stabbed on the towpath in Etruria early morning. Found on his person was the letter E – a magnetic, plastic letter.'

He pointed at the board again, this time at the photo of a woman with long blonde hair. 'Then we have Suzi Porter – original name Sandra, maiden name Seymour. Wednesday, January seventh. Also forty-two, married twice with two young sons. Also went to Reginald High School, and at the same time as Mickey Taylor. She's been in the city mostly too, except for four years when she moved to London. According to her second husband, Kelvin Porter, she's been back in Stoke for the past seven. He was at work and was seen on camera at the time of the murder. Ex-husband, Joseph Tranter, has an alibi but we're looking into that. Nick, you still working on his girlfriend?'

'Yes, I gave the job to Allie,' said Nick.

'I caught up with her this morning,' Allie explained. 'Apart from having a bit of doubt in her mind about the relationship Joe Tranter might still have with his ex, she came forward with nothing else. I'll leave her to stew and then chase her up again. I know she's hiding something.'

Trevor nodded. 'Also, when we were questioning Tranter about his whereabouts, it came to light that he looks after the offices of Car Wash City for Terry Ryder.' A murmur went around the room and he held up his hand. 'Yeah, we knew about it, but we don't want Ryder to gather that. Suzi Porter was murdered in her home two days after Mickey Taylor was killed. There were signs of a struggle downstairs – things on the coffee table knocked to the floor, drops of blood in front of the fireplace – before she was tied to a chair in the kitchen. She could have known her killer as there was no forced entry.'

'Or he could have forced his way in,' Sam piped up. 'If she opened the door to him.'

'Indeed.' Trevor nodded again. 'Now, Joe Tranter says he was at home with his girlfriend, Rhian Jamieson, which is the woman Allie is questioning. The magnetic letter found on Suzi was a red V. Did I mention that the E found with Mickey Taylor was green? I'm not sure if the colours are significant – do shout out if you can think of anything.' Trevor then pointed to a photo of a man lying on a cream carpet. 'Frank Dwyer.'

'Sam's been finding and collating his info,' said Nick. 'Sam?'

'Frank Dwyer was sixty-seven, never married. Long-term male partner moved out years ago and he's been living alone since. He was a P.E. teacher at Reginald Junior School in the eighties. Known to us since he behaved inappropriately with one of the pupils at the school in 1983. There was no forced entry into his property either. Still trying to trace next-of-kin. Also, we're looking through photos and emails on his PC.'

'Thanks, Sam. And here's the strange thing.' Trevor circled a photograph of a pizza box with a marker pen. 'A pizza from Potteries Pizza was either delivered to Dwyer's address in Queens Road, or he brought it back himself. Then it was smeared all over his face. What was left ended up on the floor – not sure what that was all about. Who's checking out pizza places?'

A hand was raised at the back of the room. 'There's eighteen of them in the city, three in each town. The nearest outlet is too far for Dwyer to walk to, and neighbours say he didn't own a car. He walked to the local pub most nights.'

'Good. We need to check with the owners of ones nearby to see if they can recall who came in to buy it. And rule out Dwyer as well – he could have gone for a late-night walk if he was hungry.'

'They also do online orders too, sir, so we're looking in to the timing of those,' Sam added.

'I wonder why he left the pizza box there,' said Perry. 'Wouldn't you take that with you?'

'Maybe he forgot it in the spur of the moment?' a voice shouted up.

Perry shrugged. 'Possible, I suppose.'

'Would you like me to collate all the information once I have it?' asked Sam.

'Thanks. Keep me informed.' Trevor looked at the photo of Frank Dwyer. 'Only one stab wound this time but a purposely placed deadly one to the neck. Found on him was the letter E. Blue.'

'Eve,' Allie spoke quietly.

'Yes, it could be,' Trevor concurred. 'And if it isn't, it might be the beginning of another name.'

'Or an anagram,' added Nick.

Trevor nodded. 'So – links. Each victim had a coloured letter about their person.' He ticked off with his fingers. 'Each victim was stabbed. Each one has a connection to Reginald Junior or High School. Mickey Taylor was killed outside but neither of the other two murders had forced entry into their homes. Anyone?' He looked around eagerly.

'Forensics are due back to see if sexual intercourse took place with Suzi Porter before she was tied up,' said Nick. 'Although we know it's not looking likely, we need to rule it out.'

'So if it wasn't rape, what's the motive for the killings?' asked Allie. 'More often than not, murders are carried out quickly, on the spur of the moment. Maybe whoever killed Suzi knew that her husband wouldn't be back until late – knew he could spend some time with her?'

'Someone he works with?'

'Someone *she* works with?'

'Both are options.' Trevor raised his hand as another murmur went around the room.

'Beside the wounds that killed her, there were no defence marks,' noted Allie. 'She had a cut to the face but nothing else.'

'So he most probably punched her to unconsciousness, tied her to the chair –'

'With binding he could have brought with him.'

An involuntarily shiver coming from Sam to her right caught Allie's line of sight.

'Some sort of revenge attack?' added a detective constable at the back of the room. 'Most people think she's a diva. She's probably upset more people than *we* have.'

A little canned laughter.

'If Joe Tranter wanted to get back at his ex, don't you think there are better ways than killing her?' said Allie. 'For instance, she gets paid for her looks. Why not maim her physically in some way? I think that would be more of a punishment to her.'

'Good point, Allie. We won't rule anything out yet.' Trevor pointed at her. 'Keep me in the loop when something positive comes to light.' Another pause as he straightened the knot in his tie. 'Before I go ahead with the press conference, has anyone any more ideas about the letters E, V and E and what they mean?'

'They could be part of a large number of words, too,' noted Perry. 'In which case we're looking for a needle in a haystack.'

Trevor raised his hand one last time for hush as groups broke off to chat. 'There's going to be a lot of phone calls to follow up on, guys, so let's keep our wits about us. Everyone is going to be talking serial killer even without knowing of the magnetic letters but we still need to keep that information back for now. Nick, Allie, I'd like you along with me.'

The press interview was with the police only. The families involved would all know about the letters found on their loved ones and Allie knew that the DCI couldn't risk anything getting out just yet.

'We're looking for anyone with the name Eve, or Evelyn, who has any connection, no matter how slight, to any of the named victims – Michael Taylor, Suzi Porter, previously known as Sandra Seymour, and Frank Dwyer – to come forward.' Trevor picked up a photo and held it up for the camera. 'This is Frank Dwyer. Does anyone know him? He was sixty-seven years of age and lived in Queens Road in Sneyd Green. We're still trying to locate his family.' He looked directly into the camera. 'Do you know any of the victims and their connection to a woman named Eve? Have you any connections to anyone called Eve? If so, can you check with them to see if they have any information, to see if they are missing? Is your name Eve? If anyone has any information, it's vital that they contact us on the number shown on your screen right now, so that we can talk to them.'

'Before there's a fourth victim?'

Trevor's eyes shot quickly to the back of the room where a small man in a brown crumpled suit stood with his Dictaphone.

'There are no concrete connections yet . . .' He raised his eyebrows questioningly.

'Pete Simpson, *Staffordshire Post and Times*. Is it likely there will be more?'

'Let's keep to the facts we have rather than make any kind of speculation, Mr Simpson.' Trevor turned away from him sharply. 'We're looking for a woman called Eve for now.'

'Why is the name Eve important to you?'

'We're not at liberty to discuss that further at this moment.' He pointed to a woman to his right. 'Next question.'

'Do we know if Eve is old or young?'

Allie stared into the crowd of press as the DCI answered the questions one by one, admiring his cool once again. Christ, he was good at it. She knew she'd probably slip up if she had to face such a barrage on something so serious while keeping back vital evidence.

A few minutes later, Trevor called a stop to it. As everyone began to leave, Allie beckoned to Simon Cole, from *The Sentinel*, standing at the back of the room. They'd known each other as long as she had worked in the force. Simon always had a smile on his face unless the story he was working on was sombre. He was a cheap date, getting drunk on only a few pints of lager on the occasions she'd gone out with him as part of a larger group. Extremely well-liked and good at his job, unlike Pete Simpson from the *Staffordshire Post and Times*, whom Allie wouldn't trust with anything, Cole was always professional. She wondered what his thoughts were on this case.

'I don't think it has anything to do with the schools,' he said as they stood in the corridor afterwards, chatting. 'People dislike me as much as the police because of my job, I reckon. Any one of us could be next.'

'It's a connection we have.' Allie wouldn't be drawn into speculation. 'I'm not sure how relevant it will become.'

'Should we be worried?'

Allie didn't reply at first. A commotion along the corridor gave her a bit of breathing space. Ahead of them, the custody desk was dealing with a noisy problem.

She glanced back at him. 'People are getting tetchy.'

'Want me to run anything specific in the paper?'

'Not yet, but you'll be the first to know.' She looked at him; his blue eyes were attentive. 'A murder every other day – we don't want the public to think there is another one likely.'

'Okay, I get your gist.' He nodded. 'Everyone's suggesting links but I'll try and keep it from being too obvious.'

Allie smiled her gratitude. *The Sentinel* had a daily circulation of forty-two thousand print copies – with many more thousands of hits online. How that could fuel the fires of the rumour mill if this case were reported improperly or irresponsibly, she mused.

'This thing – that "Eve" could be the beginning of a word,' she said to him quietly as people came along the corridor and past them. 'It might be something and nothing so we need to keep the emphasis on that away from the public for a while longer if we can. It's bad enough having three murders in a week without anyone panicking that there are going to be more.'

Simon looked up from his notepad. 'You think there might be another one soon?' With nothing more forthcoming, he nodded. 'Okay.'

Allie nodded too. It was a mutual sense of understanding that they had. She would get details kept from the press: he, in return, would get first call once a story became hot. It had worked out well over the years as trust had grown between them.

'You have a bigger story brewing?' he probed one last time.

Allie sighed in frustration. 'I have a feeling that we're likely to find out sooner rather than later.'

The noise was ear-splitting when Allie entered the incident room again. Phones ringing, officers talking, officers shouting, hands waving, paper flapping about. All available staff had been drafted in – calls were being answered and logged as quickly as possible.

Nick beckoned Allie across to his desk before she went to sit back at her own. 'Can you take stock of what we have as it comes in?'

'Yes, sir. I'll transfer the incident number to my desk so I can take some calls too.'

'And can you see to it that anything important is listed and on my desk?'

'Of course.' Allie recoiled slightly, putting his overreaction down to the urgency of the case rather than assuming he felt she was incapable of thinking for herself.

'There's a lot of pressure on us right now. Let's just hope there's something useful before . . .' Nick stopped.

Allie nodded. 'Better get to it, then,' she told him. 'I have a feeling it's going to be a long night.'

Chapter Eighteen

Joe heard about Frank Dwyer when he arrived at work, and it had shaken him. There was no doubt about it: he knew all three victims.

Frank Dwyer had been his P.E. teacher. Dirty Dwyer, they'd called him – he'd had a problem keeping his hands to himself, if the rumours at the time were true. He racked his brain for any connection with someone named Eve, but he couldn't recall anyone from school.

It played on his mind for the rest of the day and it was the first thing that Rhian mentioned the moment he got in that evening.

'Have you heard the news?' She followed him into the kitchen once he'd hung up his jacket. 'I can't believe there's been another one. It's beginning to get a bit scary.'

'Yeah, I heard. I'll catch up with it on the TV once I've had a shower.' Joe opened his wallet and pulled out a few notes.

'What's this for?' she eyed him suspiciously as he gave them to her.

'I have to go to London tomorrow for a couple of days.'

'But you've only just got back from a night there!' Rhian's shoulders drooped as much as her face. 'What for now?'

'The usual.' He kissed her on the forehead. 'Nothing to bother your pretty head about.'

'And when will you be back?'

'Tuesday – Wednesday at the latest. Thought you might like to go shopping.'

'Money's not the answer to everything. I do make some of my own too,' she whined, wrapping her arms around his neck. 'And I'd rather not be on my own right now. The press conference on the TV earlier said that everyone should be extra vigilant.'

'I'll be there and back before you know it.'

'Couldn't I come with you? I promise I wouldn't get in the way of whatever it is you're doing.' She smiled, licking her top lip suggestively. 'I could make sure we had some fun too.'

'Don't you have any appointments booked?'

'Yes, but I could always rearrange them.'

Joe shook his head. 'Sorry, business is for the boys.'

'Don't be so bloody sexist!'

'You know what I mean.'

'So, what if the police call?'

'Why would they?'

'They might want to question you again. What will I say?'

'Tell them I'm away on business.'

'But you still haven't told me what you were doing on Wednesday evening, and I'm not comfortable lying to cover up for you when I don't know what you were up to. I –'

'Rhian!' Joe pressed the bottoms of his hands to his temples. 'Stop with the whining, will you?'

Rhian folded her arms. 'No, I want to know –'

'Leave it out!' He pushed past her. 'You're becoming a proper nag, do you know that?'

'And you're becoming a proper bore, do you know that?'

Rhian took a moment to calm her temper before flouncing into the conservatory. Stupid bloody man – if he thought he was going to disappear day after day and she would stick around to wait for him, he had another think coming. But after a few minutes, she came to her senses with a huge sigh. She needed to calm down, stop her mind from working overtime and perhaps try and get to the nitty-gritty of what Joe was really up to.

Flicking through that evening's edition of *The Sentinel* while she waited for him to come down from his shower, she read about the recent murders. Mickey Taylor: early Monday morning. Joe had gone out that day at six o'clock. And he'd definitely been out when Suzi had been murdered. She read the article again, noting in particular any times. This Dwyer fella had been killed this morning . . . what time had Joe come in last night? Around midnight?

'Stupid bitch, putting doubt into my mind,' she muttered, her thoughts turning darkly to Allie.

This was all to do with that sergeant this morning. She must have it in for Joe, for some reason. And even though she felt wary of him at times, he had never hit her. Of course she'd heard he was handy with his fists too, but that didn't mean he had murder in him.

Did it?

Allie wasn't enamoured with a visit to the city morgue first thing on Sunday morning but welcomed the response from the press conference the night before. Since the victims had begun to pile up, she'd barely found time to sit down and think about the case. Everyone at the station was getting antsy: if the killer was meticulous about detail, there would be another magnetic letter tomorrow, meaning someone else was going to die, and the police still had no idea who. But she was determined to find the killer. She didn't need another unsolved case hanging over her head for years.

Several leads had come through after the press conference. One of them was a woman claiming to be Frank Dwyer's sister. Perry had also brought in Charlie Lewis to see if the rumours he recollected were true. She left him to it as she went to meet Colleen Hulton.

As soon as the woman walked towards her, there was no doubt in Allie's mind about whether she was related to Frank Dwyer. Colleen had the same facial features as her brother: strong nose, thin lips and brown eyes that stared back exactly the same as the photograph they had of Frank. Her hair was dark, though, where his had been grey. She seemed a few years older than him, but dressed well to seem much younger. Allie warmed to her instantly.

Once the formal identification of the body had taken place, Allie sat down with Colleen in a private room and waited until she was ready to speak.

'Frank and I hadn't spoken in a while,' Colleen admitted, wiping at her eyes. 'But it still upsets me that he's gone. He's the only family I had left. It makes me realise how precious life is – and that maybe I should have kept in touch with him, tried to patch things up.'

'Can you recall roughly how long ago it was that you saw him?' asked Allie, opening up her notepad.

'I can tell you exactly. December 1983. Frank was working at Reginald Junior School and there was an . . . incident with a boy, one of his pupils. He touched him inappropriately, if you get my meaning.' Colleen grimaced, shaking her head vehemently. 'I was disgusted by it. I don't know how long he'd been doing that sort of thing. When it all came out in the newspapers, Frank was sacked from the school. The school didn't name the boy but they did name my brother, and his neighbours hounded him out of his house. So I let him stay with me.' She looked at Allie then. 'It was the worst thing I could have done. Because then everyone started hounding me too.'

'Everyone?'

'All my neighbours and so-called friends.' Colleen blew her nose before continuing. 'Frank ruined my life, and my family's life.

I nearly lost custody of my kids. I was going through a bitter divorce at the time. My husband went ballistic when he realised Frank was staying there. It would only have been for a few weeks, until things had calmed down. I have two boys, you see. How can you tell them that you don't want them to be alone with their uncle?'

'Did he ever –'

'No, he didn't.'

'Are you sure they would tell you?'

Colleen ripped the corner from the tissue and rolled it in her fingers. 'I asked them when they were older and I'm sure they told me the truth.'

'What happened then?'

'Frank appeared in court, and lost his job. He was struck off the teaching register.' Colleen sniffed. 'Not exactly the kind of role model I thought he would be for my boys. In the end, we moved to Newcastle. I – we never saw him again after that. Not until I saw his picture on the news last night.'

Allie wrote down what she had said. 'Did you know Frank was homosexual, Mrs Hulton?' she asked next.

'Yes, and I accepted that, but what I couldn't accept is what he had done to that boy.' Colleen breathed in deeply and sighed. 'It was wrong. He shouldn't have done that.'

Allie showed Mrs Hulton out of the building and then went back to the room. While it was unoccupied, she sat and wrote up her notes. Then she headed back to the station to catch up with Perry. She wanted to hear what Charlie Lewis had told him.

'It's something I'd blanked out until I heard that Dwyer had been murdered,' Charlie Lewis said as he sat opposite Perry in an interview room. 'I tend not think of school days much now.'

'I try to forget them as much as I can, too.' Perry couldn't help but smile. 'I had braces on my teeth and terrible acne.'

'I imagine I wasn't much better.' Charlie's smile was faint.

Perry took out his notebook and looked across at him awkwardly. 'I'm sorry – this is going to be uncomfortable to discuss, but I need to know what happened with Dwyer when we were at school.'

'Right.' Charlie shuffled in his seat and coughed to clear his throat. 'Luckily for me, I was young and what he did – well, I didn't let it change me, nor my outlook on life. Compared to what other children go through, I suppose you could say that I got off lightly. It was after a P.E. lesson one day. I'd been running around the athletics track and had an asthma attack. Dwyer was looking after me and had taken me into his office. It was lunchtime so I waited it out while I got my breath back.

'Dwyer was at my side. He gave me a drink of water and he rubbed my back while I calmed down. I didn't really think anything of it at the time. I thought he was comforting me. But when I turned round,' he cleared his throat again, 'there's no easy way to say this without being vulgar, but he had his cock in his hand and was masturbating.'

Perry could hardly look at the man. It wasn't something he hadn't heard before but because he remembered Charlie as the quiet ten-year-old he was back then, it seemed more perverted than usual.

'I stood up quickly, went for the door, but he blocked my way out. It was then he told me that he'd been watching me, knew that I'd been watching him – as if – and that he was showing me what I wanted to see. He kept asking me to touch him but I wouldn't. I was terrified, I can tell you. And all the time he talked dirty, he was wanking. And he didn't stop until he'd finished.'

Perry kept his head down as he took notes rather than show Charlie the blush spreading over his cheeks. 'What happened afterwards?'

Charlie almost growled. 'He just popped it back in his trousers, the dirty bastard, moved from in front of the door and let me out. But as I ran, he grabbed my shoulder and whispered into my ear. "This had better be our little secret, Charlie boy," he told me. Then he licked my fucking – my ear. I couldn't get out of there quick enough. Ran like hell, all the way home. Near on had another asthma attack. Lucky I didn't live too far away.'

Perry knew he was trying to make light of the situation. The look on Charlie's face wasn't one of embarrassment anymore; it was one of hurt.

'Did he try anything again?'

'Hell, no. When I got home, my mum took one look at me and it all came tumbling out. She was on to my father soon after – and the school were informed. But we kept things quiet because my father was a local councillor then. He didn't want any scandal and I didn't want to be known as "the boy who had been touched in the changing rooms" or else I would never have been able to live it down. Luckily for me, it never did get out either so I carried on pretty much as before. Dwyer was suspended soon after that – sacked a few months later after an enquiry. He tried to deny it but people actually believed me – that was a great feeling at that age. I wasn't a troublemaker and I was a quiet boy, as you know.'

'Not like me.' Perry couldn't help but smile to lighten up the mood.

His smile was barely returned as Charlie composed himself again. 'Sorry – brings a sour taste to my mouth just thinking about it now.'

'It's all just helping us to build a better picture of who his killer might be.'

'And the killer of Mickey Taylor and Suzi – Sandra Seymour?' Charlie asked. 'They're linked in some way, aren't they?'

'You know I can't tell you that.'

'Which leaves me to believe they are. Can you tell me if I'm in any danger?'

Perry shook his head again. 'For all we know, it could be anyone next. It could even be me.'

Chapter Nineteen

Rhian stood at the bottom of the stairs, barefoot in a skimpy nightdress, a long-sleeved cardigan falling off one shoulder in a way that she knew looked sexy. She had decided that getting Joe on side was the best way to find out what had happened, and they'd made love twice that morning. Normally at nine o'clock on a Sunday morning, they'd still be asleep, recovering from a skinful the night before. But as Joe was driving to London, he hadn't wanted to touch a drop and she'd stopped after a couple of glasses on her own. She hadn't had such a clear head at the weekend for ages. Definitely a bonus for what she had planned to do for the rest of the day.

'Do you have everything?' she asked as Joe came downstairs, carrying a small bag. 'Toothbrush? Toothpaste? Deodorant?'

'Yes, Mum,' he grinned, reaching the bottom.

'Someone has to look after you.' She pulled him close. 'I'm going to miss you.'

'I'll be back before you know it.'

'Erm, that was the part where you should have said that you would miss me too, you big jerk.'

Joe laughed. 'I'm going to miss that cute little ass of yours. You're a dicktease, wearing that thing.' He put his hand up her nightdress and gave her bottom a squeeze, pressing him to her as he kissed her deeply.

'Just in case you forget me while I'm gone,' he said afterwards as they broke apart. 'It won't be long and this will all be over.'

'Until the next time?' Rhian pouted, shiny eyes full of lust.

'There'll always be a next time. That's what you love about me. You can't deny that.'

Rhian tried to keep her face straight but failed miserably. 'Your modesty. *That's* what I love about you.'

'Not my charm and good looks?'

She shook her head with a cheesy grin. 'Nope.'

Waving him off moments later, she closed the door behind him and grinned even more. One thing was certain: she wasn't going to miss him tonight. She reached for her phone and sent a text message to Laila to say the coast was clear to come over. Then she raced upstairs to pack her own bag. She and Laila were booked on the eleven-ten train to Manchester to do some real shopping: Stoke would never be able to compete with that. She'd booked a room at the Midland Hotel and they were going out that night too. She couldn't wait!

When she arrived at the station following the identification of Frank Dwyer, Allie was just about to head upstairs when she spotted someone in the reception area. It was the oatcake man. He delivered the Staffordshire delicacies across the city, stopping off at their station every Friday morning. She doubled back quickly, hoping that if a breakfast order had been placed, someone from her team would have thought to add her usual two filled with bacon and cheese to the list.

'Graham!' She smiled as she walked towards him. 'I'm starving. Did anyone order anything for me?'

'Hi, Allie. Yes, I think so.'

Allie studied him as he checked over his list. His clothes were clean, beiges and browns. A plain man in all senses of the word. He had a full head of blonde hair, greying slightly at the roots; his face was neither attractive nor ugly.

'Two bacon and cheese oatcakes, with extra crispy bacon,' he told her when he looked up again. 'I've only just dropped them off. They should still be warm.'

'Oh, thanks. You're a good one.' Allie turned to head back inside the main building.

'I've been following the news,' he said.

She turned to him again.

'Well, I expect everyone in Stoke has.' He looked sheepish. 'I can't remember ever hearing anything like this before. They're all connected to the schools, aren't they?'

Allie remained straight-faced. No one had given that information out but it was clear that the public would make their own assumptions.

'I went to them too,' he explained.

'Did you?'

He nodded. 'You don't remember me?'

She shook her head. 'No, sorry.'

'I knew Mickey Taylor and Suzi – Sandra Seymour and, well, everyone knew dirty Dwyer. He was a teacher there. P.E. was never my favourite subject. I hated sports,' he said with a grin.

'And the others?'

'They were in my year. So was Karen Baxter – she's your sister, isn't she?'

Allie took a sharp intake of breath. She didn't really talk about Karen outside of her immediate circle of family and friends anymore.

'I can still remember finding out she'd been attacked,' he went on. 'Sorry, it must have been awful for you.'

'I don't remember much of her school years now,' she said, avoiding his question.

'Yes, I blanked out a lot of them too. All those weird clothes and haircuts.' He smiled. 'I – I just wondered if you'd thought that maybe Eve might be a nickname for a person.'

Allie wondered if anyone had already thought of that. 'It's a line of enquiry we're looking into,' she assumed. 'Do you have someone in mind?'

He shrugged. 'Not anyone in particular, but you remember us kids? We all wanted to be different so we made up names. Maybe Eve was someone without any reference to Eve in her name.'

Allie's mobile phone rang. She pulled it out and checked the screen but it was an unknown number. She smiled at Graham apologetically and headed back upstairs while she took the call.

The aroma of bacon wafted towards her as soon as she opened the door to the incident room. She made her way over to her desk, relishing the small parcel she could see waiting for her. She scooped it up quickly.

'I've just had a call from the Co-op,' she told Sam as she turned to leave again. 'The boy named Danny – he's there with his mates. I'm going there now, see if I can catch him.'

Twenty minutes later, Allie parked as near to the top of Sneyd Street as she could and walked up the bank towards the Co-op. On a corner and opening up on to Hanley Road, it was a busy shop at any time of the day or evening. As she drew level with the building, she spotted a boy fitting the description that Mrs Green had given her. He was sitting on a concrete bollard opposite two other boys, who looked similar in age.

'All right, lads,' she said as she approached them.

None of them spoke.

'I'm after Danny. Is that you?' She looked at him deliberately.

'Depends what you're after him for.'

'I'm Detective Sergeant Allie Shenton and I'm investigating the murder of someone I think you know.' She looked at the other boys too. 'Someone you *all* know.'

'It's about Frank, isn't it?' Danny stood up. 'It had nothing to do with us.'

'I don't bite,' she told him, hoping she could gain his confidence before he legged it.

The other two boys followed suit and all three began to move off.

Allie reached for Danny's arm. 'Look,' she lifted a foot up, 'don't make me chase you in these heels. I'll break my bloody neck.' She smiled. 'I only want to ask you a few questions. You're not in trouble of any kind.'

'We haven't done anything,' he said.

'I know.' Allie nodded her head. 'Two minutes, that's all I need.'

Danny shrugged. 'Why me and not them?'

'Two minutes.'

Eventually, Danny nodded. 'Okay.'

Over the road was a church with a low wall around its front. She pointed to it and they crossed to it in silence. Then she sat down and showed him her warrant card.

'What's your surname, Danny?'

'Am I under arrest?' he asked.

'No.'

'Peterson. It's Danny Peterson.'

'Will you sit for a moment? I'll get neck ache looking up at you, and the sun is in my eyes.'

A pause.

'Where do you live, Danny?' she asked once he was in her level of sight again.

'Greenbank Road in Tunstall.'

'With your parents?'

'My gran. Mum moved to Rhodes last year. I don't know who my dad is.'

'Did you not want to go with your mum?'

He shook his head. 'She didn't want me to go with her. She says I'm a troublemaker and she can't deal with me.'

Allie tried not to feel too sorry for the boy. It wasn't right that some children got pushed aside for new relationships, but equally he might be putting on a front.

'Danny, you do know that Frank is dead?'

'Yeah.'

'And that he was murdered in his home.'

Danny nodded.

'Where did you meet him?'

'Here.'

'At the Co-op?'

When Danny nodded, Allie held in a sigh. 'Is that where you hang out?'

'Mostly.'

'With those two? Are they your friends?'

'Yeah, but I'm not telling you their names.'

She took the mobile phone he was more intent on giving attention to and placed it on the wall in between them. She expected him to reach it back but he didn't.

'I don't want their names, Danny,' she told him. 'I'm only after information about Frank, anything that might help me to find out what happened to him on Friday night.'

'It wasn't me! I didn't do anything!'

'Do you think I'd be sitting here with you if I thought you had?'

Allie could see the boy's appeal to predators. His looks made him seem a lot younger than his sixteen years. Jet black hair, clear olive skin and sparkly eyes. He was obviously not sleeping rough, as his clothes were clean and so was he. His jacket was expensive, looking out of place with his cheap jeans and trainers. She wondered if he had saved money for it or if it was a knockoff from a market stall.

'Did you visit him a lot?' she questioned over the thunder of a lorry roaring past.

Danny shook his head. 'It was pissing – chucking it down with rain one night, and he said we could go to his house to keep dry. We thought we'd have a laugh, and being three of us, we knew we'd be okay. Safety first, and all that.'

Allie nodded. 'So you went to his house. What happened there?'

'He made us tea and some toast. We watched the telly for a bit and then we left.'

'Anything else?'

'No.'

'Did you ever visit on your own?'

Danny looked more interested in the cars coming past on the road.

'Danny?'

'Yeah, a couple of times.'

'And Frank behaved okay with you?'

'He didn't touch me. That's what you want to know, isn't it?'

'I need to check.' Allie nodded. 'It isn't common for men to invite boys into their homes like that.'

'Well, I'm okay.' Danny shrugged off the comment.

'Did he ever give you money?'

'Just a fiver.'

'Just the once?'

He nodded. 'He didn't ask me to do anything for it either. He just said I could treat myself but I wasn't to tell the others or they'd all be trying to fleece money from him. He bought me a pizza too.'

'Can you remember where he got it from?'

'I think it was Farm Fresh or something like that. It wasn't very nice – too thin.'

Allie frowned. Of course, she supposed pizza didn't have to be brought in. Frank was a pensioner and until they'd looked into his financial records, she'd have to assume he was on a pension. It probably only cost a pound or two from the freezer shop. Maybe a takeaway pizza was more of a treat.

'Danny, did you ever share a pizza with Frank from Potteries Pizza?'

Danny shook his head and reached for his phone. 'I liked Frank,' he said. 'Was there a lot of blood?'

Allie tried not to smile at how his sentence had flipped from caring to grisly in a matter of a second. 'I'm glad to hear that,' she replied. 'But you need to be careful. I don't want to hear of you going into anyone else's house, do you hear? People won't always be as nice as Frank.'

'Okay.'

His head was down over his phone again. Allie watched him for a moment and then stood up. She couldn't tell him that what Frank had been doing seemed like a perfect grooming trick. Lord knows what might have happened to him if Dwyer hadn't been murdered. She made a mental note to find out where Danny lived and see if she could see his gran. He seemed a decent kid; she hoped he'd stay that way.

His friends were walking back to him now. Allie crossed the road to her car. Glancing back before she opened the door, she looked at all three, laughing about something on Danny's phone. Innocence and youth, she mused. And after the indecent images they'd retrieved from Dwyer's computer overnight, Allie was glad that none of them had been hurt too.

This old man, he played four.
He played knick-knack on his door.
With a knick-knack, paddy-whack,
　　Give the dog a bone.
This old man came rolling home.

1988

Patrick walked along Leek Road as quickly as his feet would allow him. It was ten minutes to eleven and he was late: his dad would backhand him if he wasn't in by eleven and he had at least a thirty-minute walk from Abbey Hulton because he didn't have enough money for the bus fare home now. But he didn't care. What he had spent his money on was worth every last penny.

He staggered along the pavement, careful not to step out onto the road. Blurry vision made him realise how drunk he was. His old man would backhand him when he saw that too. But he couldn't stop grinning, recalling the evening with Melissa Stout.

She'd given him his first blow job. His first taste of a woman's lips around his cock. Okay, she'd pumped a bit hard at his shaft, as if it were a bottle of ketchup, but who was he to complain? He was still a virgin: he'd take what he could.

Fifteen years old and never been shagged but he'd had a girl suck his cock. As memories came flooding back, he felt himself getting stiff again. He tried to quicken his step, get home while it was all fresh in his mind and relive it, fantasise with his eyes closed that she was kneeling in front of him again. It had happened so quickly. One minute, he was sitting with his mates – 'the outcasts,' they called themselves: him, Daz and Lefty. The next, he was buying her a drink at the youth club with the last of his money from his paper round. Half an hour later, he was behind the shops in a doorway with her hands down his pants.

Melissa Stout wasn't anything to look at, everyone knew that. But everyone also knew that she put out whenever she fancied. Besides, she was the only girl who had shown any interest in him. No one would come near him, usually. He'd only decided to go to the youth club at the last minute because Daz wanted to get off with one of the fifth-years.

He pulled his wrist closer to his face. What time was it? It was nearly eleven. Fuck: he was going to be in for it. Maybe he should run.

Footsteps thundering towards him made him turn quickly. Four lads were running along the pavement. Patrick's heart sank when he saw them up close. It was Mickey Taylor and his cronies. Well, he wasn't going to let them spoil his evening.

He hadn't spoken a word when a fist punched at the side of his head.

'What the fuck was that for?' he cried out.

'I've been told you were ogling my girl at the youthie, Shorty,' said Mickey, squaring up to him.

'You weren't even there. How would you know?'

'You wouldn't catch me there. Not ruining my street cred.'

'Yeah,' said Johnno. 'Youth clubs are for geeks like you and the fucking outcasts.'

'More like you've probably been banned.'

Patrick wished he'd kept his mouth shut as soon as the punch landed on his nose. It happened so quickly that he couldn't have moved out of the way even if he'd been sober. He put a hand to his face, unsure if the stars he could see were above him in the night sky or inside his head.

'I know everything that goes on.' Mickey prodded a finger into his shoulder. 'I know you were looking at Sandra.'

'I wasn't.'

Johnno sniggered. 'I heard you got your end away with Slag Stout. I hope she didn't catch anything. Or rather I hope you didn't catch anything from her, the dirty whore.'

Patrick grimaced. He was never going to live that down now. It was one thing to think about what she had done but another to have it thrown in his face for the rest of his time at school.

The boys surrounded him. Patrick tried to run through them but they pushed him back. He tried again, but they pushed back more forcefully this time and he fell, landing heavily on the pavement.

'Are you an item now, then?' Mickey laughed cruelly. 'Slag Stout and stupid Shorty!'

Hearing the rest of the boys laughing, feeling brave thanks to the lager he'd drunk that evening, Patrick spoke back.

'If you were by yourself, Taylor, this would be a fair fight. You're nothing but a coward on your own.' He pushed himself back up to sitting. 'Why do you get your kicks from picking on me?'

Mickey bent down and leered at him. 'Funny you should mention kicks, you cheeky fucker.'

For days after, all Patrick could remember was a boot coming towards his face. And the feeling that his dad would do far worse by the time he finally got home after they had finished with him.

Chapter Twenty

Malcolm Foster unlocked the front door to Winton Insurance Brokers, glancing quickly over each shoulder before stepping inside. Luckily, Tower Square wasn't too busy at this time of night, and it was dark, although he knew he'd probably be picked up by someone's CCTV camera. He hurried up the stairs and pushed open the next door that he came to. Through this and his office was at the end of a long corridor.

He'd been working there for twenty-two years, always coming in to catch up with any outstanding paperwork on a Sunday evening – not that he would ever class himself a stickler for routine. Like a lot of people, he tolerated a job he was good at because he didn't have the inclination to try and do something better. Steady Eddie was his game, no rocking of the boat for Malcolm. But today wasn't any ordinary day. Today, he had a lot of cleaning up to do.

In the quiet of the room, he switched on his computer and, while it booted up, thought about what was on it. More to the point, what he needed to erase. If he wasn't quick, and the police could somehow link him back to Frank Dwyer, he'd be jailed, he was sure.

He'd only heard of Frank's murder that morning. Malcolm had been in Dubai for a fortnight's holiday with his wife and had caught up with the news on the way home. The taxi driver had given them a blow-by-blow recounting of events pointing to what he thought was a serial killer at work in Stoke, and how he thought that the police had done nothing and had no idea who it was. By the time they'd arrived home, Malcolm was already imagining the worst: that he'd be next. It would be some sick fucker who'd come to get his revenge on the sick fuckers who'd made him that way.

He drummed his fingers on the desk. What if the taxi driver was wrong and the police were keeping evidence back until they had more to go on? The enquiry could lead them to him and he'd be well and truly screwed. Perspiration burst over his top lip; his shirt was wet to the touch.

He opened the drawer and took out the desk tidy, littered with its many bits of paraphernalia. Underneath it was a manila folder. He pulled that out too. Not even bothering to look inside it, he threw it into the metal waste bin. Using the box of matches he'd bought at the Spar supermarket across the square, he lit one and dropped it on top. Heart pounding, he watched as passwords to websites that he didn't want anyone to see went up in flames.

He ran a hand over his chin: if only everything was as easy to get rid of. It was going to take an age to delete it all. Thank God none of it was on his home computer. His marriage had survived only because of the images that he looked at, kept hidden away from everyone. But they had come attached to emails from Frank Dwyer, and he'd paid good money for them: if *that* came out in the open, all their lives were ruined. If the police dug deeper still, everything might come out about Nigel. He'd left Stoke fifteen years ago now. There was no point in opening up old wounds. It wouldn't be good for any of the family.

Malcolm turned his attention back to the computer, his hand moving the mouse over the screen, clicking quickly to delete everything he could think of. Christ, what a mess. He thought back to the time he'd met Frank online in a chat room, about five years ago. For a while he'd been careful what he said: you never knew who you might be talking to and he'd heard the police were setting up a lot of stings locally. But when Frank had offered to meet up with him, it had seemed far too good of an opportunity to miss.

They'd chatted like old friends for a while, the atmosphere between them light and bantering. All at once the suggestion to take things further had been aired and soon Malcolm was embroiled in everything that Frank was.

Paedophile.

Shit, even the word in his head was enough to bring him out in a sweat all over. How hard he had fought the urges, tried to control himself after what he'd done to Nigel. In the end, it was easier for him to accept what he was and try to quell his appetite for youngsters another way. Stored on his computer were photos of boys as young as nine. Indecent images, filth, call them what you may, but they were all the same to him. They were what he enjoyed.

They were also a prosecutable offence.

Things had turned sour with Frank just over a month ago now. He'd stormed upstairs after first harassing the receptionist downstairs, threatening to tell everyone what Malcolm was involved in if he didn't cough up the money that he owed. Frank had given him access to a set of photos and a few online videos but the quality hadn't been as good as Malcolm was expecting so he'd refused to pay. Luckily, the situation hadn't got out of hand. Frank had left when he said he'd get the money to him. Once Malcolm had seen his nasty side, it had been worth it to get him off his back.

But now Frank had been murdered. He wondered, was this someone after 'his sort' or just a random stranger who had followed Dwyer home? A one-night stand gone wrong?

It was less than twenty minutes later when he heard a sound coming from downstairs. He jumped to his feet, sneaking quietly over to the window to look down onto the street below. It sounded like someone had rattled the letterbox, he was sure. It was dark, the square lit up with a few streetlamps, and an icy mist was settling in for the night, frost already freezing up car windows. Malcolm pressed his face to the glass but couldn't see the door from where he was standing. The square below seemed empty.

Then he sniggered. Damn his imagination. It was Sunday, for Christ's sake: no one should be calling in today.

He sat down at his desk again, started deleting more files. A minute later, he sniffed. What the –?

Petrol.

This time he walked back along the corridor towards the stairs. From the top, he could see a pool of liquid on the mat. He watched as the letterbox rattled again, saw a piece of paper in flames pushed through.

'Hey!' Malcolm shouted out.

The paper fell onto the raffia mat below, igniting the liquid. With gusto, it erupted into an inferno. Malcolm ran to the bottom step but there was nowhere safe that he could put a foot down to run to the front door. He covered his mouth with his hand. Fuck, how much petrol had been poured through? The whole area was alight.

Seeing no other way out, he ran back upstairs, closing the door at the top of the landing, hoping to keep the flames at bay until he could summon help. In his office, he dialled 999.

'Fire. Someone has poured petrol through the door of the building and I can't get out. I'm trapped upstairs!' he told the emergency operator. 'Yes. No. Tower Square. Yes, Tunstall, that's right. Yes. There's a fire exit at the back. I'll get out and wait at the front of the building. Hurry up!'

Malcolm put down the phone and rushed to the door. If the fire were to take hold, it would be better for him if it all went up in smoke. Feeling a little exhilarated at the thought, he went to the end of the corridor, pressed down hard on the handle to open the fire door and stepped out on to the small balcony.

The bang to the back of his head knocked him completely off his feet. He dropped to the floor, seeing a pair of black boots before he lost consciousness.

Patrick dragged Malcolm back through the building to the other end of the corridor. He was a dead weight already, he thought, laughing at his own joke. Before opening the door, he covered his face with his scarf.

This was the riskiest one yet. He had minutes before he might become overwhelmed by smoke, and the fire engine he'd heard Foster call could arrive at any moment. He pushed the handle down on the door, shouldered it open and, keeping his head down, dragged Malcolm to the top of the stairs. Once there, he slapped him around the face a couple of times until he came to again.

'What – what . . .' Malcolm spluttered.

Watching the man try to sit up with Patrick's foot on his chest was the best laugh he could have hoped for. The smoke was coming thick and fast now, the flames below heading up the stairs. Oh, how he wanted to stay and have some fun, but he needed to get away too.

'What do you want?' Malcolm coughed. 'Get off me. We need to get out.'

Patrick lifted his foot and stamped down hard on Malcolm's chest.

Malcolm groaned, curling up into a ball.

From the look on his face, Patrick could see he'd realised his mistake. He'd made himself into a perfect shape.

'No! Please!' Malcolm cowered.

One last kick was enough to propel him down the stairs.

Malcolm threw out his arms, trying to slow himself, but the momentum pushed him forward and he fell face first into the flames. Even his screams as he tried to reach the door didn't put Patrick off. It was even better than listening to the racket coming from the next-door neighbour's house.

He kept his mouth and nose covered as he watched Foster burn with the same pleasure he had taken shoving the knife into Frank Dwyer. Sadly, there wasn't time to hang around like he'd done at Suzi Porter's place but at least he knew that Foster would have suffered.

When he could smell singeing flesh more than smoke, he turned and ran back to the fire exit. As he got to the ground, he heard the sirens in the distance and legged it down the alleyway behind the building.

Chapter Twenty-One

Around eight thirty that evening, Perry arrived home exhausted. The case was beginning to take its toll on him, not least because of the nagging feeling that not only had he known the victims, but there was a good chance he'd known the killer too. All three deaths were linked to schools where he had been a pupil in the past – surely that wasn't just a coincidence? Was it someone he knew from junior or high school? Could it even be one of the younger teachers that was doing this?

More to the point, he wondered as he shrugged off his coat, should he be worried for his own safety? Of course there were lots of pupils from the schools but even so, his job made him more vigilant, always wary and careful not to trust. He made a pact with himself to take extra precautions until the case was solved.

'Lisa?' he shouted up the stairs, finding the rooms downstairs empty. There was no reply, so he went upstairs. Her car was on the driveway so if she had gone out, she hadn't gone far. But usually she would text him to let him know where she was going and what time she was expected back.

'Lisa, are you up there?'

At the top of the stairs, in front of the bedroom door, sat a large, white fluffy bunny. Frowning, Perry picked it up. Around its neck was a ribbon; tucked inside it was a note:

I am the bearer of good news.

A smile appeared on his face.

'Lisa?' He opened the door and saw that she was asleep on the bed. Gently, he roused her.

She opened her eyes. 'Hey,' she said, stretching out with a yawn. 'You just got in.'

'Yeah.' He lay down beside her and brandished the bunny. 'Either you're going to accuse me of having an affair and are going to boil this bunny up for supper or . . .'

'I'm pregnant!' she screamed and jumped into his arms.

'Really?'

'Really.'

'But –'

'Don't you dare say how, you big daftie!'

'I was going to say that we'd only just started trying. Is that normal?'

'Well, we must be good at it.' Lisa beamed, and then her eyes filled with tears. 'Ohmigod, Perry, we're going to have a baby.'

He hugged her to him, then pulled away. 'I won't hurt you, will I?'

'Of course not.'

'So, how far along are you?' He picked up the pregnancy test on the bedside table and saw two blue lines. 'Does this thing tell you that too?'

'It does.' Lisa took it from him and looked again, as if she couldn't believe her eyes. 'I'm only about six weeks gone so we can't tell anyone yet.'

'No one at all?'

Lisa shook her head. 'No, not until twelve weeks have gone past and the pregnancy is a bit more along. I don't want to tempt fate yet.' She grinned. 'We're going to have a baby!'

'We are!' Perry hugged her again and they lay down on the bed together.

Quite frankly, he couldn't think of a better way to end the day.

The next morning, Allie walked slowly along the corridor to Karen's room. Half an hour after she'd arrived home last night, she'd received a phone call from the staff nurse on duty at Riverdale Residential Home. Karen's doctor had asked to see Allie first thing in the morning. It had led to another sleepless night, with nightmares of her sister and of Suzi Porter covered in blood.

It was just seven thirty; she tried to stifle a yawn, hoping that it would be something and nothing that Dr Merchant wanted to talk to her about. It could be a routine check-up, or maybe her sister needed extra care that had to be paid for. Maybe they needed permission to try out a new medication, something to give her an inch more towards a better quality of life.

She pushed open the door to find Karen awake and propped up in her bed. But, even as she hoped it would be nothing to worry about, deep inside she knew something was wrong. Over the past few weeks, she'd seen further signs of Karen's deterioration; she just hadn't wanted to admit that anything serious was wrong. Not after all these years of seeing her sister in that bed, in that room, in that home.

'Hey, sis, how are you today?' Allie combed Karen's hair away from her face and planted a kiss on her cheek. It was warm to the touch. As she pulled back, she saw its flushed tones.

There wasn't even a murmur from Karen. A blink of her eyes and a slight lip movement was all she could muster.

'That good, huh?' Allie smiled, trying not to let her tears spill over.

While she waited for Dr Merchant to arrive, she pushed thoughts of what he was about to say to the back of her mind and thought more about the day ahead and what she needed to do. Right now, it seemed that the whole office was bogged down in paperwork, crossing the t's and dotting the i's, or trawling through CCTV footage to find any similarities near the scenes of the three murders. Most of the forensic evidence was back but not all of it. Some of the jigsaw pieces were slotted together but not the linking ones yet. And now there were all these indecent images to get through on Frank Dwyer's computer. Luckily, Nick had delegated that task to one of the male police constables, rather than add to Sam's long list of tasks.

The press conference had brought up further information since Saturday. There were lots of things to follow up on but so far no significant leads, no worthwhile connections to Eves or Evelyns. There were masses of connections to Mickey Taylor and Suzi Porter, though, and every one of them had to be interviewed where necessary. It would take them forever at this rate before they got that break. There just weren't enough hours in the day.

'Can you remember Sandra Seymour from school, I wonder?' she spoke softly to Karen. 'I wish you could tell me. You could help me solve a crime. Would you like that? I know I would.' She smiled. 'Hey, we could have opened our own private investigation services called The Snoop Sisters.'

Allie sighed. It was all well and good joking about it but she wondered again how long their killer had been planning these murders. And how long it would be before he slipped up. It was only a matter of time before they would find something that would lead them to him, to stop him killing any more.

She looked up as there was a knock on the door.

'Good morning, Allie.'

Allie sat up straight. 'Nothing wrong, I hope, Dr Merchant?'

Dr Merchant stepped a little closer, coming round Karen's bed to stand next to her. 'I'm afraid there might be.'

Allie looked at the floor momentarily. After seventeen years of her sister living a shadow-like existence, *now* the doctors were going to give them bad news? She heard Dr Merchant clear his throat to get her attention again. She didn't want to but she looked up at him again, wishing she had taken Mark up on his offer of accompanying her.

'She's had another bleed to her brain,' Dr Merchant explained. 'It's only slight and I'm not sure entirely what damage it's done yet. But it's hard to tell with Karen being unable to communicate much in the first instance. We're going to start running some tests – is that okay?'

'Of course.' Allie nodded. 'Should I be worried?'

Dr Merchant pinched his lips together before speaking. 'I'm not sure, Allie. Only time will tell, I'm afraid. But it is the reason she has become a little less responsive as of late.'

'Are *you* worried about her?' Allie phrased the same question differently.

'Yes, but again, it is only time that will give us answers. I know you have a busy schedule – it's hard to keep away from the news about the murders,' the doctor conceded, 'but I do think maybe it would be good to spend some quality time with Karen as soon as you can.'

Once he'd gone, Allie sat still for a while, staring ahead blankly, barely able to take in what he'd said.

It wasn't until she got back into her car that she let her tears fall. Tears of grief or relief – she couldn't distinguish. There were definitely tears of guilt. Because, as much as she hated to see her sister living like she did, she would rather have that than not have her at all.

The staff in the incident room seemed in as much of a state of disbelief as Allie felt as she sneaked in to join the eight thirty briefing. It was not yet underway and as Nick spotted Allie, he beckoned her to his desk.

'I've been calling you,' he said.

Allie sniffed, knowing the redness around her eyes would be visible. She reached in her pocket for her phone and switched it from silent to normal. 'Sorry, quick visit to my sister. Forgot to put the sound back on.'

'Everything okay?'

'Yeah, I –' she threw her thumb over her shoulder. 'I'll get back to it.'

'You sure you're okay?' Nick's eyes were full of concern.

She nodded, unable to speak for fear of bursting into tears.

'There was a fire last night. Winton Insurance Brokers on Tower Square. At first we thought it was a random arson attack but a fire officer dropped this off about an hour ago.' He held up an exhibit bag with a magnetic letter inside.

Allie gasped. 'N?'

'It was left on a car down the street, tucked under the windscreen wiper. The owner couldn't get to it last night: he found it when he was allowed to go back this morning. It was wrapped up tight inside a plastic bag and shoved underneath the wiper blade. "Police" was written on a white label. It's gone off to forensics along with the bag.'

'But that spells . . . EVEN.'

Nick nodded. 'And that might be a whole new game of soldiers.'

'So we were probably wrong on the name Eve?'

'It's possible. And if so, what the hell is he getting even for?'

Allie shook her head. 'It could mean this is over too?' she said after a pause. 'Even though we still have to catch him, if he *has* gotten even, we might not have any more people getting hurt.'

'Let's hope so.' Nick moved to the front of the room, raised a hand for attention. 'Right, listen up everyone. This attack doesn't fit with our MO but now that we have another letter, we know it's our fella. I'm told there's not much left of the interior of Winton Insurance Brokers after the fire did its worst. The square was evacuated and closed off. The buildings either side will remain closed today too, until everything has been made safe.'

'What do we know about the victim?' Allie asked.

'Malcolm Foster, sixty-two, lived in Stockton Brook. Married to Sylvia with a son, Nigel, who lives in Portsmouth with his family. They'll both be in for the press conference later. Obviously there can be no formal identity yet but we have to assume it's him. Approximately nine thirty last night, Foster's wife became worried when he didn't come home as planned. She'd been calling his mobile but it had gone unanswered.' Nick pointed to the photo of Malcolm Foster, tanned and relaxed, smiling with a drink in his hand. 'This is the most recent close-up, taken from their digital camera. They'd only got back from a fortnight's holiday in Dubai a few hours before. Sylvia said Malcolm always went into the office every Sunday but she hadn't expected him to go that night. But around six p.m., Malcolm told her that he needed to deal with something urgent, said he'd only be about an hour. She couldn't understand why after two weeks away he wouldn't wait until the next morning. When she failed to get hold of him, she headed over in the car and found the building up in flames, fire brigade all over it . . .'

'Nasty,' said Allie.

'Anything to do with the schools, do we know?' asked Perry.

'No straight connection that we can find. They came to Stoke about thirty years ago.' Nick looked around the room again. 'There was no need for our killer to change his methods so drastically unless he was trying to tell us something different. So, why fire this time?'

'Accelerant used was petrol,' Sam updated them. 'It was poured through the letterbox before being set alight. The front door was locked anyway so the victim wouldn't have been able to get out the front way, plus the fire would have been at its worst there.'

'Rear entrance?'

'Fire door was open. Our killer legged it through the back alleyway.'

'Can you check with CCTV? And the back of nearby businesses too.'

'Already on it, boss,' Sam replied.

The door opened and Trevor came into the room. 'Carry on,' he said to Nick, taking a seat at the back of the room.

'The yellow letter N was found nearby in a plastic sandwich bag. A label on it said "Police." It means the owner of the car who found it under his wiper blade now knows we have a letter. It also means that if he talks, the public will know that EVE plus N is EVEN.'

Conversation erupted around the room. Nick held up a hand for silence.

'Do you think he's pissed off that we've kept the letters out of the press?' questioned Perry.

'It's possible.' Nick pointed to the whiteboard. 'So far with Foster, we have no connection to the schools and no connection to the other victims. I want to know why him and I want to know why a fire. Anything else on Frank Dwyer?'

Allie updated everyone on her conversations with Colleen Hulton and Danny Peterson, and Perry talked through his interview with Charlie Lewis, whose alibi for all three murders was watertight, although Perry had never believed Lewis had anything to do with the deaths.

'There're also tons of indecent images of young boys on Dwyer's home computer,' Allie added. 'Most are under thirteen at a guess.

There's obviously some link there that we're trying to work in, to tie in with the witness statements from yesterday.'

Nick wound the briefing up. 'I want everyone going over every tiny detail of evidence again – every statement, everything. Check every word. Go over every phone call. Step up the door-to-doors. Make sure *every* lead is followed up. Someone knows who he is.' His eyes flicked around the room. 'We need to find out what the hell he's getting even for.'

As he joined the DCI, Allie sat back at her desk with sagging shoulders. All they needed was one lousy, tiny, teeny break. Because the other alternative was too horrible to contemplate. They would be too late to save the next victim, likely to be dead by tomorrow.

Chapter Twenty-Two

At eleven o'clock, Rhian and her friend, Laila, were on the train back to Stoke-on-Trent from Manchester. Several bags of shopping were shoved in the racks above them, every single one belonging to Rhian. The night away had been as successful as the shopping trip and they'd headed for a club after hitting Deansgate Locks. A takeaway afterwards and they had arrived back at their hotel just after two that morning. Now paying for it with a massive hangover, Rhian rested her head on the window of the train, dying to get home for a proper sleep.

'I can't believe you bought three pairs of shoes,' said Laila. She pulled down the table from the back of the seat in front of her and rested her head on it.

'I can't believe I *only* bought three pairs of shoes,' stated Rhian. 'There were so many in the sale.'

'You're such a lucky cow.'

Rhian smirked. 'I know. Joe might be old but he's loaded.'

'Money's not everything, though, is it?'

'It is when I can buy three pairs of shoes.'

'I wish I could afford one pair!'

Rhian knew that her friend wasn't jealous but simply envious. Laila had a bar job in the city centre. She often moaned about how she hated it with a passion and was trying to find something else.

But with a child to look after during the day, and the baby's father gone AWOL, it didn't leave Laila with much choice. Luckily, her mother looked after the baby when she was at work.

Laila sat back up again, pushing her long hair back behind her ears. 'I can't wait to see Kyle.'

'You've only been away from him for one night.'

'I know, but . . . you won't understand until you have kids of your own.'

Rhian looked at her oddly. 'I don't want to have kids.'

'What – like, never?' Laila sounded stunned.

'No, never.'

'You'll change your mind.'

'Erm – no I won't.' Rhian dismissed the image of the baby that had melted her heart in the car that she had seen the other day.

'I can't imagine life without Kyle now.' Laila sighed.

Rhian huffed. 'Last night you were telling me how much he tied you down!'

'Babies tie everyone down. And I was drunk.'

'You're fortunate your mum is there to look after him, like she did last night. You wouldn't be able to go anywhere.'

'Well, like I said, not everyone is as lucky as you.' Laila crossed her legs and turned away.

Rhian shook her head and sighed. 'Don't go all moody on me now after I've just paid for your hotel room.'

'*You* didn't pay. Joe did.'

'It's the same thing.'

'No, it isn't. And just because *you* have a sugar daddy doesn't mean we all want one. Besides, he's only with you because you look like Suzi Porter.'

Rhian turned towards her quickly. 'Excuse me?'

The train pulled in at Stockport station. Laila wouldn't look at Rhian so she poked her in the arm.

'What's that supposed to mean?'

Laila shrugged. 'Nothing. Forget I said anything.'

'No, go on tell me. I want to know.'

But Laila wouldn't.

Rhian turned away, watching fields disappearing as the train started up again. She thought back to what that sergeant had said. Joe wasn't bothered by his ex-wife's death, not in the slightest. But then the doubt crept in as she thought about all the late nights over the past few weeks.

'What is it with everyone lately?' she said at last. 'Ever since Suzi was murdered, all anyone wants to do is put doubt in my mind about her and Joe. First, I had the police on to me and now you.'

'I haven't – '

'Is that what everyone thinks?' Rhian interrupted. 'That he's with me because I look like her?'

Laila shrugged again. 'Aren't you ever suspicious, though?'

'Of what?'

'He's so much older than you.'

'And – your point?'

'Most men say they'd like a younger woman but most don't act on it.'

'You're talking about a trophy girlfriend, aren't you?' Rhian snapped.

'Well, you've obviously thought of that too!'

'No, I happen to know that he loves me for who *I* am and that's enough for me.'

'Good.'

'Fine!' Rhian was determined to have the last word but Laila wouldn't let it drop now.

'If you're that certain, you ought to check around the house to see if he has anything of hers. If he has, he's still in love with her. Then you have your answer.'

'Do you think he is?'

'I don't know. I don't see him that often.'

Rhian cast her mind back. Had Joe seemed upset because Suzi wasn't there any more or because she'd led the police to the house and he was worried they would find something they shouldn't? Joe was a selfish bastard at times – just like her. She wouldn't put anything past him.

'What would I look for?'

'How the hell should I know?'

A woman with two young children came to sit in the seats opposite. The toddler dropped his teddy and Laila leaned forward to retrieve it. She gave it back to him with a smile.

'Aw, he's gorgeous,' she said to his mum. 'How old is he?'

Rhian rolled her eyes and turned to look out of the window as the train set off again. But what Laila had said still played on her mind all the way home, even more so as she went into the house with her shopping bags.

As she stood alone in the silent hallway, another layer of doubt grew in her mind.

Allie was on her way to the interview rooms downstairs again. Earlier, they'd received word from the pathologist. There was nothing new on Frank Dwyer's body, only the same unidentified DNA of their killer. She sighed dramatically. He was well prepared, this one.

Up ahead on a row of seats, a man sat upright, hands in his lap. She drew level, noticing the tense frown as he concentrated on a poster ahead of him. Domestic Abuse: a single red rose dripping with blood.

'Mr Foster, I'm Detective Sergeant Shenton. Thank you for coming in early.' Allie opened a door to the right of him and pointed to the table. They sat down opposite each other.

'I'm so sorry about your father,' she began.

'I'm not.' Nigel Foster crossed his arms and unfolded them. 'Sorry, I don't want to come across as hostile.'

Allie gave a faint smile of acknowledgement. 'Didn't you get on with him?'

'He was not a nice man. Well, to me he wasn't.'

'Is that why you moved from the area?'

'Partly. I was also offered a brilliant opportunity working at Portsmouth University.'

'Do you have family, Mr Foster?'

'Yes, two boys and a girl. Eldest is eleven, middle one seven and the youngest three.'

'And do you visit your parents often?'

'I haven't seen them in years.'

'Oh?' Allie knew this already after speaking to Mrs Foster, so it was good to get it confirmed. 'Too busy with the job?'

Nigel sat forward in his chair, struggling to hold back tears. She stared at him, waiting for him to speak.

'I'm not sure how much you know about my father, but he . . . he did things to me that I will never forget. That's why I won't allow my children to visit their grandparents.'

'Can you be a bit more specific?' She raised a hand as he began to protest. 'I don't want a lot of details. Just the basics will do.'

He looked away for a moment then back at her. 'My father abused me sexually from the age of nine until I was fourteen.' He gasped as if struggling for air. 'I'm sorry,' he said. 'I've tried to block it out for so many years that even thinking about it brings back the memory as vividly as if it were yesterday. He raped me repeatedly. I was powerless to stop him. He said the usual crap – made me believe that it was what I wanted. That I asked for it, that no one would believe me if I did say anything. So I didn't.' He looked up then, with dark, angry eyes. 'I never said anything, just took it until it stopped when I was fourteen.'

'It just stopped?'

'Yes. I obviously became too old.'

'Is that what you think?'

He nodded. 'I know so. I found photos. Pictures of boys, young boys, a lot younger than me.'

'Printed or online?'

'They were mostly printed back then. I bet he has tons online now, though.'

His comment made Allie look up from taking notes. 'Did you know any of the boys?'

'No.'

Allie glanced at the clock. She needed to finish this so they could go into the press conference. 'Thanks for your time. I'll show you through to the room we're using.'

'I hate myself for not doing anything about it.' Nigel's voice broke and he began to cry.

'You were a child, you have to remember that.' Allie wanted to reach out to him but wasn't sure if she would offend him. She quickly put her hands under the table. 'A child taken advantage of by his own father. There is no way you were to blame.'

'It doesn't make me feel any better.' Nigel sniffed. 'Seeing him six feet under will, though.'

Allie said no more while she waited for him to gain his composure. What could she say? She couldn't alleviate how he was feeling. Another child let down by another parent in this ideal world they all strived to create.

Eventually, he stood up. 'I'm not sure if that helps in any way but I hope that you're clearer about the man who was murdered.'

'Thank you for your honesty. That can't have been easy to share.'

'My – my wife doesn't know any of this. That's why I came to see you here at the station.' His eyes were pleading. 'I do hope it can stay that way.'

'I will do my very best, but I can't promise that, I'm sorry. But now might be the time to tell your wife. I can give you some numbers – people who can help.'

As she made her way back upstairs to the incident room, Allie wondered if the fact that Danny Peterson was hanging around with Frank Dwyer and the fact that Malcolm Foster had abused his son might be connected. Had their killer been abused as a child?

Chapter Twenty-Three

Allie tried to shut out thoughts of her sister as she got to work sifting through information that afternoon. There were so many things to look at, especially since the press conference had been broadcast. Sylvia Foster had made an appeal and Nigel had been present too. It had been uncomfortable to watch from the back of the room as Trevor worked his way through endless questions thrown at him during this one. Four victims in eight days, no matter how hard they worked behind the scenes, smacked of incompetence to the general public who just wanted the killer caught. It would have smacked of incompetence to her, too, if she hadn't known better.

As they left the room, Allie couldn't help but think back to how Nigel had reacted to his mother. Even though Sylvia Foster had cried through most of the conference, there had been no show of emotion towards her from Nigel. He hadn't held onto her hand, touched her arm, or even sat close to her. Instead, he'd refused to look up at the camera through most of the interview until it had been time for him to read his statement. At the last minute he had declined, passing it along to Trevor to read out for him. It was sad considering the circumstances and, even though Allie couldn't begin to understand what he'd been through, she could understand why Nigel wouldn't support his mother. She clearly knew more than she was letting on.

Upstairs again, Sam beckoned her over before she sat down at her desk. 'There's a couple of things I want you to see on CCTV. You got a minute?'

Allie wheeled her chair over and sat down next to Sam.

'There's Malcolm Foster going into Winton Insurance Brokers.' She pointed to a figure on the screen and they watched as he walked into the square and went into the building.

'And,' Sam pointed out a blurry figure running across the screen in front of them, 'there's our guy from the fire thirty-two minutes later.'

Allie leaned closer. 'Is that all we have?'

'Yep.' Sam sighed. 'Really informative, isn't it? This is from the cameras that pan round. I've tried the shop across the road but theirs are for show. The one next to that only catches the pavement in front and the bloke didn't run past that way. Want me to continue?'

'Yes, for a while. See if you can see anyone nearby on anything else.'

'Okay. I also have this. It might be something and nothing but there are a few cars that keep appearing. I've seen them several times now. Might be worth checking out.' Sam pressed a few buttons on the keyboard and then pointed. 'This one here. A dark blue Fiesta, old, Y reg. It was seen coming out of the street next to Red Street on the night that Suzi Porter was killed. And then again,' she pressed a few more buttons, 'here, just off Market Street on Sunday evening.'

'After the fire?'

'Yes.'

'Any others?'

'Well, there's a small white van and a blue Honda Civic. Both are in the vicinity of two of the murders but not the others, just the same as the Fiesta. I need to rule out work and home addresses.

Follow the Leader   193

And talking of addresses, we've found Malcolm Foster's email address amongst emails sent from Frank Dwyer's PC.'

'Photos attached?' Allie hazarded a guess.

'Yep.'

'Shit.'

'Indeed.' Sam paused. 'Are you okay, Allie? You don't look so good.'

Allie saw concern in Sam's eyes and her own filled with tears. 'It's Karen,' she said. 'She's not doing so well.'

Sam rested a hand on Allie's forearm. 'Anything I can do? Maybe look at some paperwork while you go off and see her?'

'I went first thing this morning – well, I was summoned for first thing this morning. That's why I was rushing in for the briefing. Her doctor rang last night just before I went home. He's going to run some tests, says he won't know much until then. But it's not . . . it's not looking good. She's barely communicating with me; she's hardly made a murmur for the last few weeks. I've known but I've not wanted to admit it to myself.' Allie sniffed and wiped at a rogue tear as an officer walked past her desk. 'I think I'm losing her, Sam,' she whispered.

'Oh, Allie, I'm so sorry.'

Allie squeezed her eyes shut to stop more tears.

'Have they given any indication of –?'

'I don't want to think about it.' Allie shook her head. 'Although I know I should.'

'Why don't you go and spend some time with her?'

'I can't.'

'Of course you can.' Sam nodded. 'We can cover for a few hours. I'll keep you informed by phone. We can –'

'No, I mean I can't bear to think about it at the moment. I know it sounds callous but I need to keep busy. Once I've gone home tonight and seen Mark and had a good cry, then I can go and see her, try to accept things. And I'm on the end of the phone if I'm needed.' Allie quickly wiped away another tear that had dripped down her cheek. 'Right, what's next?'

Chloe Winters shivered as she stood waiting at the bus stop on the outskirts of Hanley. It was nearing midnight; there was hardly any chance of a bus now but she didn't have enough money for a taxi, so she'd have to wait and see and then start walking. All her friends had gone ages ago, when they knew she'd hooked up with Daryl. She'd been looking forward to seeing him so much – what better than a night out laughing with the girls and then home with him afterwards to catch some good loving? Or some in the morning, once they were both sober.

Behind her, bushes that marked the boundary of Central Forest Park shivered in the wind, causing her to shiver too. No bus in sight, she reached inside her bag and located her purse, searching through it again in the hope of finding some money that she'd missed from before. But there was nothing. Even though there were a few cars about, it seemed deathly quiet. She hugged herself to keep warm.

She checked her phone. Nothing from Daryl since she'd stormed off fifteen minutes ago. It was all his fault. If she hadn't argued with him in Chicago Rock, then she wouldn't be waiting here for a bus that she'd probably missed. What time were the last buses, anyway? She looked down the road again, as if one was magically going to appear.

She combed her hair from her face with her hand, the wind whipping it into her eyes as a taxi raced past, passengers in the back going home to warmth and sleep. She shivered again, stamping her feet to keep her toes from numbing. Only last month they'd had a few days of snow and here she was now in a dress and flimsy jacket and strappy platform shoes. It wasn't icy – she'd stay on her feet, but . . . She cursed Daryl. She looked at the time again: five past midnight. She'd wait for another ten minutes and then she'd have to walk.

If Daryl hadn't been all over that girl he used to go out with – Chloe cast her mind back, Becky something-or-other bitch-face – she wouldn't have felt the need to argue with him. But he thought he was such a stud. She'd been happily snogging the face off him until she'd needed to pee. When she came back, he was so close to snogging Becky that he hadn't noticed her standing by his side for over a minute. She'd tapped him on the shoulder, tipped the remainder of her drink down Becky's top and stormed out. She'd hoped that he'd come after her, looked over her shoulder even as she'd left the building, but he hadn't. Becky had won, despite her having the last laugh. Her eyes filled with tears.

A few minutes later, she began to walk, her feet hurting with every step. When she heard footsteps behind her, she stopped, turned abruptly, but there was no one there. She laughed to herself.

'Stop scaring yourself, you daft cow.'

She walked another few yards before she heard footsteps again, closer this time, and faster. Someone grabbed her arm and ran with her.

'Stop pissing about, Daryl.' Chloe struggled to keep up with him. 'I don't want to talk to you. You can't be trusted on your own for five minutes.'

On they ran, past Walkers Fruit Shop and down the side alley next to it.

'I *saw* how you were looking at her! You're hurting my arm – let go!'

He continued to drag her along the path, then across the grass and into the bushes before she had time to say anything else. She pulled a face – he might think it was romantic to act all spontaneous but she wasn't going to let him off that easily.

When they were out of sight, he turned her to face him. It was then that she could see it wasn't Daryl.

'Who the hell –'

He stopped her with a backhander across her face. She cried out, stumbled in her heels. He pushed her and she fell to the ground. On all fours, she scrambled desperately but he grabbed her ankles and pulled her back. Soil filled her nails as she tried to get a grip, hook into the ground and stay where she was, but he was on her like a flash. He flipped her over onto her back, his hand sliding up her leg. She lost a shoe in her fight to kick him off. Pushing her dress down as he inched it up, she slapped at him as he grabbed her hands.

'You're not going to get away from me.'

At last she tried to scream, but it was silenced immediately by a punch to her mouth. He hit her twice more. Dazed, she quietened, feeling her legs go weak as he covered her with his body. He lifted off her slightly as he fumbled with his jeans. She knew she should try to scream again but it was as if she had lost the know-how. All the times she'd read about girls getting attacked and not running away or screaming for help and wondering how they could just lie back and take it. Now, here she was, powerless and frozen with fear. Tears pouring down her face, she tried to close her mind off to what was happening.

———

Patrick moved through his neighbourhood as quietly as possible. He was taking a risk going through the wooded shortcut and on to Century Street. The alcoholics would be out and in fighting mode if he bumped into any of them. But at this time of night, he could blend in with the darkness, the dreariness of the place.

Coming out into the light of the only lamp in the street that worked, he stepped into the road that would lead him across to Waterloo Road and across to Ranger Street. Ahead, he could hear the sound of a man and woman arguing, their colourful expletives coming through an open window. He pulled down his woollen hat as he ran the last few minutes home, trying to keep the negative thoughts at bay.

From the onset of the game, Patrick had wondered if he'd be in the right frame of mind to carry everything out. He'd thought that maybe killing Mickey Taylor would be all he was capable of. But one after the other? Would his mind be void of any emotion? Would he be able to kill and kill again? In quick succession, which is what he'd needed to do? And not stop until he had taken down every one of them? He was more than halfway through the game, but would his mind be capable of all of it?

He pushed himself to sprint the last few metres along Ranger Street to his front door. As he put his key in the lock, he glanced around. There was no one to see him, no one looking out of the windows, no one to make up tales about him, not like before. Only five lights on in the whole street, mainly downstairs.

In the shower minutes later, he turned the dial to high and lifted his face up into the spray, the drops stinging his skin in their race to cover him first. If he had been the religious type, he might have thought it was washing away his sins, cleansing him of his evils.

But he wasn't religious. He must just be mad.

No one in their right mind would do what he had done if they weren't.

Chapter Twenty-Four

Allie's mobile woke them at just after five thirty on Tuesday morning. This time it was the theme tune from the film *Top Gun*. Mark pulled the covers over his head as Allie made a grab for it and switched on a lamp. Seconds later, she was sitting up and wide awake.

'When did this happen?' She flicked her feet to the side of the bed. 'Any sign of a magnetic letter? But you're saying she asked for me? Okay, I'll see you there. Yes please, email me. Thanks. Bye.'

'Shit, has there been another?' Mark asked as she reached for her dressing gown and pulled it around her shoulders.

'I'm not sure. Some girl has been raped, badly beaten and left . . . I have to go and see her.'

Mark sat up immediately. 'Are you sure you have to be the one to talk to her?'

'She asked for me by name.'

'Yes, but you have a team of officers. Get one of them to interview her.'

'No, they might miss vital evidence.'

'They wouldn't do that.'

'They might. Everyone is so busy at the moment, I want to be sure that everything is looked into, and as soon as possible.'

'That's ridiculous! Surely it doesn't take priority over murders?'

Allie ignored his jibe. 'Of course it doesn't, but that doesn't mean we can't do our best for her. I don't want anything to be missed, that's all.'

'You can't keep on thinking everything you do will bring justice for Karen just because her attacker was never caught.'

Allie recoiled. 'You make it sound as if this kind of thing is a regular occurrence!'

'You know what I mean.'

'Luckily for you, I do.'

Mark ran a hand through his hair and then sighed. 'I hate to see you like this,' he said. 'Seeing how all the memories come flooding back to hurt you. And then I'm left to deal with the aftermath. I can't keep doing it. It tears me apart. I –'

'For fuck's sake, this isn't about us,' Allie interrupted. 'This is about some poor girl who has been attacked. Have you any –'

'Don't patronise me!'

Allie pinched the bridge of her nose and closed her eyes for a moment before looking back at him. 'Mark, let's not do this again now. You know this is my job.'

'Yes, and always more important than our marriage.'

'What the hell did you just say?'

Mark went quiet.

Allie didn't have the time to spare. 'I need to go,' she told him.

Mark flopped back onto the bed. 'Do what you like, Allie. You always will.'

She strode across the bedroom towards the bathroom. 'Well, thanks for your support,' she threw over her shoulder. 'It's great to know you're on my side.'

The door slammed behind her. What a prick!

She gasped for air, only now perceiving how erratic her breathing had become. Sensing she was on the brink of a panic attack, she tried to control it. Breathe in slowly, breathe out slowly, stop it boiling over.

She took a shower, hoping the water would wash away her fears. Ten minutes later, she came out of the bathroom a little calmer. All she could see of Mark was the shape he made underneath the duvet and the top of his head.

'Mark, I don't want to fight,' she spoke quietly into the room. 'But I don't need you to whine either. This is my job.'

When he didn't reply, she switched off the light and left.

Forty minutes later, Allie tapped on the door of the rape crisis suite before entering the room. Although the room was clinical, it had been created to look as homely as possible. Two large settees, squishy cushions, rugs and pictures on the wall adding a splash of colour to the cream-coloured paint. A female police constable sat across the room from the victim, Chloe Winters.

Allie smiled her acknowledgement. PC Angela Butler: a woman in her late forties who had a daughter just a little older than the woman who sat across from her. Allie was glad that Angela had been on duty at the time.

Details of the attack had been emailed to her and she'd checked them in the car park downstairs before coming into the building. Deciding not to say who she was for fear of upsetting Chloe, she smiled at her too.

Chloe was twenty years old but with her make-up cried away, knees tucked into her chest, and arms wrapped around them for comfort, she looked barely older than a schoolgirl. She wore a dressing gown and slippers, the kind found in spas to throw away after one use. Already she had some impressive bruising to her face, a swollen eye that seemed to be closing by the second, a thick lip and a cut to the side of her right cheek. Allie's heart went out to her. Lost, vulnerable and in shock, she looked exhausted too, having had no sleep. And Allie was going to make things worse by asking her once more about the attack.

'Hi, Chloe,' she spoke softly. 'I –'

'Please don't make me go through it all again.' Chloe's voice could barely be heard. 'I can't do it.'

'I'm so sorry for what happened to you, but we need to get to the bottom of this as quickly as possible and then you can go home.' She sat down next to her, far enough away not to cause offence.

'I've told the other officers everything.' A lone tear rolled down the young girl's bruised cheek.

'I need to see if you recall any more details about your attacker.'

A sob broke loose. 'I don't want to remember.'

Allie paused. She wished she could tell her why she needed the information. The bodies in the city morgue were piling up quicker than her team could gather information about them. Yet, even though they had four victims who hadn't been so lucky, Chloe wouldn't see that as anything to be grateful for, that she was fortunate to be alive.

'Can you tell me why you were on your own?' she asked gently.

'I – I had an argument with my boyfriend. I stormed off and then realised I didn't have enough money for a taxi.'

'Where had you been?'

'Around the town, then finished in Chicago Rock.' Chloe dabbed at the swollen eye with a tissue. 'I waited for a bus for ages. I thought maybe I'd missed the last one so I had no choice but to walk.'

'And you can't recall anyone around nearby?'

Chloe shook her head. 'That was when he – he ran at me, grabbed my arm and kept on running.'

'And you thought it was your boyfriend – what did you say his name was?'

'Daryl – Daryl Harvey.' Chloe started to cry. 'I thought he'd come to make up with me, say he was sorry. I thought we'd be able to flag down a taxi and get home. It was freezing.'

'And the man pulled you into the bushes then?' Allie saw the balled-up tissue clenched in the girl's hand and passed her a fresh one.

Chloe nodded. 'He came out of nowhere. He had a balaclava covering his face and he ran at me.'

Allie gave her a bit of time. Although she knew Chloe was upset, she had to find out more. If this was their killer, why hadn't he finished the job? Had he been disturbed? She looked at the young girl again.

'May I ask something that is going to be hard to answer?'

Chloe gnawed on her bottom lip.

'Did he say anything once he . . . after?'

More tears fell. 'He said "all men are not idiots." And then he punched me in the face.'

Allie gasped. But it wasn't just Chloe she was thinking of now. Images of what must have happened to her sister flashed up clearly in her mind. She tried to keep her thoughts on the job in hand.

'Can you remember anything about him? Was he tall or short?'

Chloe shook her head.

'Well, how about was he thin, or fat? He ran a while with you – was he out of breath when you stopped?'

Chloe remained silent.

'I know it must be hard, but we have to ask lots of questions. We want to find this man and lock him away. Anything at all you can remember might help,' Allie continued. 'When he spoke to you, did he have a local accent?'

'I think so. I just lay there as quiet as I could,' Chloe began to cry again, 'so that he'd stop and leave me alone. I'm so ashamed that I didn't scream.'

Follow the Leader 203

'Don't be ashamed. Not many women would have in your position,' Allie soothed. 'Fear often takes over, sweetheart. Did he walk away then?'

'Yes.'

'Did you see which way he headed?'

'No, I kept my eyes closed. I waited until I was sure he was gone and then I walked back to the police station. I didn't know where else to go, what to do. But I couldn't go home – not like this.'

Allie touched her arm, hoping she wouldn't flinch. 'Thank you, Chloe. I know it's hard to go through these things over and over but they are so important to us.' She stood up. 'I'll leave you with Angela until we can take you home.'

She turned to leave. Angela stood up too.

'One more thing,' Allie said. 'You asked for me by name, is that right?'

'*You're* Detective Sergeant Shenton?' Chloe cried out.

'Yes, that's right.'

Chloe pointed at her. 'He left a letter there for you.'

Allie drew in her breath, glancing quickly at Angela.

'He said he'd taped it underneath the nearest rubbish bin to where he – where he . . . He said I was to tell no one but you about it or he would come and finish off the job next time.' Chloe prodded herself in the chest. 'Did he attack me,' she cried, 'to get back at you for something? Did he? Did HE?'

Allie shook her head. 'I have no idea who this is, Chloe. I'm so sorry. I'll do everything I can to –'

'I want to go home.' Chloe began to cry again.

It took Allie less than ten minutes to get to Central Forest Park. She turned off Chell Street and parked haphazardly in a space by the side of the lake. As she got out of her car she could see, in the distance, yellow crime scene tape flapping in the wind. She counted two officers gathering evidence, marking the spot where Chloe had been attacked.

Running, almost scrambling over the grass in her haste to get to the letter, she headed up towards the bin. It had been raining for a couple of hours; she knew everyone would work quickly but evidence would still be lost.

A sob caught in *her* throat this time. It was too close; she wouldn't be able to stop an image forming of the man dragging Chloe Winters out of sight, intent on harming her, violating her.

The path was at the back of the park, far from the main entrance. As she approached the bin nearest to where it had happened, she took sterile gloves from her pocket and snapped them on. At its side, she stooped and ran her hand over the bottom of the metal container. Feeling something, she dropped to her knees on the wet path and pulled at the tape it was secured with.

An envelope. She turned it over. Handwritten in black ink was *DS SHENTON*.

Before she opened the seal, she beckoned one of the officers at the scene across to her.

'Over here!' she shouted. 'DS Shenton. I need an exhibit bag!'

She carefully ripped along the edge of the envelope. Inside was a single piece of plain white card. Two letters this time, large and handwritten in black ink again.

Y. N.

Chapter Twenty-Five

Rhian had just got out of the shower when she received a call from Joe to say that he wasn't returning home as planned.

'But you said you'd probably be back by today,' she whined.

'The job's going on a bit longer than intended.'

'So, tomorrow then?'

'No, we won't be finished by then.'

Rhian sighed.

'I'll definitely be back on Thursday.'

'Okay, fine. I suppose I'll see you whenever.' She disconnected the phone with a stab of her finger and threw it down on the bed beside her. Bloody men, she fumed. What the hell was she going to do with herself until he got back?

'Hello?' Joe waited but there was no reply. 'Rhian?'

Cursing, he disconnected his phone with a shake of his head. Damn that bloody woman – she was so childish at times. Why the hell would she hang up on him just because she couldn't get her own way?

'Trouble at t'mill?' Chris asked, eyeing his face. Chris was one of the young mechanics that he'd got to know well over the past few days.

'Let's put it this way,' Joe replied. 'I'm quite glad I'm not going back to Stoke as early as planned now for another reason.'

'Moaning at you for staying away, is she?'

'She's always fucking moaning about something.'

'You don't have much luck with women, do you?'

Joe shook his head. Chris was referring to Suzi too. He'd told him what had happened to his ex-wife last night.

When Ryan had suggested staying until the job was finished, until the original plan to seek seven cars rather than five finally came to fruition, he hadn't anticipated how much he'd want to stay on. Working with a good team of blokes rather than the boys who washed the cars at Car Wash City had been a good experience. He'd felt part of a team here, even though the work they were doing offered its fair share of risk. He'd enjoyed getting his hands dirty again as well but, more so, he'd had a laugh working with Chris. They'd been out for a beer a couple of times too. For the first time in ages, Joe had felt free, able to do what he wanted without having to answer to anyone.

In turn, it made him realise that he wasn't that excited about getting home to see Rhian. Especially with her obsession of watching or reading anything she could about Suzi. Over the past week, the woman had turned into a walking encyclopaedia of knowledge about his ex. She seemed to have a morbid satisfaction over her death – or was it just satisfaction?

He'd been keeping an eye on the news since he'd been away too – couldn't believe there had been another murder. Surely the police could link them all together now? To him, it seemed to be the work of one person.

'If you're not married, I can't see your problem,' Chris continued. 'Dump her if she makes you miserable.'

Joe smirked. 'I wish it was that easy at times.'

'What's so hard about it?' Chris shrugged. 'Life's too short to be miserable. And I, for one, know that I'd rather keep the wad of cash we're going to get for this job for myself if I wasn't happy with my woman. You worked hard for it, man. What does she do for a living?'

'She works for herself as a nail technician – which would be good if she actually showed me some of the money once in a while.'

Chris frowned. 'Seriously? Why do you put up with it?'

Joe paused. 'I have absolutely no idea.'

Chris raised his hands in surrender as he walked off. 'I rest my case. Not worth the hassle. Get rid.'

'When will you be done with these?' Ryan came over minutes later, pointing to two cars waiting to be spray-painted.

'They'll be finished later tomorrow,' Joe told him. 'And great that we managed to get all seven too,' he added.

Ryan paused as he looked at the row of cars that had already been finished. 'You've done a good job there, mate. You're good at your trade.'

'Cheers.' Joe grinned.

'You in the line to do any more?'

'Yeah, I might be. As long as I don't get any heat from Ryder.'

'Why would you?'

'You're right.' Joe shrugged. 'The compound's hard to see from the road.'

'What he doesn't know won't hurt him. I don't give a shit if –'

Chris came back with three mugs of coffee. 'You two fancy coming out for a curry tonight?'

Joe nodded as he took a mug from him. 'Sounds like a plan to me.'

'Yeah, count me in,' added Ryan, taking one too.

'Sound.' Chris grinned. 'Be good to drink the old fellas under the table afterwards too.'

'Cheeky bastard.' Joe pretended to swipe for his head, but already he was looking forward to the evening. At least he would have some fun before heading home to Rhian's nagging.

Downstairs, Rhian flicked through channels on the TV, unable to watch the midday news. Despite the other murders, Suzi Porter's name was still all over the first story. Although Rhian had to scoff – this killer on the loose was making a mockery of the police. There had been four in the city now and they still hadn't caught anyone. Not that the police were giving away that they were connected, but Rhian knew. Everyone was talking about it. Four in eight days – that had never been known before.

With more time to stew, she thought again about what Laila had said. It had hurt when she had suggested that Joe only wanted to be with her because she was a younger model of his ex. But now he was staying away longer than originally planned, she couldn't stop the jealous thoughts tumbling around her mind. Was he having too much fun without her? Most likely, he was visiting some seedy laptop club with his so-called 'business associates.' She frowned. What if he was seeing someone else but it wasn't Suzi?

She stared at the television, not actually taking on board what was on the screen. Then she jumped up quickly. This might be her only opportunity to be sneaky, have a search around. If she didn't find anything, there would be nothing to worry about. At the very least, she tried to convince herself, it might put her mind at rest.

Rhian looked in the obvious places first: in coat pockets, through Joe's clothes drawers, inside a suitcase on top of the bedroom wardrobe, in the drawers underneath the bed. She checked downstairs, in every cupboard in the kitchen, on top of the cupboards, in the sideboard, amongst the junk and magazines piled underneath the coffee table.

She moved back through to the kitchen, noticing his laptop on the table. Rhian didn't know Joe's password, but she switched it on anyway. After trying several words that she thought might be associated with him, she gave up. As she stood at the breakfast bar, drumming her fingers on its top, her eyes fell on the door to the integral garage. She went across and opened it, stepped down inside and switched on the overhead strip of lighting.

Christ, it was a mess. Metal shelving along each wall was filled with what seemed to her like junk, but she bet Joe would say that about her boxes of make-up stashed upstairs. Tins of white paint, brushes in old turpentine, paint stripper, floor varnish. Screws, nails, a drill set. Old blankets and towels, a rolled-up remnant of the bedroom carpet. Bathroom tiles, an old tyre and a box of light bulbs with one missing.

Disheartened by the number of things she'd need to trawl through, she turned to leave. Her leg caught on the side of a pile of 4x4 magazines, and she watched as the glossy covers slipped from the shelving, flopping to the floor. Bending to pick them up, she caught sight of an old biscuit tin behind them. She reached it out and forced open the lid.

Then she wished that she hadn't.

The selfish, conniving bastard. Tears of rage welled up in her eyes. Despite all of her suspicions and her relentless hounding, never in her wildest moments of jealousy had she really believed that Joe would still be in love with his ex-wife.

'Chloe Winters, twenty years of age.' DCI Barrow pointed to a photo on the whiteboard as he joined them again for the evening's briefing. 'Just after midnight last night, she was dragged from Town Road and into bushes at the top of Central Forest Park, where she was beaten and raped. When interviewed, she then informed DS Shenton that her attacker had left a letter for her. It turns out it was a written letter in an envelope rather than a magnetic one this time.' He held up two fingers. 'Two letters, Y and N. If we're looking at this as a word and not an anagram, add that to E.V.E.N. and it doesn't spell anything. Any thoughts? Random attack or linked to our killer?'

'It doesn't fit.' Allie shook her head fervently.

'The letters would suggest it does.'

'Not consistent. Two of them, and handwritten on paper.'

'But the fact that our suspect left the note for you to find makes me assume that it has to be something to do with this case.' Trevor glanced surreptitiously at Allie.

Or something to do with me.

Allie knew that must be what they were all thinking. After all, she hadn't stopped thinking that since she'd found the note. She hadn't stopped thinking about the bollocking she'd received after opening the note, too. Although she'd worn gloves, she knew she should have brought the envelope back to the office first. Both Nick and Trevor had gone berserk at her actions. But she'd been so wrapped up in emotion that she hadn't been able to stop herself.

'Allie?'

She looked up to see everyone staring at her.

'Sorry?'

'I was just saying that our man would have had less time to do what he did to Chloe,' Trevor continued, thrusting his hands into his trouser pockets. 'They were outside; even in the bushes they were more open. He would have been running on adrenaline, knowing that someone might have come past and caught him at any time.'

'At midnight?'

'Monday night is student night,' said Nick. 'Lots of young ones around who wouldn't be afraid to walk through the park.'

'Or maybe some a little worse for wear who wouldn't see the danger,' said Perry.

'I reckon all the more reason to separate Chloe from this investigation,' Allie piped up again. 'It could be a random attack.'

'So what would Y.N. mean, then?' asked Sam.

A murmur went round the room.

'Maybe the fact that he didn't rape Suzi Porter before he killed her got to him,' said Perry. 'So he attacked Chloe Winters to do the deed and was going to kill her afterwards. But maybe because he raped her, he was unable to kill her? Long shot, I don't know – but do you see where I'm coming from? Maybe by raping Chloe, he couldn't kill her afterwards.'

Allie wasn't convinced. She stood up and walked to the front of the room, grabbed a marker pen and wrote down the capital letters they had received so far.

E. V. E. N. Y. N.

Treating it like a game of hangman, Allie then struck through the letter Y and the letter N.

'Chloe Winters isn't part of his game,' she said, turning to the room. 'She's too young.'

'We need to keep an open mind.' Nick moved to her side.

'He's playing with us.' Allie blew out the breath she had been holding and glanced at Trevor. 'And he's going to kill again unless we can work out the next victim.'

'But can we rule out Y and N straightaway?' someone asked.

'It's a handwritten note. It's two letters, not one,' Allie repeated. 'You wouldn't link them to this case, surely? If so, why not plastic letters in a bag stuck underneath the bin?'

'Let's keep that in mind but stick with the job in hand for now.'

'But, sir, I think we –'

Trevor held up a hand. 'Sit down, Allie.'

'But –'

'I said sit down!'

Allie shuffled back to join the rest of the team again, a blush spreading across her cheeks.

The briefing went on for another few minutes before everyone broke off. Sam and Perry went to get something to eat in the canteen before it closed. Allie wasn't hungry so was back at her desk. She fiddled with the pen in her hand, flicking it open and closed, eventually irritating herself. Her original thoughts around a word being spelt out were worrying in themselves: the series of letters could mean there were going to be more killings unless they could work out who the murderer was, or they could point to who he was going to go after next. Yet, why were both Sam and Perry thinking that Chloe Winters' case wasn't related to their alphabet-letter man too? And if they were right, was Chloe even relevant in this case, or had she just been in the wrong place at the wrong time?

She decided to go and speak to Nick.

'Could I have a quiet word, please,' Allie said as she approached his desk.

Nick nodded and stood up. 'Let's see if the meeting room is free.'

A few minutes later, they were seated at the table in the room.

'Look, I hear where you're coming from regarding Chloe Winters,' Nick began, 'and for what it's worth I agree. But the last thing we need is for everyone to think there is some sort of vendetta being carried out until we're more certain.'

'It's not that, sir.' Allie paused for the briefest of moments. 'I think it could be something to do with the attack on my sister.'

Nick frowned. 'Surely not.'

'My name was on the letter.'

'Your name was mentioned at the press conferences and in newspaper reports.'

Allie shook her head. 'Someone wanted to give me that message personally. What if he's still out there and he's – he's starting up again? You know how brutal the attack was on Karen. What if . . .'

'Allie, stop.' Nick held a hand up. 'I know it's brought back painful memories but it was a long time ago that Karen was attacked.'

'Maybe so.' Allie took a deep breath before spitting out the thought that had been bothering her. 'I think . . . I think he's setting up all these killings to put us off the scent and then he's going to go after Karen again. It makes sense to try and kill her and –'

'To you, maybe,' interrupted Nick, 'but it doesn't make any sense to me whatsoever. It was years ago.'

'She went to Reginald High School and she was in Mickey and Suzi's year.'

'There've been two murders since then. And Frank Dwyer and Malcolm Foster have been linked via emails to images of young boys.'

'There's a photograph on Karen's wall in her room. It's a group of teenagers and I recognise some of them. Mickey and his wife and Sandy – Suzi Porter – are three of the names in a list written on the back of it. The photograph clearly shows my sister knew them all well.'

'They hung around together – so what?' Nick shrugged. 'I might be in a few photos like that but I haven't seen the majority of people I went to school with for years, if at all.'

'She knows our killer, I'm certain!'

'You don't know that for definite!'

Allie gasped. 'Only because she can't tell me.'

'Let's think about it logically. Why come back now? After all these years?'

'To show that he can.'

Nick shook his head. 'I don't buy that. And this investigation is too intense to concentrate on anything else at the same time. We have people pulled in from everywhere possible before this bastard strikes again. I can't have you thinking of other things.'

'But –'

'Look, if he is after revenge, or some sort of vengeance, we need to continue trying to work out why.'

'Revenge – exactly!' Allie lowered her voice a little before she spoke again. 'We have four of those letters in the word EVEN.'

'Do you have some reasoning around your theory?'

Allie frowned. 'I don't follow you.'

'Why our killer would be after revenge on your sister?'

'I'm not sure, but I think –'

Nick shook his head again. 'I know you want closure on what happened to Karen but this isn't the way. You're not thinking straight, Allie. I need your mind to be focused on this case entirely.'

'So we're just going to ignore the fact that Chloe was raped and left for dead?'

'Of course not.'

'It's part of this case!' Allie slapped her hand down on the table. 'He's going to come after Karen.'

Nick raised his eyebrows and stared at her. Allie knew she was close to the mark.

'We'll wait for forensics to come back from the letter,' Nick continued, 'and . . .'

'Match the DNA against our killer's!'

'*If* we have his DNA. You know it's all down to funding – and time. Things are piling up as it is.' He stood up. 'Chloe Winters' case is with PC Butler and she is looking into everything and keeping us in the loop as first to know. It's crucial that we gather information as quickly as possible but I need you to concentrate on the murders first and foremost.'

'I know, sir.' Allie nodded. 'But she's my sister. And her attacker is still out there.'

This old man, he played five,
He played knick-knack on his hive.
With a knick-knack, paddy-whack,
Give the dog a bone.
This old man came rolling home.

1989

Dressing for the school-leaving disco, Patrick was certain he'd never make a good impression in his old jeans and school-blue shirt, but at least they were clean. And, even straight after his shower, he already felt sweat patches forming underneath his arms. He opened his bedroom door and crept into Ray's room, where he liberally sprayed some of his aftershave over his neck. Ray wouldn't know: he hadn't seen him since this morning. He must still be out at the pub.

The disco was in full swing when he arrived there with Daz and Lefty. The three of them stood in a corner together. Patrick could see a girl from his class giving him the eye as she danced to The B-52s' Love Shack. He ignored her – he wasn't going to fall for that again. There was no way he'd be beaten up now that he was leaving school, not after last month's attack.

Just as he was starting to relax, in walked Mickey Taylor and his gang. Kath Clamortie was holding Mickey's hand, even though she wasn't leaving school that year. Sandra Seymour was hanging onto Johnno's arm. Alongside them were Whitty and another girl from their class, Belinda Evans. At the back of the group, Matthew Thompson had teamed up with Karen Baxter. Patrick checked his watch: quarter past eight. The disco was nearly over so if they started any trouble, he would leg it before it got out of hand.

But Mickey and his gang stayed away. Patrick watched the girls dance for a while, kept an eye on the boys. Thirty minutes later, Lefty nudged him, tried to tell him something, but he couldn't hear above the music. When he looked again, Johnno, Whitty and Mickey were making their way across to him. Patrick braced himself for one last thump.

They stopped in front of them and Mickey held out his hand. 'Truce?' he shouted. 'Now that we're leaving school.'

For a moment, Patrick hesitated. He glanced at Lefty and Daz, who must have been thinking the same as him, surely? Mickey was never nice to them – it didn't have anything to do with it being the last time at the school. But as Mickey held out his hand, and the other guys behind him seemed to be mellowing, he shook it too. While Mickey shook hands with Daz and Lefty, Johnno followed Mickey's lead; so too did Whitty.

Then the lights went down and the up-tempo music slowed.

Sandra grabbed Patrick by the hand. 'Come on – dance with me, then.'

'No! Wait. I can't!'

She pulled him into the middle of the floor. 'Yes, you can.'

Patrick turned around to see Johnno egging him on. As Sandra wrapped her arms around his neck, Patrick held his breath and waited for the knife to stab him in the back. But it didn't come. Still uncomfortable, he danced with Sandra but, after a couple of minutes with no mishap, he began to relax. It was strange to dance with a girl. His hormones getting the better of him, he tried to think of football as she pushed her body closer.

Once the record had finished, Sandra dragged him over to where a bunch of teachers were chatting. She tapped Miss Roper, their biology teacher, on the shoulder.

'Patrick would like to dance with you.' She smiled innocently.

Patrick couldn't speak. Miss Roper was hot. He reckoned she was the woman in most of Reginald High School's boys' wet dreams right now.

'Just this one, Patrick,' Miss Roper smiled.

As Patrick followed her back on to the dance floor, he wondered if the plan to humiliate him had backfired. Sandra had returned to Johnno now. Had they thought Miss Roper would say no and make a fool out of him? Well, who was laughing now?

To his right, he could see Whitty walking onto the dance floor with another teacher, Mrs Berry. Patrick was happy inside: he had bagged the best-looking one by far. As he walked past, Whitty patted him on the shoulder, twice in succession. 'Lucky bastard,' he grinned and then carried on.

They danced for another minute before Patrick saw someone point at them and start to laugh. He looked around; there were other people laughing. Were they pointing at him too? When he caught Johnno's eye, he saw him make the shape of an L with his hand. He didn't understand. Above the music, he heard someone shout 'loser!' And then they all joined in.

'Loser! Loser!' he could hear them chanting.

Miss Roper looked a little puzzled. 'What's happening, Patrick?'

He couldn't speak to her, just held on to her. If he didn't stop dancing, he wouldn't find out what they were laughing at. This moment could go on forever if he let it.

'Patrick!' Miss Roper cried. 'Please, I'd like to leave the dance floor now. Patrick! Let me go.'

She pushed him away and he landed hard on the floor with a thump. More laughter. It was then that Mr Andrews, the maths teacher, marched across to them.

'For God's sake, stand up and turn around,' he said.

Patrick did as he was told. He heard a peeling noise. The teacher turned him back to face him and held out the sticker.

'I assume this is yours, Patrick? It's on the back of your shirt.'

Patrick took the sticker. Written in colourful capital letters was the word 'Loser.'

The chorus, the chant: loser, loser. It started again. Patrick ran towards the exit. If he could get out, it would all be over and at least he'd never have to face any of them again. But he might have guessed that Johnno wouldn't let him off that easily. He didn't see him stick out his foot until it was too late.

He tripped, tumbling forward, landing heavily on his face. Glancing up, he saw everyone laughing; even Daz and Lefty had joined in. When they saw him watching, Lefty stopped, turning his head away for a moment, but Daz carried on.

Patrick got up again and ran.

It was the ultimate humiliation.

Chapter Twenty-Six

Nathan Whittaker, Whitty to all his old friends, drove into the car park on Waterloo Road and parked up. He turned to his wife, Mia, in the passenger seat.

'Our first family outing,' he grinned, squeezing her shoulder tenderly.

Mia smiled. 'Don't be long.'

Nathan climbed out of the car. He looked back over his shoulder, waving at Mia before hopping over the low wall and disappearing onto the walkway that would take him down the side of the Indian takeaway. He'd already placed their order before they left, so hopefully it would be ready when he got there.

As he approached the back of the building ahead, the brightness of a security light lit him up in the middle of the pathway. Before it went off again, he took out the small photograph that Mia had slipped into his wallet only the day before. He ran a finger over the image, a huge grin appearing on his face. Ridiculously cheesy but he was so in love. Casey Rae Whittaker, born December thirty-first 2014. Three point four five kilos, she'd certainly ensured they'd started the New Year with a bang. Fourteen days old as of today and boy, how she'd changed their life during those two weeks. It was the reason why they were all in the car now. Casey had been screaming since she'd woken an hour ago and Mia didn't want to be left alone with her.

It was his last day off; he'd managed to tag a few days' holiday onto the Christmas break to be with Mia, and he wasn't looking forward to returning to work in the morning. He'd been at Machine Mart for nearly twenty years and although he enjoyed it, since Casey had been born he felt like he wanted so much more for his family. Before he'd left, after a frantic call from Mia as she'd gone into labour, Nathan had been fairly content with his life. Working as a sales rep behind a counter wasn't a glamorous job but it was safe by today's job security standards, and steady with a regular income. They were comfortable, and able to cover all the bills. They only had three years left to pay off their mortgage; they drove a car apiece. Life was good, made all the better by Casey's arrival. So why now did it feel inadequate?

And then it hit him. Now, with the responsibilities of a father, he didn't want his daughter to grow up thinking her old man had no ambition. Nathan grinned, still unable to think of himself as a father after all this time. Even though he had only just left them, he pulled out his mobile phone and sent Mia a quick text message.

How is my girl doing?

Fine – so is Casey ;)

Nathan laughed. He and Mia had been married for nearly fifteen years and had wanted to start a family almost straight away but things hadn't gone smoothly for them. Whereas his brother's wife had gone on to have three children in quick succession, Mia hadn't been able to stay pregnant, suffering five miscarriages before finally carrying Casey to full term. She was their little miracle.

Five minutes later, the takeaway in his hands, he made his way back along the walkway to their car. The security light came on and went off shortly afterwards as he passed. The smell of curry from behind filled his nostrils as he reached for his phone to send another silly text message to Mia. He grinned: he had never texted Mia this much, ever. They were one of those couples who never felt the need to repeatedly check up on each other all day, every day.

Head down as he pressed buttons, the blow to the back of his head came completely out of the blue. Nathan stumbled forward, dropping the bag of food on the ground, his phone sliding along the pathway. Only just managing to stay upright, he turned around to face his attacker. A man stood before him holding a piece of 3-by-3 wood in his hand like a cricket bat. He was dressed in dark clothes and a beanie hat pulled down to cover most of his eyes, and Nathan couldn't see him clearly.

'What's the fuck's wrong with you?' Nathan put his hands up to protect himself. He was no fighter, but he would have a go to defend himself if necessary.

'Loser.'

'What?' Nathan frowned. Silence except for the sound of traffic from the road.

He stole a fleeting glance at Mia. When the man made no further moves, he made a run for it, but he was pulled back by an arm and twirled round with force. He threw a punch but it missed its target. He tried again, connecting with the man's shoulder this time.

'What do you want?' It was then he saw the glint of the blade. 'Hey, wait. I –' He put up his hands as the man lunged at him and stepped backwards. He avoided him twice until his luck ran out. The man ran at him again, pushing the knife into his stomach.

Nathan groaned, winded by the force of it as the blade penetrated his jumper. Before he had time to react, he felt a fiery heat as the knife swished out of him. All he could do was gasp as it was pushed in again, further this time.

He stumbled forward when the knife was removed for a third time, felt something being shoved into his pocket before the man moved away again.

When his attacker made no attempt to do anything else, Nathan shuffled his feet until he had managed to turn back to face the car park again. If he could just get to Mia, she could raise the alarm.

Clutching his stomach, he took slow, faltering steps, all the time knowing that his attacker was behind him. But a weird sense of optimism washed over him. He held on to a concrete post and stepped gingerly over the low wall, first one foot and then the other. He could feel a burning in his stomach, blood oozing between his fingers. Why hadn't he put a coat on instead of braving the cold night in a jacket? He didn't dare look down. He didn't dare look back.

Mia was looking at her phone, her mouth moving as her fingers pressed the keys. She must be singing. She was texting someone – was it him?

He took another step, then another. He pulled his hand away from his stomach as he fell to his knees. The release of pressure nauseated him, but he got up again. Nearly there. He stretched out a hand.

Mia had spotted him at last. Thank God, she was getting out of the car. He was safe. She would get help.

He began to shiver.

'Nathan?' She opened the door. 'Nathan, what is it?'

'Mia.' He held out his hand.

She ran to him, took his hand, screaming as he dropped to his knees. This time he couldn't get up.

'Nathan? Nathan!'

No more steps.

'NATHAN!'

From the walkway, Patrick watched as the woman screamed, looked around helplessly and then spotted him.

'Help me!' she cried, looking at him. 'He's been attacked. Help me. Please!'

Patrick smiled to himself and stayed where he was. Would she remember him later, and then wonder why he didn't rush across to her? Would she realise that he was the killer? He'd like to think so. He liked that she'd noticed him too, knew he wouldn't go to help.

From where he was standing, the woman seemed attractive. Lovely long dark hair she kept pushing away from her face as she knelt beside her man. He'd picked a good one there; he'd give Whitty credit for that much. Patrick wondered if she was his wife.

He listened: beyond her screaming, he could hear something else. A baby crying – was it coming from the car? He had a family. Even better.

His view of the scene didn't last long. A couple walking back to their car ran over to help. Patrick moved into the shadows and down the path in the opposite direction. He rounded the corner to flashing lights from an approaching ambulance and put his head down. They wouldn't spot him; no one would remember him until later, when he'd be long gone. And there were less than three days left now before he would have completed the game anyway.

Leaving the chaos behind, Patrick started running, happy in the knowledge that he could tick number five off his list. A few minutes later, he threw down the piece of wood he'd tucked inside his fleece, got into his car and drove off.

He was behind her, she could hear him; she could smell *him. She scrambled up the path, her feet slipping on the wet grass as she tried to get ahead. Footsteps, a twig breaking, a kick of a can. She tripped in her haste, falling on one knee, keeping in the gasp of pain as it shot through her and into her spine. She heard him again, pushed herself to her feet and ran.*

Ahead, she could see the road, lights of houses in the distance. If she could just make it to one of them, she would be safe.

She felt his hand clasp her ankle. Screaming, she kicked back at him. He loosened his grip, allowing her to think she was safe for a second, letting her crawl a few feet further away until he grabbed it again, pulling her towards him and over onto her back. He straddled her legs, pinning her down with the weight of his body, quickly moving to grab hold of her hands with his. He held her there for a moment as she bucked underneath him, screaming out, knowing that no one could hear her.

His breath was rancid, disgusting. She heaved, her own breathing becoming raspy at the thought of what he was about to do, what she was powerless to stop. Oh, God, she didn't want to end up like her sister.

'Look at me,' he said.

She wouldn't, kept her eyes to the left.

'Fucking look at me!'

She turned her head slowly but all she saw was an outline of a face. It had nothing to do with the darkness enveloping them. The man had no features, except a mouth that was sneering cruelly at her. She would never be able to tell anyone what he looked like, help with enquiries. He would get away with whatever he was going to do.

When she realised there was no escape, her rigid body went limp beneath him.

He administered the first punch. A full-on hit to the centre of her face. She tasted blood almost immediately, felt it trickle from her nose, groaned as lights exploded inside her head. A knee on each arm now, yet still he could stop her legs from moving – he knew what he was doing: had he done it before?

Now he had both of her hands above her head, held in his one. Should she struggle or let him do it – let him violate her, get it over with? Maybe she could get away if so. She felt a lone tear fall from her eye as his free hand reached for the button on her trousers.

'Hey.' A hand on her shoulder.

Allie screamed. Lashing out in the darkness, she sat up with a jolt. 'Mark?' she cried. 'Mark – where are you?'

'I'm here, Allie.' Mark sat up too, his voice soft, soothing. 'I'm here.'

She laughed with relief. Tears threatened to fall but she held them in. For a moment, she pulled her knees to her chest and hugged herself. Thank God – she'd been dreaming.

She heard the bed creak, a click. Allie squinted as her eyes adjusted to the bright light. When she could see properly, they flicked to the clock. Ten past one: they'd only been in bed for an hour.

'It's hardly surprising you've had a nightmare after your day,' Mark said gently.

'I didn't think I'd dropped off fully.'

'It's bound to play on your mind.'

Allie turned her face towards his and nodded, reached for him. He pulled her into his arms and they lay back down together while their breathing returned to normal.

'I thought we'd seen the back of your nightmares,' he stated, rubbing his fingers up and down the length of her arm.

'So did I.' Allie faked a yawn and snuggled into him some more. She didn't want this conversation now, didn't want to think of Chloe Winters.

A few minutes later, Mark switched off the light. Allie knew sleep wouldn't come to her again for a while. The dream had been vivid; her heart was still pounding. She could feel her fear, still smell his rancid breath.

But she couldn't talk to Mark about it. Because then he would know that she hadn't told him about the note she'd received three years ago.

Chapter Twenty-Seven

Overnight, the details of the attack on Nathan Whittaker, along with the orange plastic magnetic letter they had found inside the pocket of his jacket, had come into the station. The fact that it was a letter G introduced the idea that the killer could be spelling out the word *revenge* if the letters Y and N weren't taken into consideration, although Nick still wanted everyone to keep an open mind. With no letter R forthcoming, it wasn't a certainty that they had missed something, but Allie wondered if that was part of the game too. She also couldn't stop thinking that *if* a letter R did show up, that would mean another victim. She shuddered involuntarily.

After the team briefing, she was asked to visit Nathan Whittaker in hospital. She decided to take Sam with her. Before leaving the station, she phoned to check with the ward sister for the latest update on his condition.

'How is he doing?' Sam asked as they went downstairs.

'He's undergone several hours of surgery but he's stable.' Allie held the door open for her to walk through. 'We can't talk to him as he's still sedated, but his wife is there. She was with him when it happened.'

'Oh, God.'

'She didn't see the attack, I don't think. Not that it's any consolation for her.'

At the Royal Stoke University Hospital, they walked along the main corridor towards the emergency admissions wards.

'We have to contain this, don't we?' said Sam.

'I think it's gone beyond that now,' Allie replied. 'Even if we kept the magnetic letters to ourselves, the bloody killer isn't giving us time to think. We'll never join the pieces together at this rate.'

'I know. There's not enough time to check everything for one victim before he's off taking out another one.'

'It's preposterous. Callous too.' Allie moved aside as a man in crutches hobbled past them. 'And even though we think he might be spelling the word *revenge*, it's beginning to feel like Alphabet Spaghetti pouring out over a plate.'

'And it's not an acronym, as far as I'm aware. E, V, E, N, Y, N and now G – I've Googled it but come up with nothing.'

'It's bloody frustrating,' said Allie.

They walked the final corridor and turned right onto the ward. All around them was a smell of disinfectant, a sharp whiff of ammonia, a hint of lemon. A woman shouted out sporadically, followed by the voice of a man trying to soothe her.

The ward sister whom Allie had spoken to earlier was still on duty.

'You can speak to his wife but, like I mentioned to you on the phone, for now Mr Whittaker is still recovering from surgery. He's heavily sedated.' The woman pointed to a side room. 'Ten minutes, Sergeant,' she said.

Allie pushed on the door handle and was met by the sight of a young woman with the tiniest of babies curled up asleep on her chest. Puffy-eyed, she sat in a big comfy chair by the side of the hospital bed, her eyes moving from her husband's face for only a second as they entered before they were back to him again.

Nathan Whittaker lay on his back. His eyes were closed, his face flushed. For such a big man, he seemed helpless wired up to so many machines. Images crept into her head of Karen taking her last breaths, and she immediately pushed them away.

'Mrs Whittaker?' Allie stood at the end of the bed. 'I'm Detective Sergeant Shenton and this is my colleague, Detective Constable Markham. May we speak with you, please?'

'Aye.' Mia pushed herself to the edge of the seat, cupped the sleeping baby's head and stood up.

'She's so tiny,' Allie said, hoping that the pink baby suit was the right colour. 'What's her name?'

'Casey. She was two weeks old yesterday.'

'Beautiful.'

Mia squatted and laid the baby gently back in her car seat. 'She is when she's asleep. I hope she stays that way for a while.' She stood up again and looked at them. 'I only have that seat and I didn't want to leave to fetch the travel cot. My parents are travelling down from Scotland at the moment.' She started to cry.

Allie put a hand on her elbow and guided her back to her seat. She pulled out two chairs from a stack of four in the corner and she and Sam sat down too.

'He's doing well, I hear,' said Allie.

'I just want him to wake up.' Mia looked at them through swollen eyes. 'Just to know that it's him lying in that bed and not some . . . some replica that I'm left with.'

'Were there any other injuries apart from the stab wounds?'

'A bump to the head. The surgeon said he's going to be fine but I can't see that yet.'

Allie gave a half-smile. 'I know it's tough but I need to run through what happened with you again.'

'I could hardly speak last night.' Mia rubbed her hands together. 'And Casey began screaming when I started screaming. In the end, one of the nurses came in and took her to the maternity block where they watched her for a couple of hours. I'm not even sure they're supposed to do that. Wasn't that kind?'

Allie nodded.

'It was about half past six. Casey had been niggling for most of the day so we'd both fallen asleep on the settee. We went for our usual takeaway: we have one most Wednesdays. The ridiculous thing was that for some reason I wanted to go with Nathan. Casey was snuffling again and I suppose I didn't want to be on my own, despite it taking forever to get her ready to leave the house. They cause so much work, don't they?'

'They do,' Sam empathised. 'My little girl is five – not as messy but still a lot of work.'

'We rang the order through and went to collect it. He sent me a silly text, which I replied to. Then a few minutes later, I was listening to the radio in the car, looking out for him, and decided to send him one too.' Mia paused to catch her breath. 'I looked up and there he was walking towards me. Except he was staggering, as if he was drunk, and clutching hold of his stomach. I raced over to him. He put out his hand for me to steady him and I felt it all slippery. It was covered in blood.'

As she gasped, Sam leaned over to squeeze her hand.

'He – he dropped to his knees,' she continued, 'so I sat down beside him. I tried to cover the wound, pressed on it, you know, like you see people do on the television. But he kept on groaning. Then he kept saying my name over and over and then he said "Casey." And then nothing.' She looked at them then, wide-eyed. 'I thought I'd lost him. I was still screaming, looking around to see if anyone was near. And then I saw him.'

Allie frowned. 'You *saw* him?'

'I think so. He was across on the walkway. I shouted to him to help but he just stood there. I grabbed my phone and called for an ambulance. A few minutes later, a man and a woman came back to their car. They stayed with us until the ambulance arrived.'

'Can you recall what he looked like?' Allie probed, glancing at Sam. This was the closest they had come to their killer so far. 'Often in times of trauma, our minds pick up on all sorts of details,' she added. 'It really helps to go over everything again.'

'He was white, thin, medium build and height. He was dressed in dark clothes, a black jacket, and he wore a dark woollen kind of hat.' Mia paused for a moment before shaking her head in dismay. 'It could have been a teenager, I suppose.'

'Mia,' asked Allie. 'Did Nathan go to Reginald High School?'

Mia frowned. 'Yes, he told me the other day when he realised the people in the newspaper . . .' She stopped. 'You don't think that was the killer, do you? Is it something to do with that coloured letter Nathan had in his pocket? Because that wasn't there before he was attacked.'

'It's possible there is a connection. We're looking into it now. Has anyone fallen out with Nathan recently? At work, or a friend or neighbour? Anything you can thing of – no matter how tiny?'

Mia shook her head. 'He's such a great guy. Really – he is. People genuinely like him when he's around them. He's a bit of a joker so he's always getting people laughing. I – I hope he doesn't lose that now.'

Allie looked at the man lying on the bed in front of them, praying that he would make a quick recovery so that he could go back to his family. She hoped he'd survive the attack as unscathed as possible, even if he did have the trauma to deal with afterwards. She knew from bitter experience how hard it was to live through.

Mia sensed the conversation had come to a close and reached over for Nathan's hand. She moved her chair in closer. 'I hope he comes back to me soon,' she whispered. 'I told him to wear his bloody big coat too; at least he might have buttoned that up. But he said he'd be warm enough in his thin jacket.'

Allie blinked away tears as she stood up. She left with Sam, their two sets of shoulders sagging.

'Wow, so sad,' said Sam.

'Indeed. If this is our man, then Nathan Whittaker is one lucky bastard if he survives.'

A further press conference was held that afternoon to ask anyone who had left Reginald High School in 1989 to contact the station. It brought in another deluge of calls. Allie went out this time with Perry to check up on a few things of interest, but nothing useful came out of it. It was after eight p.m. when they stopped in the car and grabbed something to eat.

Perry ate a few mouthfuls of his burger before throwing it back in the plastic carton.

Allie was just about to take another bite of hers. 'It's not like you to be off your food,' she joked.

'It's all this stuff with Foster and his son,' he told her. 'And Charlie Lewis, and then that lad, Danny Peterson. All kids. It's doing my head in.'

Allie put down her food, her appetite suddenly dwindling too. For the first time, she noticed how weary Perry looked. Dark rings under his eyes, hair a mess, shoulders sagging. She didn't think it was just the usual tiredness they were all feeling.

'You want to talk?'

'I can't stop thinking of the connections to our school, either.' Perry sighed. 'Especially after Whitty was attacked.'

'Who?'

'Nathan Whittaker – we used to call him Whitty.'

'Oh – did you have a nickname?'

'Lefty,' Perry sniggered. 'I reckon everyone with the surname of Wright would be called that.'

Allie smiled back at him. 'So, this Whitty. What was he like?'

'A good laugh, from what I remember. We caught up at a stag do a few years ago. It was Lisa's sister's fella who was getting married. I wasn't looking forward to going as I didn't know anyone but I had a really good night because he was there. He seemed as well liked then as he was at school, too.'

'Nigel Foster didn't go to Reginald High,' Allie pointed out. 'And Danny Peterson wasn't even born.'

'No, but he was being groomed, wasn't he?'

'I would have to say yes if I was guessing.'

Perry shook his head. 'The more this case goes on and the more I think of the people involved, the more I wonder if it *is* someone I went to school with.'

'Is there anyone who stands out to you?'

'No. How about you?'

Allie shrugged. 'I'm not sure I'll remember anyone you know, unless they used to hang around with Karen. And even then I'd only know of them vaguely. Being twelve when you were sixteen, I'd hardly take any notice of you, would I?'

'What do you mean?' Perry looked confused.

'Well, at that age, weren't we only interested in the kids in our own year? I might remember a few names, I suppose, if I had a crush on an older boy every now and again, but he would most probably be in a year above me, maybe two. But definitely not four years. And it's so annoying that there are no registers now that the school is closed.'

Perry opened a can of Coke and took a big gulp. 'We do have lists of exam results to go through, though.'

'Great,' mocked Allie. 'Let's hope the killer was clever enough to sit any.'

Perry sighed and shook his head.

'Would it help if we made a list of people who you got on with and ones you didn't?' Allie suggested.

'I've been trying to do that since Frank Dwyer's murder. And the more I think about it, the more I know that anyone in our year could be in danger.'

'Don't even go there.' Allie put a hand up to stop him, although she knew they were all thinking along those lines since the team brief. 'I'm just glad I'm that little bit younger, so I wasn't in your class,' she joked afterwards.

'Yes, a psycho after Allie Shenton,' Perry teased. 'Now that would be unheard of, right? After all, you haven't upset anyone in Stoke over the past few years.'

'Only by doing my job!' Allie protested. 'If people break the law, we have to go after them.'

'It really could be personal to anyone in my year, though,' Perry said again. 'I could be next for all we know.'

'It won't be you.' Allie shook her head.

'How do you know?'

'For starters, didn't you say that you used to get on well with everyone at school?'

'Well, I thought so. I did get whacked a few times for not joining in with Mickey's gang, though. I hate bullies. But then again, who knows if I went over the top with someone and they thought I was a bully too. It was such a long time ago – surely that wouldn't lead to someone committing murder?'

'It could have contributed to it.' Allie shrugged. 'Who knows what state of mind a killer could be in, what makes them do what they do?'

'But why now? It's twenty-six years since we left school.'

'What if *he* thinks he was being bullied but you don't, so you don't remember him?'

'I'm not with you.'

'People have different ways of reacting to things, different trigger points and thresholds. I'm just clutching at straws.' Allie wiped her hands on a paper napkin. 'I don't know about you but I'm ready to call it a night and get home to Mark before he forgets he has a wife again. How's Lisa, by the way?'

'She's good, thanks.' Perry sat forward and put his rubbish into the bag at his feet.

Allie caught the grin on his face as the harsh light of the streetlamp coming in through the side window lit it up.

'That's a big smile,' she told him.

'It is.' Perry laughed. 'But I'm sworn to secrecy.'

'About what?' Allie stared at him. 'Perry, you can't tell me half a story! And after the week we're having, if it's good news, then I want to know.'

'You promise not to say anything to Lisa?'

'I promise!' Allie almost shouted. 'Wait, she's not . . .' She looked at him and his grin widened. 'She is, isn't she? She's pregnant?'

'Yep, I'm going to be a dad.'

'Ah, that's great news! Come here.' Allie gave him a hug across the seats.

'She's not too far along, though. That's why I can't tell anyone, just in case anything goes wrong.' Perry grinned again. 'But I've been bursting since we found out at the weekend.'

'Well, congratulations, Daddy.' Allie smiled. 'Now, let's go home.'

Both of them kept their thoughts to themselves about how close Nathan Whittaker's daughter had come to losing her father.

Patrick sat up quickly, jolted from a fitful sleep. He'd woken several times that night, real fear from his dreams keeping him on constant alert. Any minute now, the front door would be kicked in and he'd be dragged from his bed, handcuffed and arrested for murder. He couldn't get away with killing all these people, could he? But he must – he must stay away from the police for as long as he could.

He lay back in his bed, drenched in sweat, breathing rapidly and waiting for the swell of his chest to slow. The panic that took over him after dreams, memories shooting to the forefront of his mind – was it any wonder he was dreaming of everything? He shook the negative thoughts aside. It *wouldn't* go wrong. He was too far into the game. He had planned this meticulously since Ray had gone to prison.

But it had gone wrong, hadn't it? Because Whitty had survived. Simon Cole had reported it on the front page of *The Sentinel* and it had been all over the news. He was serious but stable, but Patrick wasn't really bothered about that. He was more concerned that he hadn't done what he'd set out to do. He'd thought three stabs would be enough, got cocky and let him walk away. He thought Whitty would die before he got help.

He hadn't killed him.

It made him look weak.

An image of himself cowering under his bed came to his mind. He used to hide anywhere he could – different places so that Ray would give up looking for him. But he'd always find him, pull him out by a leg, an arm, an elbow – often by the hair. If he was lucky, he'd drag him into the middle of the room, administer a beating there. If he was unlucky, Ray would drag him down the stairs and into the living room, his back taking the brunt of bare runners on the stairs as they descended.

He pushed aside more memories of his childhood, threatening to send him off the rails. Ray didn't control him anymore.

Once his breathing had returned to normal, he got up, showered and made his way downstairs. As he walked into the living room, he took another look at the map on the wall. All yesterday he'd made sure his planning was in place for today. He'd gone over and over his schedule, ticking it all off, ensuring everything was good to go.

Lying flat on the sideboard was the framed photograph he'd brought back from Suzi Porter's house. He picked it up – couldn't understand how she hadn't known which one was him. It was easy to point him out. He was the one who made himself look small, whose smile didn't reach his eyes, whose trousers were too short and jacket too tight. The goofy one – the waif. The one who took the brunt of all their jokes. He screamed out, threw the frame against the wall, enjoying the sound of shattering glass as it fell to the floor at his feet.

Well, who's having the last laugh now, hmm?

He was. And he would be laughing all the more soon.

Just one more day and two more nights until 10.53 a.m., Friday 16 January.

Chapter Twenty-Eight

At half past nine, Rhian tiptoed downstairs and into the kitchen. Ignoring the empty wine bottle on the side, she filled a glass with water, took two headache tablets and swallowed them greedily. She shuddered as the cold water hit her stomach.

In the living room, she searched out her phone and flopped down onto the settee. Three text messages from Joe, the last one worrying about her lack of response. She'd refused to answer his call yesterday, plus several texts he'd sent because of it.

At her side, the coffee table was littered with personal paraphernalia, photos from years gone by. But none of the photos were of her. They were all of Suzi Porter; several were topless poses, suggestive and provocative. Rhian had fanned them out last night, lost count at twenty-seven and thrown them up in the air like a pack of cards, screamed when they had come down again like confetti. How could he still have them all? It was beyond a few holiday snaps he'd saved as mementoes over the years. And besides, this was his ex-wife. His *dead* ex-wife.

His last message said he'd be home by midday and, sure enough, she heard his car pull into the driveway as she checked her watch for the umpteenth time. Normally, she would be dressed and racing to the door to greet him, all smiles and hugs and making up for lost time. This time, she gathered all the photos, threw them back in the tin and put them out of sight behind a pillow.

She heard him come in through the garage door, and then he appeared in the doorway.

'What's up?' he asked. 'Aren't you feeling well? Is that why you didn't answer when I rang?'

Rhian paused for the slightest of moments. 'Do you love me, Joe?' she wanted to know. 'You've been away for four days and I've been here alone, bored out of my brains.'

'Look, I'm knackered.' Joe pinched the bridge of his nose. 'So if you have a problem with that, you know where the front door is.'

'Oh, I'm not *that* bothered about being lonely.' Rhian pulled the tin out from underneath the pillow and slammed it down on the coffee table. She lifted the lid and tipped the contents out. 'I'm more bothered about you still being in love with your ex-wife!'

Joe's face contorted as the photos scattered to the floor. 'You nosy little bitch,' he snarled.

'Were you still in love with her?'

'Leave it alone.'

'Were you still in love with HER?'

'You have no right to go through my personal belongings!'

'I have every right. I live here too and –'

'You don't own this place. It's mine!' He prodded himself in the chest. 'Fuck, I must be out of my mind to still be with you.'

'You *do* still love her, don't you?' Tears pricked at Rhian's eyes.

Joe looked down at the photos and then back at her. 'Pick them up,' he said.

'No.' Rhian folded her arms.

'I said pick them up.'

'Why? Do you want to masturbate over them? Is that what you do?'

'The woman is dead, for fuck's sake. Put them back in the tin.'

But Rhian wouldn't. 'Is that where you were on all those late nights? Were you fucking her? You had lots of opportunities to screw her when you were off seeing Jay. Were you seeing your son or were you seeing her? You still won't tell me where you were on the night she was killed. I've a good mind to get in touch with the police and tell them to check out times and dates. You could easily —'

'Oh, so now you're accusing me of murdering her as well as fucking her!'

'I know you're involved in her murder somehow.' She stood up quickly. 'What happened — did you make a pass at her and she turned you down so you got mad?'

Joe swiped the back of his hand across her mouth.

Rhian dropped to her knees, tasting blood as her top lip split. She cried out in pain. 'What did you do that for?'

'You drive me crazy, do you know that?' he seethed.

Rhian pointed to the photos. 'Have you any idea what it feels like to be your girlfriend and see that you have photos of your ex-wife spreading her legs?'

'She's not spreading her legs.'

'She might as well be!'

'They're things I kept to show Jay when he was older.'

'And you expect me to believe that?'

'Believe what you want.' In silence, Joe collected up the photographs and placed them back in the tin. He closed the lid and put them underneath his arm. Then he stood for a moment before sighing loudly. 'I've had enough of you and your childish antics. I think it's time we called it a day.'

'Wh — what?' Rhian faltered.

'You heard.' Joe bent to retrieve a photo that he'd missed.

'But why?'

'You really want me to spell it out for you?' He glared at her. 'You don't contribute in any way to this relationship except to moan and spend my money.'

'I do! I have my own business and I –'

'You paint nails for your friends when you can be bothered. And let's face it – you're not interested in earning any money because you don't need to. I pay for everything, which I wouldn't mind if you weren't such a fucking nag.'

Rhian was still too shocked to speak.

'I should have listened to everyone's warnings. They were right – you *were* just after a sugar daddy and I fell for it. Well, not anymore. Go back to Mummy and Daddy. That's where you belong.'

'No!' Rhian rushed to him and threw her arms around his waist. 'I'm sorry. I shouldn't have accused you of anything. Don't you see? It's because I love you so much that I can't stand the thought of you with her.'

Joe pushed her away.

'I've said I'm sorry. Tell me what else I can do!' Rhian grabbed his arm, held on to it as he walked away. But he pulled it from her grip, leaving her standing there in dismay.

'It's over,' he said. 'I want you out.'

'No! Joe!'

At the sound of the front door slamming behind him, Rhian ran to the window. She just about had time to see him screeching off in the car.

At Car Wash City, Joe went into his office and slammed the door. He put the tin on his desk and sat down, head in hands. Damn that stupid bitch. Thank God, he'd come to the conclusion that he needed to finish things with her before he'd gone home today.

Coming back to her sneaking around behind his back had been the last straw.

The photos were laughable. Although he hadn't seen them in years, they weren't hidden away. He'd relegated them to the garage because he didn't want to be reminded of happier times before everything had gone sour, plus he'd been saving them for Jayden. And now Suzi had gone, they would be even more personal to their son.

He picked up one of the photographs. In their early twenties, he and Suzi had been on holiday to Benidorm. Suzi was lounging on a sunbed in a bikini, eating ice-cream, a large sun hat hiding most of her face but not her infectious grin. He'd taken the photo and then lain down next to her, kissing her long and hard he'd become so horny that he hadn't been able to stand up for half an hour. And now she was dead. His eyes watered. He sniffed, wiped his nose on the back of his hand and sat up straight.

Joe would need to pick the right time to show Jayden the photos. Once the police had found Suzi's killer, and they were able to bury her, afterwards it would be good to sit with Jay, remove the topless images and share memories with him. Father and son time sounded good to him. He hadn't had much of that.

He stopped. Perhaps this could be a second chance for him and Jayden. If Rhian wasn't around, he could spend more time with him. He'd have more bloody money to spend too; it was definitely time to get rid of the freeloader.

How wrong he had been to think that he could be satisfied with someone who looked like Suzi. It wasn't the same – it would never be the same. He should have listened to other people. He reached for his phone and brought up Rhian's number, paused over the connect button. He didn't need her whinging at him. A text would suffice. Quickly, he tapped out a message and sent it to her. Afterwards, feeling much better about things, he made the decision that if Rhian was still there that evening when he went home, he would throw her out himself.

He stood up, stretched and looked around his office. Everything seemed to be as he'd left it. He marched over to the forecourt to chat more to the lads, see if anyone had been sneaking around while he'd been away. If not, the coast was clear and he had money in his pocket again.

Chapter Twenty-Nine

Rhian read the message as soon as it came through. Then again, and again.

'*Meant what I said. It's over. Pack up your things.*'

How dare he – how fucking dare he! She was the one who had been wronged yet she ended up being thrown out?

She flopped down onto the settee, her recent upset turning quickly to fury as she pressed a hand against her split lip and winced. She wasn't ever going home with her tail between her legs for anyone. And if their relationship was over, then she would seek her revenge first. And she knew exactly how.

Allie received a message to say that Rhian Jamieson had asked to speak to her urgently. She tried to hold in her surprise when the young woman opened the door with a swollen lip and a bruise appearing on her face.

'What happened?' she asked as she followed her into the living room.

'Me and Joe had a bit of a disagreement. That's why I called you.'

'We have other officers who can deal with this,' Allie informed her. 'Sorry to sound harsh but I deal with more serious cases than common assault. I'll call this in for you and –'

'It's to do with one of your cases.' Rhian moved to stand in front of the window. She turned her back to Allie for a moment and then faced her again. 'I found some photos that Joe had taken of Suzi Porter. I think he might have been blackmailing her.'

'Do you have these photos?'

'No.' Rhian sighed. 'That's what the argument was about, and why he hit me. I found them and wanted to know why he had them. He lashed out and then he left with them.'

'How do you know he was blackmailing her?'

'He told me.'

Allie raised her eyebrows inquisitively. 'And you'd say that in court, would you?'

Rhian wouldn't look at her.

'Because that's what would happen if we looked into this further. We have to have evidence and you know –'

'I think he's involved with her murder too!'

Allie sighed. 'This had better not be a get-your-own-back-on-your-boyfriend conversation, Miss Jamieson.'

'It isn't!'

'So your evidence is?'

'He has the photos. That's *your* evidence.'

'What kind of photos are we talking about?' Allie moved the conversation on.

'Well, they weren't holiday snaps!'

'Are you talking indecent images?'

Rhian nodded.

'Of Suzi Porter?'

'Of *dead* Suzi Porter.'

'And how is that relevant?'

'I don't know!' Rhian tutted. 'You're the detective – you work it out.'

'If you think that you're getting one over on Joe by telling me this information,' Allie took a step towards the door, 'then I'm going to book you for wasting my time.'

'There are other things too!'

Allie closed her eyes momentarily. 'Go on,' she said when she opened them again.

'He wasn't with me watching *The One Show* like he told you.'

'Like you *both* told me,' she remarked. 'Do you know where he was? What time he came in?'

'He came in about eight and no, I don't know where he'd been. He wouldn't tell me – he won't even tell me now.' She shrugged. 'Maybe he'd gone over there after work. And when that other man was killed – that Mickey Flynn?' Rhian continued. 'Well, he was out then too.'

'Could he have been at work then as well?'

'Well, it was really early.' Rhian folded her arms. 'He says he was but how would you know?'

'Indeed.'

'He knew them all at school – he used to hang around with Mickey, told me he was thick as thieves with him. I bet he knows that man who's survived too.'

'Nathan Whittaker? So where was he when that attack happened?'

Rhian looked away sheepishly.

'Oh, for God's sake, Rhian.' Allie turned to leave. 'Don't call me again unless you have something that is relevant to the murder of Suzi Porter or I really will arrest you for wasting police time. Do you hear?'

She'd got as far as the door when Rhian shouted.

'There was blood!'

Allie stopped.

'That night – he came in and ran upstairs to have a shower. There was blood on the front of his T-shirt. I panicked at first because I thought it was his. But he told me one of the blokes at work had had an accident and that he'd given him first aid. It could have been Suzi's blood.'

'And you didn't think to tell me this before?'

'Why should I?'

'Oh, possibly because you're lying to cover up where he was.' Allie looked on incredulously. 'And that you're now trying to frame him for the murder of his wife.'

'She's his ex-wife,' Rhian corrected.

'Do you have the T-shirt?' Allie snapped.

Rhian shook her head. 'I haven't been able to find it.'

'You mean he's washed it or he's got rid of it?'

'I don't know. It was a plain white one – he's got loads.'

'Blood is hard to get out of white items. I'm sure you would have spotted it.'

'Well, he must have got rid of it, then.'

'So you have no evidence whatsoever?'

Rhian shook her head.

'Did Joe hit you?'

'No, he didn't.'

'He *didn't?*'

'No, I was lying.' Rhian said. 'I tripped and fell, landed right on my nose. I'm such a clumsy cow.'

Allie stormed off down the hall and opened the front door.

'Aren't you going to check out his office at Car Wash City?' Rhian shouted after her.

'I don't have time to go on a wild goose chase.'

Allie got back into her car and started the engine. Even though she knew Rhian was after making trouble for Joe, she wouldn't have put it past her to panic and ring him if she thought she might be on her way to see him.

She headed for Car Wash City.

Rhian sat at the breakfast bar, her foot tapping on the side of the stool. Why wouldn't that woman take her seriously and act on what she had told her?

It had been on the tip of her tongue to spill that she knew more than she was letting on about his past. But for once, she'd been smart enough to keep her mouth shut. She ran upstairs and into the back bedroom. With a big heave, she pushed aside a chest of drawers and dropped to her knees. Catching hold of the carpet, she tugged at it until it gave way from the grippers again and pulled out the envelope that she had slipped underneath. Inside it were two photos she had removed from the batch in the tin.

Joe thought he'd been clever taking all the photos but he'd have to be smarter than that to catch her out. The press would be interested in some of them, she was sure, and they might pay a hefty sum for them too, especially as Suzi was still so prevalent in the news.

She smiled, wincing as her lip split again. If Joe wanted her out, those images might be her insurance.

Patrick sat in The White Cafe in Stoke tucking into a large plate of shepherd's pie, chips and gravy. With a branch of Potteries Pizza situated in the next street, people were used to him coming in here. Even though he was later today, it was often a stop he'd call at before heading to Morrison's if he was down that way. Their breakfasts were good and cheap too and for the best part would fill him for the rest of the day.

Already, it was full of the regular dossers. Over in the far corner, a man who seemed no more than twenty and in need of a decent bath was trying not to fall asleep in his coffee. Patrick reckoned he was putting off the inevitable, letting the demon spirit invade his veins and head at The Wheatsheaf around the corner. He wondered what the draw to it was. Having a dislike for alcohol after seeing what it had done to Ray, he hadn't ever been addicted to anything. He hadn't smoked either – too many memories of cigarettes put out on his bare arms and legs when he was younger.

Belly full, he slid his plate to one side and drank his tea. The tea was good here too. He slurped, couldn't help himself. Grinned like a five-year-old, so did it again. He picked up his copy of that day's *Sentinel* and opened it out. He was already splashed all over the front page but inside there was more about what they knew of him, which seemed all speculation.

He read Simon Cole's name again in the by-line. Patrick was leading on every part of the story now, even though there were no photos of him. He'd quite grown to like Simon over the past two weeks. He seemed to report fairly, always equally, showing both sides of the story.

By the side of a report on a young girl who had been raped earlier that week, most of the letters on page nine were critical but hilarious. People blaming the police for not catching him, accusing them of keeping quiet. He read too of an incident earlier in the week when two blokes who had been in his class at school had attacked each other, both convinced that one or the other was involved.

Patrick was glad people would remember him. He'd stayed invisible for long enough, and now it was time to do the final act. Just like the red herring in a book, his story had the capacity to be explosive or a damp squib. He sniggered to himself. This game of his *was* like writing a novel. Making sure he was one step ahead of the police all the time: twists, plots, an ending to die for. Plus had he not killed most of the victims, had the timing not been right or had something gone wrong at the last minute, such as Nathan Whittaker surviving, then he'd always known he was going to move on to the next victim at the allotted time. Killing everyone was his goal but finishing the game on time was his main priority.

He would be all over the newspapers again tomorrow, he was sure. Ray would be too.

Ray had been begging him to visit him in prison for the past couple of years now. But he didn't fool Patrick with his words of apology. All that talk in those letters about how he wanted forgiveness – he knew it was lies. Fibs to lure him into thinking that everything was okay. Ray would never change: the drink would never let him go. Patrick was certain that if he let him back into his life, the torment would start all over again. What was the saying – a leopard never changes its spots?

Ray hadn't fooled him. He would never believe him. Never.

When it was time to leave, Patrick folded up the newspaper and left it on the table. He pulled on his woollen hat and headed out of the pub. It was ten past three. He reckoned it would take him a good hour to walk over to Longton. He didn't want to take the car and he wouldn't run there as he'd have to run back – he needed to keep his strength for tomorrow.

Joe groaned when he saw Ryan's car pull up on the forecourt. He plastered a smile to his face as he showed him into his office.

'Everything good, I hope?'

'Yeah, not so bad.' Ryan moved to the window and leaned his back on the sill. 'Yourself?'

'Yeah, yeah. Good.'

'Can't believe the police haven't caught this serial killer yet, though. You heard anything since you got back? Anything on your ex-wife?'

'Nothing new. Bunch of tossers.'

'Right. I was wondering if you might want to continue our arrangement straightaway rather than wait around?' Ryan questioned. 'I reckon, with the right people, we could get a lucrative operation going.'

'Sounds good, but I need a bit of time, yeah?' Joe ran a hand through his hair. 'The Missus is giving us grief already and we've only been back a few hours.'

'I thought you were all for dumping her.'

'Oh, I am.' Joe nodded. 'These things take time. I'll have her gone by the end of –'

A rap on the open door had them both looking up. Joe groaned inwardly and sat down at his desk.

Allie was surprised to see Ryan Johnson in Joe's office, but she did her best to hide it. Johnson was on the police radar as one of the men who were now keeping an eye on Terry Ryder's businesses while he was in prison. She also knew of him because he and his brother Jordan ran Flynn's, a nightclub on the outskirts of Hanley that was owned by Ryder's daughter, Kirstie.

'Gentlemen,' she addressed them both with what she hoped was a friendly smile.

'DS Shenton,' Ryan addressed Allie with a smile, charm personified. 'To what do we owe this pleasure?'

'Not here for you today, Mr Johnson.' Allie walked right in. 'I just need a word with Mr Tranter.'

'If that bitch has been saying anything . . .' Joe cried. 'She fell, all right?'

'Oh!' Ryan grinned. 'Trouble at home?'

'I'm not here about the assault on Rhian Jamieson, although it would be good if she could make up her mind whether you hit her or she fell.'

Joe ran a hand over his chin. 'Well, whatever else she said, it isn't true either.'

'She claims you have photographs of your ex-wife.'

'Photographs?' Ryan cocked his head inquisitively.

'There's no rule against it, if I have,' Joe replied.

'If they've been used for blackmail, there is.' Allie held his gaze.

Joe scoffed. 'Is that what she told you? She's such a kid.'

'Is she, Mr Tranter?'

'Is she what?'

'Is she telling the truth?' Allie continued. 'Were you blackmailing your ex-wife?'

'Of course I wasn't.' He held up his hands. 'Rhian likes to make things up if she knows it will cause a row. She's a make-up sex kind of girl, if you know what I mean.'

'Not sure that I want to.' Allie glared at him.

A silence fell between them.

Ryan broke it with a snigger. 'So, what are you going to do now?' he asked Allie.

'Not that it's any of your business.'

'You don't have a warrant, though.'

'I can get one.'

'But you know that anything detrimental will have been moved by then, don't you?' Ryan pushed himself from the windowsill.

'There had better not be anything detrimental.' Allie met his gaze.

'There isn't!' said Joe.

'Are you talking photographs now, Sergeant?' Ryan laughed.

'Of course.' Allie turned away from him and back to Joe, before she lost her temper.

'Well, in that case,' Joe pushed the tin towards her, 'these are what Rhian found. I was keeping most of them for Jayden. Feel free to peruse at your leisure.'

Allie opened the lid and took out a few of the photos.

'You see?' he shrugged. 'Lots of couples take these kinds of photos on holiday. Lots of women go topless on beaches. These are no different.'

'So this bruising on Rhian's face?' Allie wouldn't be put off.

'You don't give in, do you, Sergeant?' Ryan laughed again. 'She fell, didn't she, Joe?'

'She did.'

'Rhian also mentioned that you'd come home with blood on your T-shirt,' Allie said, 'on the night that Suzi Porter was murdered.'

'She did what?' Joe stood up quickly.

Ryan gasped. Allie ignored him, kept her eyes locked on Joe's.

'You know, on the night that *you* said you were watching *The One Show* together.'

'*The One Show*?' Ryan burst out into laughter. 'Really?'

'Mr Johnson,' Allie barked. 'Either leave the room or be quiet. This has nothing to do with you.'

Ryan held up his hands in mock surrender.

'I told her it wasn't my blood.' Joe went to the office window and pointed. 'Do you see the boy there, in the blue top? The one with the grubby bandage on his hand? That's Luke and he fell off a low step, trying to reach the middle of a Land Rover roof, the soft bastard. Landed on the corner of the bumper and sliced his finger.

Nothing to worry about but it didn't half bleed. He had it glued at A&E – you can check their records. That's where the blood came from on my T-shirt.'

'Where's the T-shirt now?'

'It'll be in the wash. Or it will have been washed and shoved in the basket waiting to be ironed. You can check that too, if you like. Rhian isn't good at getting chores done around the house.'

'How twenty-first century of you to have a woman to do your ironing.'

'I pay her in kind.'

Ryan laughed again. When Allie glared at him, he put a finger to his lips.

Allie sighed. 'Where were you really on that night, Mr Tranter?'

'I was home, like I said. Rhian is lying.'

'And how do I know that if you don't have an alibi now?'

'Her word against mine.' Joe shrugged again. 'You'll have to prove otherwise.'

'Yes, you're good at that, from what I heard,' Ryan spoke again.

Allie stiffened as Ryan stepped closer to her.

'How far did you go to get the truth out of Terry Ryder?' he asked.

Allie swallowed as she glared at him. For a moment, they stood with eyes locked together, but she was determined not to rise to his bait. Instead, she turned from Ryan to look at Joe again. 'I repeat, Mr Tranter, where were you on that night?'

'I was at home, with Rhian.'

Allie stood for a long moment, looking from one man to the other. 'Fine,' she gave in finally. 'I'll get an officer to come and take a statement to that effect. See if you can recall any further details by that time.' She took out her card and handed it to him. 'One more thing, before I leave. We're making sure that everyone who left Reginald High School in 1989 is aware of the importance of taking extra precautions with their safety at the moment. So, I'd watch your back if I were you. We might not be the only people interested in your whereabouts.'

Joe stood up quickly. 'Are you saying this killer might come after me?'

Allie yielded. 'We're asking people from that time who knew any of the victims to be extra careful. Can I trust you to look after yourself for a while?'

Joe watched as Allie marched out of the door and across the forecourt, feeling a nerve twitching in the side of his temple.

'She's a feisty bitch, that one,' Ryan said as he, too, watched Allie disappear. 'Does she think she has something on you?'

'No, they're obviously panicking since this guy has been killing everyone. Bit worried about being told to look after myself, though,' Joe laughed nervously.

Ryan stood for a moment, then nodded. 'Let's talk again when there is less heat on you. Let me know how you're fixed. I do want you as part of my team.'

Once Ryan had left too, Joe paced the floor. That stupid bitch, Rhian! She'd sent the sergeant there because she knew they'd be after him like a shot once she mentioned the blood. How could she betray him after all he had done for her? After all he had put up with.

He swiped his keys from his desk and stormed out. 'If anyone wants me, I'm at home,' he said to the lads outside before getting into his car.

This old man, he played six,
He played knick-knack on his sticks.
With a knick-knack, paddy-whack,
Give the dog a bone.
This old man came rolling home.

1983

Patrick couldn't believe his luck when he got an invitation to Dawn Spencer's tenth birthday party. The whole of class nine had been invited. And he was going to go and enjoy himself with everyone else. He arrived at her house in a grey suit and a tie that his dad had insisted on him wearing when he'd told him about it. He'd worn it to his nan's funeral the year before. The jacket was tight across the chest and he could no longer fasten the double-breasted buttons, and the trousers were flapping around his ankles, making him realise how much he had grown.

If his mum had been around, she would never have let him go in the suit. She would have known what was best for him to wear. No one dressed up that smart for a birthday party. Everyone knew that games were played. You can't play games in a suit.

The gateposts either side of the front path had balloons tied to them, bobbing up and down in the slight breeze of a sunny day. There were banners across the front door – Happy Birthday – and more balloons too. Patrick grinned – he was so excited to be part of this. Usually he was never invited to anyone's party.

Everyone else knew to turn up with a present for the birthday girl too.

The birthday girl greeted him at the door with a look of disappointment. It made his heart sink a little.

'Where's my present?' Dawn said as he stepped into the hallway.

'I – I haven't got one,' he made up the first thing he could think of. 'My dad was working and didn't have time to get anything for you. Sorry.'

'Don't be stupid.' She folded her arms across her blossoming chest. 'Everyone knows your dad is an alkie and can't keep a job because of it.'

'No, he isn't!'

'He is so.'

'You don't know what you're talking about.'

'I do too!'

'Come now, don't fight,' Dawn's mother intervened. 'Young man, would you like to come and sit at the table? I'm sure you'll know most of the other children.'

Patrick was shown into the dining room, which had wide-open patio doors leading out onto a large garden. There, a table was set and eleven children sat around it; a brightly coloured tablecloth was almost hidden beneath plates of food. He couldn't believe his eyes when he saw the amount. Triangle ham sandwiches, sausages on sticks, quarters of mini pork pies and sausage rolls, cheese and pineapple chunks on cocktail sticks, and bowls of crisps and peanuts.

He smiled shyly at everyone until Johnno sat forward with a smirk on his face that made him sober up instantly.

'What are you dressed like that for?' Johnno pointed at him and everyone stopped what they were doing to look. When he laughed, everyone else followed.

There were two seats left and Patrick sat down on the one farthest from Johnno. He fingered the collar of his shirt, already feeling uncomfortable in it.

'There's lots of food.' Sandra Seymour handed him a plate. 'Come on, eat up.'

'Yeah, eat up, Shorty.' Johnno snatched it from her. 'I'll get it for him.'

Johnno piled his plate high and passed it to him. Patrick tucked in, all smiles. He hadn't tasted food so good in a long while.

He was on his third sandwich when another girl came in. It was Melody Edwards. The only seat left was next to him but she proclaimed in a loud voice that she wasn't going to sit there.

'Don't be rude,' her mum admonished and pushed her gently into the seat. 'He's in your class and you should be polite to him.'

'No one wants to sit with him at school.' Melody shimmied to the far edge of the seat, as far from Patrick as she could physically get without falling off it.

The girl on the other side of her pushed her away. 'You're squashing me!' she protested.

'I don't want to sit by him!'

'You shouldn't have been late then.'

'It wasn't my fault. It was my mum's. She was late, not me.'

The girl shrugged as if she couldn't care less.

'Would you like some ice cream now, Patrick?' Mrs Spencer asked as she came round to dish it out with the jelly.

Although he was full, Patrick couldn't resist. 'Yes, please,' he nodded enthusiastically.

'Have some sauce,' Johnno said, squirting lots of raspberry gloop on top. Patrick eyed it with longing and began to eat. But the ice cream took its toll. After a few mouthfuls, he put down his spoon.

'You can't leave any,' Johnno insisted. 'It's bad manners at someone else's party.'

'I can't eat any more,' he explained. 'I'm going to be sick if I do.'

'Eat it.'

Patrick knew by Johnno's harsh tone that he'd be in for it if he didn't finish it all. Grateful even to be at the party, he swallowed the rest of the dessert in big mouthfuls, feeling his stomach expand, his insides curdling as the jelly slid down his throat and the ice cream landed heavily on top of all the food he'd already consumed.

All at once, he wished that he hadn't.

'Time for games,' Mrs Spencer cried, clapping her hands to get the children's attention above the noise they were making. 'What shall we start off with? Blind Man's Bluff? Pass the Parcel? Tinned Sardines?'

'Hide and Seek!' suggested Johnno.

'I'll be "It,"' said Dawn, eagerly. 'It's my party.'

As Johnno ran off, he grabbed Patrick's arm. 'Come on,' he cried. 'I know a great place where we can hide.'

As Johnno tore upstairs, Patrick lolled after him, his insides curdling more with every step. Most of the children had gone outside into the garden or into the kitchen.

He stopped at the bottom step. 'Won't we get in trouble going up there?'

'We won't be found for ages,' said Johnno, beckoning to him. 'Come on.'

Patrick decided to follow him.

Johnno opened the door to the airing cupboard and pushed him inside. 'Quick, get to the back.'

Patrick climbed in and clambered as far into the cupboard as he could go. It was a tight squeeze but he managed to turn himself around and pull up his knees so that Johnno could get in beside him. But Johnno just stood in the doorway, a smirk on his face again.

'Bye, freak,' he said and closed the door.

Patrick found himself in the dark. He froze for a moment before scrambling to the door. He reached for the handle but it wouldn't go down. He tried again. 'Johnno!' He banged on the door. 'I'm stuck! Let me out!'

Panic took over as he heard Johnno laughing outside.

'I'm not letting you out, Shorty,' Johnno said. 'You were only invited because everyone in the class was, you stupid idiot. No one likes you.'

Patrick banged on the door again, the darkness seeming to creep up on him. 'Let me out,' he screamed, tears welling in his eyes. 'I don't want to be in here! Let me out!'

'Don't be such a baby.' Johnno kicked the bottom of the door.

'What are you doing upstairs? Come down here at once.'

Patrick heard Mrs Spencer's voice and banged on the door again.

'See you later, loser,' Johnno whispered before thundering down the stairs.

Patrick banged on the door again but no one heard him. He sat down on the floor and began to cry. Then he felt his stomach churning again – oh, no, he was going to be . . . He threw up over his trousers and shoes. As the smell assaulted his nostrils, he threw up again. Crying now, all he wanted to do was go home.

It seemed like a lifetime before anyone found him.

Finally, Mrs Spencer opened the door. 'We've been looking for you everywhere. What on earth are you doing in here?' She pulled him out by the arm and wrinkled up her nose. 'Oh, God, you've been sick. What a mess you've made!'

At the bottom of the stairs, he could see all the kids in his class laughing at him. Johnno stood in the middle of them, his laughter the loudest.

'That's enough, children,' Mrs Spencer admonished.

Patrick tried not to cry again as she led him through into the bathroom. Why did it always happen to him?

'You mustn't let anyone do this to you, do you hear?' Mrs Spencer said kindly to him as she wiped his mouth. 'If you become a victim now, you'll always be a victim. You need to stand up and fight for yourself.'

Patrick just listened. What did she know? She didn't know that Johnno and his bunch of mates were always on at him. They were just too much for him.

Chapter Thirty

Rhian was in the kitchen when she heard Joe's car screech to a halt in the driveway. She sighed: she was hoping he would have mellowed since their argument. As he came in, she stayed in the kitchen doorway. His face was void of expression but the slam of the door told her all she needed to know. She turned round and went back to the breakfast bar, picked up her coffee. She was damned if she was going to say sorry first.

'You'd better give me one good fucking reason why you sent the police round to my office,' he cried when he joined her. 'Or I'm going to do a lot worse than slap you across the face.'

Rhian's shoulders drooped. 'Oh. She visited you, then.'

'What did you tell her all that nonsense for, you stupid bitch?'

'It isn't nonsense,' she snapped. 'You do have photos of your ex-wife.'

'I have holiday pics of my ex-wife!' He gave an exasperated groan.

'I'm sorry, babe, I really am. But I love you so much that I – I guess I felt threatened and . . . what?' She raised her hands, realising she had read his silence wrong. 'I've said I'm sorry. What more do you want?'

'It doesn't change things. I meant what I said this morning, even more so now. I want you out.'

'But . . . you can't.'

Joe brought his face close to hers. 'I can do what I like,' he spoke through gritted teeth.

Rhian flinched. 'I'll change. I can –'

'If you don't leave by tonight, I'm going to chuck everything you own onto the pavement.'

'You're throwing me out because I told the police –'

'She came to my office.' He grabbed her roughly by the chin. 'Wanted to know if an allegation that I was blackmailing Suzi before she died was true.'

'Ow!' Rhian felt her lip splitting again from the slap he'd administered earlier. 'You're hurting me!'

'Have you any idea how much trouble I'd be in if it got back to Ryder that the pigs had been in there? I told you before, but would you listen?'

'But it had nothing to do with work!'

'Ryder wouldn't know that! He only needs to be told that the police were there and I could lose my legs as well as my job!'

Rhian burst into nervous laughter. 'You've been watching too many gangster programs.'

Joe slapped his hand down on the worktop next to her and grabbed the front of her jumper. 'Don't fucking laugh at me.'

'Then don't lie to me.' She tried to push his hand away. 'If you weren't with Suzi, you were up to no good with someone. All those late nights and work meetings – and on top of that, a trip to London. You don't fool me. You were up to something.'

'Well, I wasn't murdering my ex-wife. The blood that you must have taken great pleasure in mentioning wasn't mine.'

Rhian's eyes widened.

'I'd already told you it was from one of the lads from work who had cut himself. But you wouldn't listen. What were you expecting to get from that?'

'She didn't believe me anyway!' Even though she could see his eyes darkening and his fingers curling into a fist, she continued. 'But you were up to something.'

'So you thought that you'd get your own back by saying I was involved in Suzi's murder?'

'Well, what *were* you doing?'

'We've been ringing fucking cars! There's a whole bunch of us working on getting a load together. Some bloke in London was paying us top whack.' He showed her his hands. 'These have been toiling. I've been spraying the cars. It was a trade I was good at before being locked up but when I came out, I couldn't get another decent job. But you've probably put a stop to that now too!'

'Why?'

'We stored the cars around the back of Car Wash City. We won't be able to use Ryder's gaff now that the police have been around.'

'But they didn't come about him!'

'It doesn't matter – can't you see? Any suspicion that could bring in the law could topple everything and then I really would be in trouble. You've ruined it with your petty jealousy.'

Shocked by the venom in his voice, Rhian pouted. 'If you want me out, I'll go, but if I do, I'm going to make sure your precious son sees all the not-so-innocent photographs. Or maybe the newspapers might be interested in a story about how horrible Suzi was. If you're not going to give me any money, then I'll have to make some of my own. Because I sure as hell am NOT going back home to my parents.' She walked to the door.

'Get out!' He pushed her in the back. 'Get out of my house right now.'

Suddenly Rhian realised the enormity of what was happening. She held on to the kitchen doorframe as he pushed her again.

'I said fucking leave!'

'I'm going nowhere.'

Joe pried her hands away and pulled her towards the front door by her hair. He opened it and threw her out. She landed on her knees in the middle of the drive.

'Bastard!' she sobbed, getting to her feet again as he stood in the doorway. 'I hate you.'

'Yeah? Well, the feeling is mutual.'

Rhian ran at him. He pushed her away, tripping over the step in his haste. Seeing the advantage, she ran past him again. If she could just get inside . . . He pawed at her leg but she got through the door and into the kitchen. He raced after her.

'I'm not going anywhere,' she sobbed.

'Oh, but I think you are.'

Spying a small saucepan on the draining board, she picked it up and threw it at him. He knocked it away with his arm and it clattered to the floor. He came at her again and she screamed. Scanning around for what else she could use, she stepped backwards out of his grasp. Her bottom hit a drawer handle behind her. Still facing him, she reached back and opened the drawer with one hand, scrabbled inside it. Grasping the handle of the first thing she touched, she brandished her prize.

'Leave me –'

Joe ran straight into the small knife, the blade disappearing into his stomach.

Rhian let go of the handle.

Joe staggered backwards, his face contorted with pain. 'Fuck . . . what have you done . . .'

'I didn't mean it!' Rhian burst into tears. 'It wasn't my fault. Oh, God! Joe, are you okay?'

He reached for the handle.

'No, don't take it out! You'll make it worse.'

'Worse?' Joe gasped, dropping to his knees. 'How can anything be worse?' He sagged back against the wall.

'I'm sorry,' she sobbed.

He looked up at her. 'Don't just stand there, call an ambulance. Hurry up!'

Hearing the door creak open behind her, Rhian turned quickly to see a man standing in the doorway. He was wearing black running gear, muscular thighs visible through thick leggings. A black woollen hat covered his head.

'We had an argument,' she cried, 'and he ran into the knife. I didn't stab him.'

Patrick stepped into the kitchen. 'What the fuck have you done?' He screwed up his face. 'This is my game. You don't get to make the moves.'

Rhian froze. 'Who – who –'

'I'm alive, you morons,' said Joe. 'Just get me an ambulance, will you?'

Rhian grabbed for her phone on the table. Patrick got to it first and swiped it out of her reach.

'What did you do that for?' She bent down to pick it up.

Patrick brought his knee up into her face. The force of it sent her backwards and she landed heavily against the cooker door with a groan. Her head flipped back and cracked against the handle. In seconds, she flopped to the floor, out cold.

'Hey!'

Patrick turned to face Joe. 'Well, well, well.' He shook his head slowly as he surveyed the situation. 'Another minute or so and I might very well have been too late. Lucky for me that I decided to call when I did. Snazzy home you have here. I'm normally quite good at talking myself into places – it's the look of innocence I portray, I suppose – but you made my job a whole lot easier. You left your front door open.'

'I wanted her to leave.'

'Ah.' Patrick nodded and then sneered. 'Still got a way with the ladies, I see.'

'Phone.' Joe pointed. 'Pass me the phone.'

'Let me help first.' Patrick stooped over him. Before he could react, he pulled the knife from Joe's stomach.

'You silly bastard.' Joe groaned and tried to get up. Blood poured between his fingers and he sat back abruptly again.

'Oops,' grinned Patrick.

'Come on, man. Please just get me the phone.'

'I think that should be "just get me the phone, Patrick."'

'What?'

'Patrick – that's my name. You'll probably remember me as Shorty, although I'm not as short now, obviously. Do you remember me? I was in your class for most of my school years. You made my life hell.'

Joe gave a lopsided smile, his eyes beginning to glaze over. 'Yeah, that would be me. I was a right shit at school.'

'You used to call me a loser.' Patrick glared at him. 'But I seem to recall there are winners and losers in every game.'

'What the fuck are you talking about? I need help – just get me an ambulance.'

'The game we're going to play – it's just like the ones you used to play with me, Johnno.'

Joe's eyes struggled to focus again; he blinked profusely. 'What did you say your name was?'

'Patrick.'

'Ah, Shorty – yeah, I remember you now.'

Patrick's right eye began to twitch. 'Oh, I bet you do.' From his pocket, he pulled out a white magnetic letter. 'You heard about the recent murders, Johnno? Mickey Taylor – now, you must remember him. He was your buddy, and one of the ringleaders. He was the first one in the game to go.'

Joe coughed a little.

'Then there was your ex-wife.' Patrick sniggered. 'Changing her name from Sandra didn't make her attractive to me. Yeah, I suppose she was quite beautiful, until you got close up. It was easy getting into her house too. I said I was Matthew Thompson – you remember him from 5C? I showed her a photo and pretended to be him at first. She didn't recognise me either. And when she gave me some lip,' he made a fist and smacked it into the palm of his other hand, 'wham bam. Knocked her out and tied her to a chair.'

Joe had gone quiet.

'I wanted to stab her,' Patrick pointed to his own chest, 'right there in the heart. Because that's what she did to me. That's what you all did to me. You took away every ounce of confidence I had. She snubbed me too – so I finished her off as well.'

Patrick could see Joe's head leaning to one side. 'Don't go to sleep on me just yet.' He leaned forward and pushed him up a little. 'Because I need to tell you that next up was Frank Dwyer – you remember him, Johnno? The dirty fucker. One afternoon after games had finished, he asked me to stay behind. Said he wanted to give me extra lessons. Took me into the showers and made me undress. He . . . Never mind what he did.' Patrick closed his eyes as he fought to keep away the images.

'Malcolm Foster – now you won't know him at all, Johnno. The reason I killed him, I hear you asking? Simple, really. As I was doing my research on Dirty Dwyer, I found out Foster was buying images from him – filthy, disgusting photos of little boys being made to do despicable things. It wasn't hard to put two and two together, the dirty bastard. So, as a little bit of fun – and to throw the police off a bit – I thought I'd get rid of him too.'

'And then there was Nathan Whittaker. You remember Whitty, Johnno? He made me look a prick at the last school disco. I fucked up with him because he survived. But I'm not going to fuck up with you.'

Joe held out a hand and groaned.

'I've been following you all for months – years, some of you. So when it came time to put the game into play, everything was meticulously planned. Everything was in order. I'm sure the police worked out that the word I was spelling was *revenge* but they weren't quick enough to know who I was going to come at next.'

Joe coughed.

'E – Mickey Taylor. V – Suzi Porter – Sandra Seymour, to you and me. E – Frank Dwyer. N – Malcolm Forrester. G was Nathan Whittaker. And now you.' He held up the letter so that Joe could see it, tapping on his leg to get his attention.

'Pain. Heat,' whispered Joe. 'Help.'

'Certainly.' Patrick pulled his own knife from the inside pocket of his jacket and stooped over him. Then he rammed it into Joe's stomach, into the wound that was already there, and drew it up. Next he reached for the knife that was on the floor, lifted it up above his head and, holding it with two hands, drove it down into the side of Joe's neck.

'Pity your woman is still sparked out. She's missing the best part.'

Chapter Thirty-One

When Rhian opened her eyes, she groaned as a pain shot across the front of her face. Her vision blurred, she rubbed her head, gasping as her hand came back bloody. Had she hit it on something? She focused more and saw a saucepan on the floor and then Joe's feet. She sat up slowly.

Joe was sitting on the floor, his back to the wall, staring at her with a blank look. His head had dropped to one side. Blood seeped from his neck on the other, soaking his T-shirt. By his side was the knife she had accidentally stabbed him with.

'Joe!' Scrambling across the floor, Rhian lifted his head. His eyes were glazed. 'Joe,' she whispered, tears pouring down her face. 'Joe!' She shook his shoulders. 'No, no, NO!' She pulled him into her arms and screamed. 'Help me! Somebody, help me.'

She looked closer at where the knife had been sticking out of his stomach. There was a wound, about an inch in length. But then she noticed a bubble coming from the pool of blood on his neck. She peered at it, saw blood escaping from there too. She sobbed; she hadn't done that as well, had she? No, she would have remembered. One was an accident, but two knife wounds? No one would believe she hadn't inflicted both, would they? Shit, she was in so much trouble.

Where was her phone? All she could remember was bending down to get it and then darkness. Wait, there was a man! Where was he? Oh, God – had the man who had murdered Suzi killed Joe too? Was he still in the house? She sat still for a moment and listened. She couldn't hear anything. And wouldn't he have come back to attack her again if he'd heard her screaming? Well, she wasn't about to go looking. She was staying put – here with Joe.

She glanced at him again, her breathing erratic as the reality of how much trouble she was in began to hit her. What if the police didn't believe that someone else had done this?

Allie and Perry had been over to Waterloo Road to chat to some of the shopkeepers around the car park where Nathan Whittaker had been attacked. They were just grabbing a quick coffee when Allie's phone rang. Perry smirked as it played Plan B's *Welcome to Hell* this time.

She handed her coffee to him and answered it, pressing her spare hand to her ear so that she could block out the traffic.

'Yes, we'll check it out. Back-up going too? Okay, we're on our way.' She disconnected the call and turned to Perry. 'There's been a call from Rhian Jamieson. She says there's been an intruder.'

'Fuck! You're sure it's not another cock and bull story?' Perry quickened his step as they approached the car.

'No, I gave her a right bollocking this morning. I don't think she'd dare to make something up. She is asking for me, though.'

On the drive over, Allie couldn't help thinking that this might be a trick after the conversation she'd had with Joe Tranter a few hours ago. There'd clearly already been another domestic between them, but . . . no. Rhian wouldn't, surely? And with a killer on the loose, they wouldn't chance anything anyway.

In Smallwood Avenue, the front door of number four was ajar as they walked up the drive, the Focus and Joe's Range Rover parked next to each other. Allie reached out her baton and lobbed it out full; Perry did likewise. She pushed the door open fully, allowing them both to see into the hallway.

'Rhian,' she shouted through. 'Miss Jamieson? It's the police.'

Directly in front of them, Rhian appeared in the kitchen doorway. She was barefoot, her clothes and hands covered in blood.

'It wasn't me!' Rhian started to cry. 'There was a man – he came in through the door. He knocked me out. And I – oh, God, it wasn't me!'

'Are you alone?' Allie needed to know.

'I – I think so. But Joe, he's . . . I think he's dead.'

'Where is he?'

Rhian pointed at him with a shaking hand.

Allie assessed the situation and stepped inside. At the kitchen doorway, she stopped for a moment in shock when she saw Joe Tranter lying on the floor. Quickly snapping on sterile gloves, she took two quick steps and dropped to her knees beside him. Gut instinct told her that he was dead but she had to make certain. Rhian started to cry again as she came closer but she wasn't her concern for now. Uncomfortable with the blood around his neck, screwing up her face while she tried to keep her dinner down, she lifted his wrist to feel for a pulse. There was nothing.

She shook her head at Perry. 'Call it in,' she said. 'Get an ambulance, too, for her. And get her out of here.'

'I'm not leaving him!' Rhian screamed again. 'He's not dead. Please tell me he's not dead!'

'Rhian, I just need you to go into the living room for now.'

'But I didn't do anything! You have to believe me.'

'Come on.' Perry took her arm. 'We need room for the professionals to do their job. And you can help by giving me a description of this man.'

'But it's your fault! It was him. Can't you see that?' Rhian screamed. 'You didn't catch him when he murdered Suzi and now he's – now he's killed Joe!'

While Perry led her away, Allie stood up and surveyed the room, trying to figure out what had gone on. Even though Rhian had mentioned another man, she needed to see for herself. There were no signs that anyone else had been here, no sign of a forced entrance, but that didn't mean anything either.

Where was it?

And then she spied it, over on the worktop, stuck to the side of the toaster.

A white magnetic letter. E.

Nick arrived thirty minutes later; the forensic team was already on the job. The street had been cordoned off and uniform were being debriefed about starting house-to-house.

'Another magnetic letter, sir,' Allie told him as she stepped out of the hallway to see him shrugging on a white suit.

'Yes, I was told. An E – which confirms your thoughts. The DCI is on his way over.' He nodded. 'And you say you were on your way here anyway?'

Allie brought him up to speed with the events of the day as Rhian was taken to the station to make a statement. All around them, a scene of chaos changed into one of an order and near routine.

She looked down the street as she removed her gloves and shivered in the January air. As of only last week, she had never visited Smallwood Avenue. Now it felt so familiar.

Allie turned when she heard Nick call out her name.

'He wants to be caught, doesn't he?' she said before he had a chance to speak again. 'Everything is happening so quickly that he's playing with us. He's giving us clues but not enough time to piece them together. Why Joe Tranter? For me, it's like going round in a circle. We know that he went to Reginald High School. He was married to Suzi Porter when she was named Sandra. Maybe that's the connection. What do you think, sir?'

'It's possible, but there could be one more, simpler explanation.' Nick pulled on shoe covers before zipping up his suit. 'He's after killing as many people as he can before he's caught.'

Patrick let himself in to his house, raced up the stairs and into the bathroom. He stripped, shoved his clothes into the laundry basket, not caring about them this time. He jumped into the shower, his heart racing as he tried to catch his breath. He loved running for clearing his mind. During his exercise sessions, he couldn't concentrate on much more than breathing and getting to the end in an equal or even quicker time than the last session. But his mind would still work on other things while he ran. Problems would be solved, worries would be resolved.

He smiled to himself, remembering that afternoon's events. It couldn't have gone any better if he had planned it. Then, he sniggered. Okay, he *had* planned it, but getting into the property and putting Johnno down had been one of his biggest worries. He'd intended to sneak into the garden and, when they were both home for the evening, throw a brick through the kitchen window, or make some sort of noise, to bring Johnno outside. He'd hoped to startle him, run at him quickly. Killing Johnno would be his most dangerous kill yet. If Johnno had recognised him, said his name, laughed even, Patrick knew he might not have had the courage to kill him. He might not have had the strength either. Johnno had always been bigger than him and, looking back at his body slumped on his kitchen floor – the closest he'd been to him since following him around the city to learn his routine – he knew there would have been strength behind his punches, even though he would have been agile enough to avoid them. Luckily for him, his woman had done a number on him before he'd arrived.

At first, he'd been pretty angry when he'd seen what she'd done. But afterwards, running home, he'd been pleased with the outcome. And he *had* been able to inflict death on Johnno. She hadn't done a good enough job, leaving him to take great pleasure in finishing it off.

Joe Tranter – dead. Before leaving, he'd made certain of it this time. Whitty's survival had been a mistake – he should have died and there was no way Patrick could make that happen before the end of the game now – now that the police were all over him and he was in hospital. Whitty would have to be known as the one that got away. But Johnno, his penultimate killing – perfect.

Back downstairs later, Patrick turned up the volume of the television to drown out next door's slanging match. He sang along to a car advert, tapping on his knees to the tune. He wasn't bothering with work tonight – well, what was the point? He only had another day, not even that now, before his game was over. He'd need a clear head too.

It was time to put the last part of his plan into action. He picked up the phone.

After the devastating news of Joe Tranter, Allie's mind wouldn't rest, not even while she was lying in bed in the still of the night. Everything about the case was going round and round inside her head. Mickey Taylor. Murdered out in the open, but the killer hadn't just stumbled across him on the towpath. How long had he been following him? How did he know that Mickey walked that same stretch of pathway every day? Mickey most probably spent a lot of his time at the factory, followed by his home, no doubt. Their man must have known that was the best place to attack. And how the hell had he got away undetected?

Suzi Porter. The killer gained entry to her house without force – did he know her? Or did he, like Sam had suggested, push his way in somehow – a foot in the door. And if so, how did he keep Suzi quiet long enough to attack her? There was no blood found in the hallway, and only a few drops in the living room; most of it had been in the kitchen around the area of the chair. Had he talked his way in because of the school connection? Or had she never known much about it?

Frank Dwyer. Again, someone had got into his house without force. His sister seemed to think that Frank attacking one boy meant that he could have done it to more boys. Charlie Lewis had helped corroborate this with his story of events. Dwyer was also linked via emails and indecent images to Malcolm Foster. And the whole business with the pizza was weird. No one in the pizza places recalled seeing Frank Dwyer collecting it. Most of the places run by Potteries Pizza didn't take many online orders, and tracking their phone records had so far been inconclusive. CCTV images were few and far between, none showing Frank. None showed Danny Peterson either.

Malcolm Foster. The only one in their long line of victims who wasn't stabbed. Why? Their killer had obviously made the connection between him and Dwyer, and Foster had abused his own son when he was a child. Had their killer been abused as a young boy too?

Nathan Whittaker. Allie couldn't think of him without conjuring up the image of his wife, sitting at his hospital bedside with their daughter curled up on her chest. So tiny, so vulnerable – it

Follow the Leader   281

was great that her father had survived. He was more stable now, and awake longer too. Sam had been sent to question him, but he hadn't recalled anything significant about the night. They'd need to question him again soon.

Getting to Malcolm's attack had left them with the letters spelling out EVEN, something to fool them, keep their man from being caught. But now with the other two plastic letters, G and E, it had to be the word *revenge*, even though they had every letter but R. So what was he trying to get revenge for? Also, the attack on Nathan – had he been left for dead or attacked that way so that he could live?

And Joe Tranter – he knew Mickey and Nathan, so what did that mean? He had also gone to Reginald High School, had been married to another of the victims, not to mention the indirect connection to Terry Ryder and Ryan Johnson, who was known to be associated with Ryder. Allie couldn't help feeling guilty that she had snapped at Joe earlier that day, but, hell, she was only human.

His girlfriend, although not squeaky clean enough for Allie's liking, had been ruled out as his killer. After being questioned, Rhian had given them a description similar to the one Mia Whittaker had offered up – a lean, white male. This was the first time anyone had come so close to him. Rhian thought he'd been dressed in running gear. Was this why they couldn't find any cars in the vicinity of the murders? Allie made a mental note to get Sam to go back over the CCTV footage, widening the area to see if he came up anywhere as a casual runner.

Trying not to wake Mark as she fidgeted, she turned to lie on her back. Yawning now, she went over the attack on Chloe Winters. Despite having it fast-tracked, they were still waiting for the DNA report to see if there was a match on the database. But every time another magnetic letter was added to the puzzle, that investigation was being pushed back. They'd managed to get camera stills at the time of the attack but there had been no sign of him afterwards, only Chloe staggering back the way she had come. Did he know Central Forest Park well or had he cased it to figure out the best possible vantage point from which he could sneak away unseen? And why had he handwritten the letters Y and N instead of using plastic letters?

Everything added up to callous, calculating and very devious. It was as if he wanted to inflict as much pain on his victims as they had on him, but for what reasons? Had she been right when, after talking to Perry, they had come to the conclusion that it could be something to do with bullying? But then, that would mean only victims connected to the school, surely?

Slowly, she turned over onto her side, closing her eyes again, hoping somehow sleep would come. But the whiteboard kept coming into her vision, the plastic letters moving around in front of her eyes.

She stared into the darkened room – what was the killer doing now, what he was planning next? They had everyone they could spare working on this case. What were they missing?

Finally, she sat up and pulled back the duvet. The clock by her side illuminated the time: five fourteen a.m. Tiptoeing out of the room, she closed the door quietly behind her and went into the bathroom. She might as well put her active mind to work. She could get to the station for six.

It was now Friday morning, twelve days after the first body of the six had been found. If the killer was spelling the word *revenge*, it stood to reason that some sort of clue to the letter R would be there – to give them a chance to win or lose. Because the one thing she couldn't get off her mind was that their killer was clearly playing a game.

So what were they missing?

Chapter Thirty-Two

Sam had arrived at her desk minutes before Allie, so after catching up with what had come in overnight, as well as continuing with the work that the press conference had brought in, Allie also tasked Sam with going through CCTV again, this time looking for runners nearby. Perry arrived shortly before seven.

'Hey,' he said, flopping into his chair, covering a yawn as he switched on his computer.

'Hey yourself,' said Allie. 'What time did you get off last night?'

'Not long after you, but I couldn't sleep. What's new?'

'There's been a call from Potteries Pizza. The manager says one of the delivery drivers from the Hope Street branch recalls something now. The pizza that was shoved into Frank Dwyer's face wasn't collected. It was a delivered order. He recalls dropping it off, said a guy came to the door. You're never going to believe where it was. Number 4, Smallwood Avenue. Joe Tranter and Rhian Jamieson's address.'

Perry frowned. 'But surely that could mean Joe Tranter killed Frank?'

'Doesn't make sense to me either. After this morning's briefing, I'm going across to Hope Street, see if I can fathom out the mix-up. The manager lives over the shop. Also, Nathan Whittaker has remembered something. Nick wants him questioned, so can you go to the hospital to speak to him?'

'Sure thing.'

'Sam,' Allie added, 'can you check to see if anything has come up on Car Wash City lately? See if you can find anything out from there about Joe Tranter. And Ryan Johnson.'

'Ryan Johnson? As in one of the Johnson brothers?'

'The very one. He was with Joe Tranter when I questioned him about Rhian yesterday.'

'It will be my pleasure.' Sam's face lit up. 'Nothing I like better than having a mess around Ryder's gaffs.'

At quarter past nine, Allie parked up in Ranger Street. She had just spoken to the manager of Potteries Pizza and, although he'd been friendly, what he'd told her hadn't been any help at all, so she'd decided to go and see the driver herself. It was only a minute's drive from Hope Street to the address she'd been given. Once there, she updated Perry and Sam with her findings via text message and got out of the car.

With terraced housing on either side of a narrow road, Ranger Street wasn't a place that she had frequented much since she'd been promoted to detective sergeant, but she knew its type of residents from her earlier days. There were always lots of incidents that uniform were called out to, but nothing major as yet, although the underlying current always made her sense it could happen at any time.

At the far end, she could see a playground, vandalised and mainly unused, so a handy place for the down-and-out alcoholics who congregated there, no matter how many times they were moved on. To her right, a woman sat on a doorstep, the door to her house open wide. Despite the icy cold temperature, she was dressed in black leggings and a dirty white, long-sleeved T-shirt. She eyed Allie suspiciously, unfolding her arms only to take drags of her cigarette.

Allie knocked on the door of number twenty-seven.

'Mr Thomas?' She flashed her warrant card at the man who answered. 'I'm Detective Sergeant Shenton.'

'Yes, my boss has just called me. Sorry, I wasn't working last night.' He opened the door wide. 'Do come in.'

Allie stepped into a long hallway and was ushered into the living room, two front rooms knocked into one large one. A quick glance and she would have been no detective if she couldn't tell that he was a single man. One leather armchair, which he sat down in immediately, and a large flat-screen TV with a games console that looked as if it were permanently attached, dominated one side of the room. At the back of the room, the main area had been made out into a gym: a treadmill, an exercise bike, various weights in front of a mostly mirrored wall.

Allie flipped open her notepad. 'Your manager says you've remembered something about delivering a pizza on the night that Frank Dwyer was murdered. Can you tell me what you recall, please?'

'Can I get you a chair to sit on?'

'I'm fine.' She shook her head. 'I won't keep you that long.'

'Okay.' He looked up at her. 'It was about midnight. I had a call to visit number four, Smallwood Avenue, with two pizzas – pepperoni and a ham and mushroom. Oh, and a bottle of Coke too. Mustn't forget that, now.'

'So you had two pizza boxes?'

'Yes, and a bottle of Coke.'

Allie made a note to check the rubbish bins at Smallwood Avenue for the packaging. It was possible that they might not have been emptied that week yet.

'Go on,' she urged.

'As I was walking up the drive, a man came out to me. He gave me some money and I left.'

'Can you describe him for me?'

'Tall, dark hair, early forties at a guess.'

Allie wrote it down. 'How long have you worked for Potteries Pizza?'

'Two years, give or take a few days. Got made redundant from the city council – had a job for life in the benefits section but it turned out to be a big fat lie. I got hardly any severance pay so I work as a driver – I wanted to see a-pizza the action.' He laughed at his own joke.

Allie didn't.

'I have a work diary in the kitchen. I write down everywhere I go.' He stood up. 'Mileage claim, you see, as I'm self-employed. I'll get it for you – won't be a moment.'

He moved forward but instead of going through the door into the kitchen, he closed it and turned back to the living room, giving Allie a clear view of the wall that had been hidden behind it. The hair on the back of her neck began to prickle, not just because as an officer she needed to have a clear escape route, but because now, in full view, she could see a map of Stoke-on-Trent. Several circles had been drawn on it in thick black marker pen.

Allie didn't need to count them because she knew how many there would be.

Letters of the alphabet that she had become familiar with over the past few days were written inside each circle.

All except for one.

―――

Perry was pleased to see Nathan Whittaker sitting up in his hospital bed when he went into the ward. His wife was with him too.

They exchanged smiles and a few pleasantries before he drew up a chair and took out his notebook.

'Congratulations on the birth of your daughter, by the way,' said Perry.

'Thanks!' Nathan grinned. 'You got any?'

'Not yet. One on the way, though.' He grinned too.

'Will you look at the pair of you,' laughed Mia. 'It's us women that do all the hard work! Congratulations, by the way. When is it due?'

'End of August. It's early days. I'm not supposed to say anything yet but I can't help it.'

'Good luck with it.' Nathan looked at him then. 'This attack was personal. I'm sure I know him.'

Perry's stomach flipped over. 'Do you know his name?'

'I can't remember. I've been trying to think of it for the past hour.'

Mia took hold of the hand Nathan was clenching into a fist and banging on the bed. 'It will come to you,' she soothed.

'Tell me how you think you know him,' said Perry. 'What was it about him that you remembered? His mannerisms, his look? Do you think you've seen him recently?'

'I might have seen him at work. That's the problem with my job. I work on a sales counter. I see loads of blokes every day.'

'So he could look familiar because he visits the shop. Do you think you might have recognised him more if he was a regular?'

'Possibly.'

'So, let's say that he isn't a regular. Where else would you know him from? We've been questioning people from our year at school after asking them to come forward. Can you think of anyone we all knew?' Perry probed further. 'Maybe that would be why the face was vaguely familiar?'

'You know I spent half my time there outside the headmaster's office. I was always clowning around, always up to no good.'

He stopped. 'I told Mia that I knew all of those people who died.' He looked at Perry. 'Fuck, was he out to kill me too?' His head came off the pillow and then he collapsed back with a groan.

'You mustn't move too much,' Mia told him.

Perry waited a moment while she helped Nathan to get comfortable again.

'Did he say anything to you?' he continued, his pen tapping on the notebook.

'He called me a loser.'

'And could you tell with that one word, was it a local accent?'

'Yes, he was from Stoke.'

'Good.' Perry wrote this down and looked up again. 'Have you any idea why he would call you a loser? Any significance to anything in your past? Or just a throwaway comment?'

'Mia would say I'm always a loser,' he grinned.

'A joker!' Mia squeezed his hand. 'I said you were a joker.'

'Hey, wait.' Nathan frowned. 'It *was* someone I remember from school, a loner who used to be the butt of everyone's jokes. What was his name? Shorty! We used to call him Shorty. Patrick . . . Patrick. Shit, what was his real name?' He paused for a fraction of a second, looking at Perry. 'Can you remember? Morgan! That's it! It was Patrick Morgan.'

'Patrick Morgan? That short guy everyone –' And then it hit him. Perry got out of the chair so quickly that it toppled over. 'Are you absolutely certain it was Patrick Morgan?' He got out his phone; scrolled down to the last message he'd received from Allie.

'Yeah. I'm sure. Do you remember him?'

But Perry was no longer listening. He was running down the corridor, phone to his ear.

Allie's phone rang, making her jump in the quiet of the room. Seeing Perry's name flashed across the screen, she tried not to show her relief.

'I need to take this call,' she said, hoping to take control of the situation until she could think of how to get out of the house.

'Of course.'

She answered it quickly, thankful it hadn't got a stupid ringtone attached to it. 'DS Shenton.'

'Allie, thank fuck!' Perry shouted. 'I've just checked back with the station. Please tell me you haven't gone in to Ranger Street yet to see Patrick Thomas.'

'I'm here now,' she said, a little shrill. 'I'm with Mr Thomas.'

'Is he in your line of sight?'

'That's right.'

'Look, hear me out, and try not to freak him out either. I don't think Thomas is his real surname. I think it's Morgan, that he's Patrick Morgan. Can you see a scar down the side of his cheek? I can't remember what side it's on, and it might not be as visible now, but it was large. About two inches in length?'

'Yes.' Allie gulped.

'You can see it?'

'Yes, that's right.'

'Fuck, Allie. He's the one. Stay calm, okay?'

'Okay.' She watched as the man in front of her – the *killer* in front of her – folded his arms and stood tall, never once taking his eyes from hers.

'Patrick Thomas is Patrick *Morgan*. He's Ray Morgan's son.'

'Right.' Allie tried not to give anything away as she met Patrick's stare. She prayed her legs would hold her weight as she felt them ready to buckle.

'I'm coming to you. Back-up is on its way. Tell him you need to leave and try to get out, but only if you can.'

'Right,' she continued. 'I'm on my way. Yes, I'll meet you there.' The phone had already gone dead.

Even safe with the knowledge that her team knew where she was and that all available units would be drafted to respond, Allie struggled to hear anything over the beating of her heart. Taking a deep breath, she put her phone away and looked up again. It wasn't the first time she had come face to face with a killer. Would he harm her to continue the game?

For a second, Mark's face flashed in front of her eyes. An image of him laughing as they were dancing together at their wedding. She cleared her throat to stop herself from crying out.

'I need to go, Mr Thomas,' she spoke directly, trying to keep the shake from her voice.

'I haven't shown you my diary yet.' Patrick took a step towards her, but staying in front of the door.

'I have to respond to something that's come in. I can send one of my colleagues to see you as soon as possible.' She took a step towards him. 'Would that be okay with you?'

'Okay, Sergeant.'

His smile caused her to shiver as she dared another step closer. When she drew level with him, he stood in front of her for a moment, staring directly, as if into her. It felt like he was reading her mind, knowing what she had found out. But then it was over and he stepped to one side to let her pass.

Holding her breath with every extra step, she made her way along the narrow hallway. If she could just get to the front door . . .

His feet on the carpet behind made her grapple with the door handle. He grabbed her by the shoulder, turned her sharply and rammed his fist into her stomach. As the pain shot through her, she dropped to her knees. On all fours and gasping for breath, all she could do was watch as he took hold of her head and slammed it into the wall.

Patrick hurried down the street to his car. He started the engine and pulled away from the kerb, foot on the pedal. Giving the police Tranter's address had been an idea he'd come up with after using the pizza to get into Frank's house. He knew they might link the delivery back to him so he'd made up an order to be sent to their address. Of course, most of it had gone in the back of the skip behind the building at work. It was just a ploy, to give him more time. While they had been working that out, he was hoping it would keep them off his tail for just that little bit longer. And it seemed to have worked.

When that woman knocked on his door and showed her warrant card, and he saw that she was alone and had no clue as to who he was, he'd had to bite his bottom lip to stop himself breaking out into a giveaway smile. Instead, he'd managed to continue his game and give out a few more clues.

It had taken a few years to get every detail of his plan right before he could instigate it. At times, it had brought back painful memories, given him nightmares and panic attacks, but he'd persevered. Except for one last hurdle, he was almost finished. Just two hours to stay free, that's all he needed.

As he drove past his open door, he couldn't help but slow down to take a look. The woman was sitting on the floor with her back to the wall, knees up, holding on to her head.

'Little miss detective,' he smirked. 'When will you realise that to catch a killer, you must follow the leader?'

Chapter Thirty-Three

It was a few minutes before Allie got her breath back enough to stand. The sharpness of the pain in her stomach began to subside along with her fear as she heard sirens, cars pulling up outside, blocking the street as they double-parked. Two cars arrived from Hanley station, followed by Sam who fussed over her like the mother hen that she was.

Ranger Street was sealed off either end, much to the annoyance of the neighbour Allie had seen earlier, who was still on her doorstep.

'What's he done, the stupid twat?' she shouted across. 'He's a right weirdo.'

Apart from one officer who was sent over to see why she was so vocal, no one took any notice of her.

Perry ran through the front door a few minutes later. 'Are you okay?' he asked when he saw Allie, holding out his hand.

'Yes, I'm fine now I have my breath back. Just a couple of bruises, probably.'

He pulled her up to standing. 'Do you need to go to hospital?'

'Not bloody likely.' She shook her head and then groaned, put a hand to the back of it. 'We're going to nail the fucker first, aren't we?'

'Spoken like a true Stokie.' Perry smirked.

'I've rung Nick – he's on to Prison Intel.' Allie had remembered who Ray Morgan was now. She pointed to the living room. 'You need to see what's in there.'

Pulling on sterile gloves, Allie followed him into the room. All around, the officers present were sifting through Morgan's belongings.

Sam was looking through a batch of papers and stopped for a moment when she saw her. 'Are you really okay?' she questioned.

'I'm fine, thanks,' Allie smiled, although a dull ache had now formed in the pit of her stomach. 'Nothing that a soak in a hot bath won't cure. Is there a call out on his car?'

Sam nodded. 'Although, I reckon he'll ditch it somewhere, don't you? He's clearly walked – or run – to most of the murder scenes. That's why we haven't been able to trace him quickly.'

'There are letters and papers everywhere.' Perry slapped a cardboard shoebox down next to them, making them both jump. 'There's so much to go through.'

Allie moved to the map. 'We have coloured letters inside large circles for all the places he's committed the murders and the attack on Nathan Whittaker. And this one here, with no letter.' She pointed. 'Stoke. One hell of a big place for a killer to strike. What's in the immediate vicinity?'

Everyone started to shout out names.

'Staffordshire University.'

'Christ, there's tons of buildings on there.'

'Yeah, the business village, science and tech centre.'

'And Sir Stanley Matthews Sports Centre.'

'And then there's Sixth Form College.'

'The railway station.'

'Royal Mail Sorting Office.'

'How big is the circle?' asked Sam. 'Could it be the Civic Centre, or the King's Hall?'

'Or the North Stafford Hotel, opposite the railway station.'

'Okay, okay.' Allie held up her hand for quiet. 'We're beginning to sound like an A-Z map.' She stepped forward to run a finger around the black line of the empty circle. 'It's a huge place if we're looking for one person. Whom I've only seen up close.' She turned round to face the room. 'Are there any photos of him around?'

A uniformed officer spotted one in a frame. 'Is this him, do you think?' He handed it to her.

Allie studied it: a woman with a young boy and girl. 'It could be, I suppose.' She looked closer. 'I couldn't be sure, though.'

'Or this one.' Perry pulled a large black and white photograph from out of the side cupboard. 'Shit, I think this must be our class in junior school. I must be on here somewhere.' He shook his head. 'I still can't believe this is Patrick Morgan doing all this stuff.'

'What was he like at school?'

'Well, you were right, Sarge. He was an oddball. I used to hang around with him every now and then, with a lad called Daz . . . Daz . . . can't think of his surname right now.'

'There was a Darren Watson who came forward after the appeal,' Sam mentioned. 'And a Darren Hawkins.'

'Yeah, Darren Hawkins, that's him.' Perry nodded. 'Patrick's nickname was Shorty. He never had up-to-date clothes and, as we didn't wear a uniform, it stood out a mile that he was wearing the same things all the time. He was clean, though, I'll give him that. Not one of the smelly kids.'

Allie's head began to spin as they continued their search. She placed an arm on the wall to steady herself until the feeling of nausea had passed.

Sam picked up a small notebook. 'See this.' She handed it to Allie. 'The writing is the same as on the map, I think. There are a few verses of a children's nursery rhyme on it. *This Old Man*.'

'*This Old Man*? I haven't heard that in ages.'

'Yes, and from one to seven. Six murders – or at least six attempts at murder. I'm sure it wasn't in his game plan to only inflict pain on Nathan Whittaker.'

Allie glanced over it quickly. 'One verse on each page. And victims' names with lines crossed through them – dates of their murders next to them.'

'And I bet he's left the name next to number seven?' Perry scoffed.

'He wouldn't make it that easy.' Sam picked up another pile of papers and sifted through it. 'But there'll be something in here. I have a feeling he's left something for us to find. Part of the game.'

Allie nodded. 'Exactly what I thought.'

'Boss.' Perry handed her an envelope. 'Letters from HM Prison Birmingham – redirected from an address in Adams Street, where Ray Morgan last lived before he was jailed. And these too.' Perry held up a fistful of newspaper cuttings.

Nick arrived, coming straight over to Allie before doing anything else.

'You sure you're okay to continue?' he asked once she'd updated him. 'You look really pale.'

'Yes, yes sir,' she nodded. 'I'm fine, really.'

Nick kept his gaze on her for a while longer. Satisfied, he nodded, turned and raised his hand. 'All right, listen up everyone. Quiet!' Once he had their attention, he continued. 'Does everyone know Ray Morgan and his background?'

Most officers nodded. Only a couple of people shook their head.

'1998, Morgan went into The Woodman, Cobridge, and stabbed a bloke, Bill Nickson, who was sitting at the bar. Witnesses said it happened so quickly that Nickson never had time to respond. In a statement recorded, Morgan told the interviewing officers that the victim had attacked him a couple of weeks before and that he'd had to practically crawl home in his own blood.

'Because he thought he'd been made a fool of, he wanted to exact revenge in as brutal a way as possible, and cold-blooded killing was the only way to deal with it. He didn't seem sorry from all accounts and was jailed for fifteen years. He had a further two years added early into his sentence for another vicious assault on a prisoner. He's been at HM Prison Birmingham for the past three years.

'Prison Intel Unit informed me and my team early last week that his release was imminent. Ray Morgan owned his property and his son supposedly lived there, but he hadn't been there for a while as the house is boarded up. Probation officers have got Morgan temporary accommodation until he sorts everything out inside – utilities, furniture, everything will be damp and unsalvageable, I reckon. They've also been trying to track down his son, Patrick Morgan, to let him know of his father's release. Or Patrick Thomas, as we now know him. I'm waiting on a call back from the prison now.' Nick turned to glance at the map again. 'I need everyone to up the search – there *has* to be something in this house that lets us know what he's going to do next.'

'He's going to finish what he started, isn't he?' Allie turned to him and spoke quietly. 'The letter R, for his father's name. Ray Morgan is the last piece in his puzzle. It must have been part of the game, to go back to the beginning.'

Nick nodded. 'He's going to go after his father. Once we've established his release time, we can –' Nick's phone rang and he held his hand up for quiet. His face flushed, he fixed his gaze on Allie as he listened to the caller, his adrenaline getting to work.

'Prison Intel have confirmed Ray Morgan was released as planned this morning,' he said after he'd disconnected the call. 'The nearest train station is Birmingham New Street so they got him a taxi to there plus a train ticket back here. His train arrives in Stoke station at ten fifty-three this morning.'

All heads went up to the clock on the wall. It was ten thirty.

'You,' Nick pointed to an officer, 'email the photo on record of Ray Morgan to everyone so we have it on our phones. It's pointless searching for one of Patrick Morgan – not enough time. The rest of you, we need to get to Stoke Station. And get a stab vest on if you have one!'

Patrick walked underneath the bridge at Glebe Street after abandoning his car on the car park in Kingsway. Ahead of him stood the sleek, white building of Stoke-on-Trent Sixth Form College. Next to it was the start of Staffordshire University campus. Patrick wished he'd been able to go on to further education after leaving Reginald High School, rather than having to get a job to bring in some money. Then he wouldn't have been at Ray's beck and call: he might have moved out of the city altogether and none of this would have happened. He wouldn't have killed all those people.

He turned left into Station Road. The Royal Mail Sorting Office was to his right, the railway station a few hundred metres in front. The automatic glass doors opened as he approached the entrance moments later, moving to one side to allow a family of five to race through with suitcases. There were people everywhere and he knew he'd be invisible here too. They were all too busy trying to get to places, visit loved ones, arrive on time for work meetings, leave bad memories as far behind as possible.

One last time, he checked that his knife was secure in his coat pocket and went inside. Moving quickly to his right in front of the queue for tickets, he looked up, checked the television screen for arrivals. Ten fifty-three a.m. Good: the train was on time.

Fifteen minutes to go.

The tannoy announced the next train – London Euston, arriving at platform one. Patrick watched people surge forward as it drew to a halt, wondered if he should just run across and jump on it. He'd be in the capital in an hour and a half. The police wouldn't find him until it was too late. They had certainly taken their time working out the clues he'd given them so far. What a bunch of losers *they'd* turned out to be.

Perspiration dripped down his back as a sentence played over and over inside his head. *Are you man enough to kill your father?*

He crossed the station and took the stairs down into the subway.

This old man, he played seven,
He played knick-knack up in heaven.
With a knick-knack, paddy-whack,
Give the dog a bone.
This old man came rolling home.

1998

Patrick jumped when he heard the front door slam shut. He rushed to his feet, raced through to the kitchen and switched on the saucepan he'd filled in readiness. He heard Ray before he saw him, cursing as he pulled off his shoes, thud, thud as he chucked them to the floor. Then he came into the room, bumping into the doorframe before staggering towards the table. He sat down with a thud, sniffed dramatically.

'I can't smell anything cooking,' he slurred.

'It's warming up now.' Patrick had no alternative but to turn his back on Ray as he stirred the liquid around the pan. 'It won't take more than a few minutes.'

'Hurry up, short-arse. I'm starving.'

'It's only soup.'

'What?'

'It's soup. I didn't have any money to buy a joint of meat yesterday. I have some crusty bread to go with it, though.'

'Soup?' Ray's voice was high pitched. 'You expect me to eat soup for my Sunday dinner?'

'It's beef broth.'

'"It's beef broth,"' Ray mimicked in a squeaky voice.

'It's all we have.'

It went quiet for a moment while Patrick poured the soup into two bowls and placed them on the table. Ray stared at his bowl and then up at Patrick. He brought his fist down on the table and the bowl flew up into the air. It landed on the floor, narrowly missing Patrick's feet, the liquid splashing everywhere, the dish smashing into pieces.

'What the fuck do you take me for – a mug?' Ray seethed. 'I know you have money from your job.'

'I don't! You took what I had last night, remember?'

'You didn't give it all to me. You said you'd kept some back to go shopping.'

'I did.' Patrick paused before continuing. 'But when I looked where I had left it, it had gone.'

'And where did you leave it?'

'In the cabinet, next to my bed.'

'So you're saying that I went in to your room and took it?'

'No, I –'

Ray reached across, grabbed a handful of Patrick's hair and pulled him near. 'Then who the fuck did? You lying piece of shit. You've spent it, haven't you? You lying bastard!'

'No!'

'You're trying to blame this on me when I know you're stashing your money away so that you can up and leave one day. Do you think I was born yesterday, short-arse?' He punched Patrick in the side of his face.

In such close proximity, his mouth took a full hit. Patrick coughed, tasted blood and put his hands out to stop Ray from hitting him again.

'I'm sorry,' he tried to say as the pain in his head intensified. Ray was squeezing hard on a fistful of his hair.

'You will be fucking sorry if you don't go and get something decent to eat.'

'I don't have any money.'

Ray laughed as Patrick squirmed, trying to loosen his grip. But just as quickly, he pushed him away again.

'I'll give you thirty minutes,' he said, swaying as he tried to stay upright. 'One of those roast beef ready meals will do, but I want a dinner.'

Patrick stood rooted to the spot.

'What are you waiting for?' Ray roared at him. 'Go on, get, you little fuck.'

Patrick shook his head. 'No.'

Ray flexed his fingers. 'Come again?' he said.

Patrick shook his head.

'Becoming quite the hero nowadays, aren't you?' Ray scraped his chair backwards on the kitchen floor before dragging himself to his feet. 'Look at you – you're pathetic. You don't even have the strength to fight off a man twice your age. And to think I fathered you. Weak, that's what you are. It's why your mother left you here with me, the stupid bitch. And now I have to put up with you, you gormless twat.'

'My mother left because she couldn't bear to be with you!'

To this day, Patrick had no idea why he'd said that.

Ray came at him. With one punch, he floored him. The strength of the man when he was sober wasn't anything Patrick could cope with, but when he was drunk, it was as if a lion had unleashed its powers. Ray straddled him and he tried to push him off, but the weight of his father's body pinned him down.

Ray punched him in the face, again and again, and again.

This is it, *thought Patrick,* my last moments. The police will find me covered in blood lying on the floor. No one will come to my funeral. No one cares if I live or die.

But he knew, in a way, that it would be far better than living the way he was.

Please let him kill me.

Chapter Thirty-Four

'Why did he let me go? Why didn't he want to hurt me?' Allie asked Perry as they sped off along Ranger Street with the other cars. 'He could have done anything to me. I wouldn't have been able to escape.'

'You weren't part of the game, were you?' Perry grimaced.

Allie's phone beeped. It was an email with a photo attachment. She opened it to see the face of an older man, gaunt and pale, staring back at her. Hair shaved closed to his head showing age spots and blotchy skin; a crooked nose and a tiny scar visible below his bottom lip. Allie could clearly see the resemblance to Patrick Morgan from his eyes alone. They were void of emotion.

A minute after they'd gone down Lichfield Street and turned right at the roundabout on to Leek Road, Perry suddenly slowed the car. Much to the annoyance of the driver behind him who blasted on his horn, he flicked on the hazard lights and parked up on the kerb.

'What's wrong with you?' Allie looked on in exasperation. 'We can't stop here!'

Perry turned up the radio. 'Listen!'

The tune playing was a song by Roxette. *It Must Have Been Love.*

'It's just reminded me of something. Oh, fuck – I –'

Allie could see that Perry was close to tears when he turned to her. 'What is it?' she asked.

'The school disco – 1989. I was messing around with Mickey Taylor and Johnno – Joe Tranter. They wanted me to play a trick on Patrick and I wouldn't. But Nathan Whittaker did. They got him to dance with one of the female teachers – and then Nathan stuck a note to his back.' He swallowed. 'It said "Loser," Allie, and I remember everyone laughed at him. When he found out, he ran from the building and Johnno legged him over, making everyone laugh even more. I think I laughed too. I only just remembered it when I heard that song.'

'I'm not with you. I don't –'

'Are we absolutely certain he's going to the railway station?' Perry broke in.

Allie nodded. 'You were with us when we worked everything out. I'm sure we're right and –'

'Lisa's at the hairdresser's this morning. The Head Station, in Percy Street, Hanley.' Perry gasped as his breath caught in his throat. 'What if it's me who's the last piece of the game? What if he's going to hurt Lisa?'

'Why would he do that?' Allie frowned. 'You said you hadn't done anything against him.'

'I know, but maybe that's it. Maybe because I didn't do anything to help him, he thinks I'm just as bad as the rest of them.'

'But so far he's come after his bullies, not their spouses.'

'Yes, but how do we know he isn't going to trick us? Think about it – he's been one step ahead of us all through his game.' Perry's eyes brimmed with tears. 'She's pregnant, Allie. What if –'

'Call her, just to be on the safe side,' said Allie. 'Call her!'

As he waited for her phone to connect, Allie prayed it wouldn't be what he was thinking. Morgan had made her think that he was going after Karen for a while, so she could understand Perry's reasoning. And even though they now knew Morgan was going after his father, she couldn't take any chances.

'Lisa?' Perry shouted down the phone. 'Are you okay? Are you sure? Are you with people? I need you to . . . no, there's nothing to worry about. NO, please calm down, honey. I need you to . . . Wait, I can –'

Allie placed a hand on his arm. 'You're scaring her,' she told him, her voice calm. 'Give the phone to me.'

He passed it to her.

'Lisa, it's Allie. I know this is difficult but please try to stay calm. There's been an incident this morning and we need to keep you safe until it's sorted. I need you to go into the back of the hairdresser's, out of sight, and away from the general public. Yes. No. Right now. I'm going to get the manager to close the shop until Perry gets to you. Can you do that for me? Yes. Now, put the manager on the line.'

'Is she really okay?' asked Perry.

'She's safe,' said Allie.

'Are you sure? He could be there, telling her what to say. He could –'

'Hey,' Allie tried to calm him. 'Hey!' When he looked at her, she continued. 'It won't take you more than ten minutes to get there.' She passed him his phone and got out her own. Removing her seatbelt, she opened the door. 'I'll leg it from here.'

Perry looked torn. 'I can't just leave the investigation.'

'Yes, you can.' Allie nodded. 'Family are more important, and for all we know, this *is* part of the investigation. I can take the rap if need be. Now, go!'

She got out of the car and Perry sped off from the kerb. As fast as her heels would take her, she ran along the road, weaving in and out of the students who were between lectures. Ahead, she could see flashing blue lights. Station Road had been cordoned off and traffic was being diverted. The traffic lights in front of her turned to red. As the cars slowed, she ran across the road, dashing behind a car that was coming to a halt. Just past the entrance to the Royal Mail Sorting Office, she climbed over the low wall and ran across the car park.

Breathless, she drew level with the North Stafford Hotel, thankful that the ground wasn't slippery underfoot today. Seconds later, she was in front of the station. Inside, she spotted Nick giving orders to two uniformed officers. She pushed through politely to reach him.

'We don't have a clue what he looks like,' Nick said, still scanning the crowd. 'Can you see him?'

'He must be here.' Allie craned her neck, checking around the station.

As more officers arrived, Nick barked out orders. 'Get this station evacuated. Now!'

Patrick stood in the subway, watching every person that came past. The knife in his pocket was open, he could feel his fingers stinging where the blade had cut through his skin.

Any minute now, he would see Ray.

He leaned on the wall to the side, watching and waiting, clocking every person that came down the stairs and into his range of vision. A man rushing through with a hand-held suitcase. A gaggle of teenage girls, their heels clattering on the tiled floor sounding similar to machine-gun fire. An elderly woman holding on to the arm of a man who looked like her son. Three men wearing red and white football shirts. A woman on her own – then another.

Then a lull.

Patrick put a hand to his mouth as he retched. What if Ray wasn't on this train? That the letter he'd had redirected to his address had been a complete pack of lies? Ray would think that was hilarious. *Stupid, Patrick!*

Two males next, then a woman with a small child. A group of women. All walking past him as if he wasn't there. Invisible again. A woman. Another woman and . . .

There.

This old man.

His old man.

How many times had Ray come rolling home, like the words in the nursery rhyme? How many times had he beaten him to take out his aggression, drunk, and angry and argumentative? Made him feel worthless, his words stinging as much as the punches.

Suddenly, he was that nine-year-old boy again, cowering on his bed because it was his fault his mother had left him behind. It was his fault that Ray drank so much, because he couldn't bear to come home to a house with only Patrick to keep him company. All lies, terrible spiteful untruths that a child would believe. Why had he let him control him afterwards? Why hadn't he been strong enough to get on with his life when Ray had been locked up, to leave him and his problems far behind?

Father and son locked eyes.

Seventeen years had taken their toll. Slightly hunched forward, Ray walked with a limp. His hair was grey, receding. Deep wrinkles around his eyes. Dark bags underneath them.

Patrick's body began to shake violently, but he closed the distance between them, his hand clasped around the handle of the knife.

There was no one left behind Ray now. Patrick watched the holdall drop from his father's shoulder, down his arm and on to the floor. Then Ray held out his arms.

'Hello, son,' Ray smiled, almost shyly. 'You came.'

Patrick took out the knife.

Ray stepped back, hands held out in defence now. 'Patrick, I –' Stumbling into the back of the steps, he lost his footing and fell, landing heavily.

'I'm sorry!' He covered his face with his arms. 'I'm sorry.'

Patrick wanted to kill the bastard, twist the knife, cut out his heart. He pulled back his hand and . . .

He couldn't do it.

Come on!

'Morgan!' A voice shouted behind him. 'Patrick Morgan!'

Patrick stopped, realising they had worked everything out. He turned to see a tall man in a suit coming down the few steps to his level at the other end of the subway. He could see the woman he'd assaulted earlier, too, and a few uniformed officers. They were twenty metres away.

'Stay where you are,' he screamed, raising the knife so they could see it. 'I'll kill him if you come closer. I'll do it!'

Watching them slow, Patrick glanced at Ray before running past him up the steps ahead and onto platform two.

Allie followed closely behind Nick as they thundered after Patrick.

'Stay away from the platform,' Nick shouted to Ray and ran past his ashen form. Allie followed, letting uniform deal with Ray. Coming out onto the middle of the platform, she stopped at Nick's side when she saw Patrick standing several feet in front of him, the knife in his outstretched hand.

'Don't come any fucking closer!' Patrick shouted, bringing everyone to a halt.

Behind them, uniformed officers moved people who were waiting for the next train, ushering them towards the exit at the far end of the platform. Several people behind Patrick stood up. A woman screamed. Allie raised a hand, hoping she would heed her warning to be quiet.

'It's over, Patrick.' Nick took a step forward, his hand outstretched. 'Drop the knife.'

'I couldn't do it.' A tear trickled from Patrick's eye as he screwed his face up. 'I killed all those people first so that I would have the courage to kill him. I *needed* to, so badly.'

'Patrick, put down the knife.'

'Why?' His face contorted again. 'Why couldn't I finish him off?'

'You need help. We can get that for you. But you need to put down the knife now.'

Patrick's hand wavered; his shoulders shook.

Allie saw a guard across on platform one looking over, powerless to do anything but watch. Her eyes flicked to the arrivals sign. There was a train due in. She hoped there had been time to contact the driver to get him to stop, or even just to go straight to the next station. Otherwise in a minute or so, the platform would be flooded with people getting off. Best-case scenario was that they would be kept on the train. Either way, it wouldn't be pleasant for people to watch Patrick be taken away. Neither would it stop people reaching for their mobile phones to take pictures, something that no one would want.

Patrick still had the knife held out in front. 'I wanted to rip his heart out.' He began to cry. 'Like he did to me. But he made me into a coward too. I – I –'

Nick took a step forward. 'He can't hurt you again.'

Patrick roared. The sound of an animal, trapped, in pain.

Nick took another step forward. As Patrick sidestepped away from him, nearer to the edge of the platform, Allie stepped closer too. If she could just reach out to grab his arm, Nick might be able to force the knife from him and push him to the ground. But then again, Patrick had shown them only too well how deceptive his build was.

She had to chance it.

'I can hear you,' he said, pointing the knife at her. 'Creeping up on me.'

In the distance, Allie could see a train approaching, knew Patrick would be able to see it too. He glanced at her and in that split second, she realised his intentions. Her heart sank as he broke out into a smile.

'I know it's not going to stop here. So what game do we finish off with?' he asked, cocking his head to one side like a small dog. 'I know. Let's play chicken.'

Allie shouted as Patrick jumped in front of the train, running forward at the same time as Nick.

Patrick's body caught the front of the carriage with a sickening thud and disappeared out of their line of sight. Allie shivered as she waited for the train to go past.

'We're too late,' she whispered.

The game really was over.

Chapter Thirty-Five

The following week, Allie sat at her desk, dealing with an endless mountain of paperwork. She always seemed to be tidying up paperwork, or filing paperwork, or sifting through paperwork. There was so much to complete or store away in her role, get right for trials. But this time, there would be no prosecution. There wasn't anyone to charge.

Nick stopped at her desk. 'You did a great job last week, Allie.'

'Thanks, sir.' She smiled. 'I'm part of a good team.'

'Indeed you are. I'm glad you remembered that. No running along on your own steam this time.'

Allie looked down. It was a back-handed compliment whose very meaning was huge. Nick was referring to her working on her own during the investigation into Steph Ryder's murder three years before. But that had only been because he'd asked her to – hadn't it?

'So when are you going to go for inspector?' he continued. 'I think you'd do a good job of that too.'

'I don't know.' Allie shrugged. 'I like being hands-on, and the further up the ladder I go, the further away I go from that.' She smiled. 'I suppose I enjoy getting down and dirty.'

Nick laughed. 'In *your* heels? I doubt that very much.' He sighed. 'It's up to you, of course, but I'd be happy to put a word in for you when you change your mind.'

He wasn't listening, expecting her to be flattered regardless. She knew his game.

'Thank you, sir,' she replied.

Perry joined her later. 'Hey, how's Lisa?' she asked.

'Still wanting to kick my ass for scaring the shit out of her.' He gnawed his bottom lip for a moment. 'I'm a prick, aren't I?'

'For going with a gut reaction?' Allie shook her head. 'Of course not.'

'But I was wrong.'

'I think you need to remember what could have happened if you were right.'

'I must admit, it shook me up. It's the closest the job's come to getting personal, I suppose, and there's a lot of guilt there too.'

'Why?'

Perry perched on the edge of Allie's desk. 'Maybe if us kids had befriended Patrick instead of making him a scapegoat, he might have turned out better.'

Allie thought back to the earlier phone conversation she'd had with Ray Morgan. She was heading out to meet him in a few minutes. He had some things to say, things that he wanted her to hear. Things to get off his chest, she reckoned.

'I doubt that,' she said. 'Whatever was going on at home was enough to take Patrick over the edge.'

'I guess,' said Perry, 'but we didn't make it any easier.'

'You can't blame yourself for any of this.'

'We were always fooling around.'

'Precisely!'

'But it must have got to him.'

Allie sat forward so that only he could hear what she was going to say. 'When I was fifteen and in my last year at Reginald High, I was friends with a girl called Sarah. She was one of those kids like Patrick. Always picked on because she was one of three sisters whose parents didn't have much money, so they were always in the same clothes – hand-me-downs, too. My parents wouldn't let me stay out late then so, as she only lived two streets away, I always used to go round to her house. We used to have such a laugh together. But she wasn't a cool kid to hang around. I started to get picked on because of that.

'All our parents went to a social club on the estate and every summer we'd go off on a bus to Blackpool. Karen was too old for it by then – it wasn't cool – so Sarah came along instead. We had such a great time together. But one summer, at the school disco the following evening, I was with another friend chatting away in the toilets about how I didn't really want to be friends with Sarah as I thought she was a wimp, a geek etcetera, etcetera, etcetera.'

Allie wasn't sure why she was telling him this, or where the memory had popped up from, but she went on.

'When we turned around, after I had blasted about her *and* told Michelle that I wanted to be friends with her instead – all down to acceptance, you know – we noticed a locked cubicle door.' Allie's cheeks began to burn. 'Guess who was in there?'

Perry's eyes widened. 'She heard it all?'

'Yes! I was mortified. Although I really liked hanging out with Sarah, I didn't want to be excluded from Michelle's friendship. Sarah came storming out eventually and never spoke to either of us again. I had a real hard time with it.'

'Did you ever see her again?'

'Around town a few times.' Allie tried to shrug away her guilt. 'But don't you see, it's kids' stuff. Peer pressure when you're a teenager is very powerful. We try our best to fit in, often not seeing who we upset to do just that. That's why we move on as adults and leave some friends behind. They were people we *had* to see on a daily basis. As we get older, we make new friends – sometimes we lose them too. But more often, we find friends who stay with us throughout our lifetime, are there for us whenever we need them and make life just that bit more bearable when we're at our lowest. They're also there for us until we're well and happy again. I guess Patrick never had that.'

'I guess.'

'All I'm saying is try not to take it to heart.' She smiled at him. 'Feel better?'

Perry smiled and nodded.

'Good.' Allie grinned back. 'Now, get your ass off my desk and do some work.'

As Perry stood up and moved away, Allie wondered about the memory. Like a lot of people, she suspected she'd pushed the incident to the back of her mind, along with all the other things she was ashamed of saying and doing in her life. Okay, everyone makes mistakes – it was part of growing up. Learning from them was the best thing to do: learn and move on. Still, although she didn't want to exaggerate her own importance for fear of sounding arrogant, she hadn't liked the thought that maybe she *had* done something to change Sarah's life, made her feel inadequate, like Perry had done with Patrick Morgan.

Allie's mobile phone rang. A few heads snapped up as Andy Williams' voice bellowed out *Can't Take My Eyes Off You* at maximum volume.

'What the . . . ?' Allie cursed.

More heads turned and people stopped what they were doing as she grappled to turn it off. The call was from Mark.

'You bastard,' she said to him, a grin forming. 'You switched my ringtone.'

'Well, someone had to.'

She was just about to speak again when Perry started to sing. Sam joined in and pretty soon the whole office had joined in.

Allie covered her eyes with her other hand as they started on the chorus.

'You see what you've started?' she told Mark. 'I'll deal with you later.' As she disconnected the call, she could still hear him laughing.

Minutes later, her desk phone rang and she picked it up. 'DS Shenton.'

That phone call had been from the DCI. He'd asked Allie to come up to his office. On the walk up the stairs to the next floor, she tried to think if she had done anything wrong. Trevor's office was on the floor above theirs and a trip upstairs was known, unofficially, as a visit to the Gods. She walked along the corridor and opened a door to see Verity, his PA, sitting at her desk.

'Go straight in,' she told her, with a smile.

Nick opened the door, his eyes meeting hers for a moment before looking away. 'Take a seat, Allie.'

Allie hid her surprise as he pulled out a chair for her at the head of a small conference table. Trevor was already seated there. Puzzled by the sombre atmosphere, she did as she was told, clasping her hands together on top of the table. Heart racing, she waited for the inevitable bollocking they were going to dish out.

When they were all settled, Trevor opened the file in front of him and turned to her, clearing his throat.

'DS Shenton – Allie – there's some information that's come to light.' He paused. 'It isn't going to be comfortable for you to hear, I'm afraid.'

'Sir?'

'When Chloe Winters was raped, you know we were running samples of blood and DNA through the database to see if there was a match.'

'You have someone, don't you?'

'Yes.'

She held up a hand, unable to cope with what he was going to say next. Why else would she be getting this treatment?

'Allie, we now know it was the same man who attacked Chloe Winters and your sister.'

'No.' Allie stood up so quickly that she shoved the chair across the tiled floor. Since the case had been resolved, she'd given up on the idea that someone was after Karen. Her vision blurred, spots of black appearing in front of her eyes. She felt like she was falling.

'Allie.' Nick stood up too.

'No.' She sat down again quickly, putting her head between her knees and hugging her calves.

Nick poured a glass of water and placed a hand on her back. When she sat upright, all the blood drained from her face.

'That means he raped Chloe Winters to get back at me, doesn't it? And that the letters Y and N – they were for me too.'

'We don't know yet.'

'You don't know or you won't tell me? He's –' She stopped, looking at them both in turn. 'He's going to come after me, isn't he? Y, N. You're next.'

'Let's hope not,' said Trevor, 'but it's a possibility we need to look into. Set in place a risk assessment for you.'

'I won't stop doing my job!'

'We're not asking you to, but we need to take precautions.'

'I can't let him win.' She looked at Nick. 'I could lure him out.'

'You mean offer yourself up for bait?' He baulked.

'If I have to.'

'Don't be ridiculous.'

'Earlier, we talked about how good the team are,' she reiterated. 'They'll help me and they'll watch my back. I'll be fine!'

Trevor closed the file in front of him. 'You know I won't allow that, and I want you to know that I won't tolerate you going behind my back to do anything, either.'

Allie left the office a few minutes later. Downstairs, she walked into her office and sat down at her desk. By her side, she could see Sam, a look of apprehension on her face.

'You okay, boss?' she asked.

Allie nodded and then ducked her head behind her computer monitor. She stared hard at the screen, hoping to contain the tears building up in her eyes. That bastard – he'd done it again. How could that be so? Had he hurt more than two women? He must have – an animal like that was predatory. He wouldn't be able to contain those kinds of urges.

She caught Sam watching her.

'I worry about you, you know?' her friend said.

Allie nodded. 'I'm okay, thanks. Really,' she added, when Sam continued to stare.

When Sam's head bobbed down again, Allie held in a sob.

She would let her think she was fine. She would let *everyone* think she was fine.

And while they thought that, she would do a bit of digging. Because she was going to find the man who had attacked her sister. She had to, for Karen.

But more so, for her own sanity.

Chapter Thirty-Six

Allie went out the front door of the station and turned left along Bethesda Street. The winter sun was warm on her back; it felt good to walk after the difficult conversation she'd just had, if only for a couple of minutes. Grab some fresh air, no matter how cold, and think about things, put them into perspective.

Hearing the results of the DNA tests had thrown her but so far, she had thought only of her sister. She hadn't wanted the two attacks to be linked – okay, more to the point, she hadn't wanted to think about the connection because it would mean Chloe Winters *had* been attacked because of her. She swiped at the tear that fell from her eye. That poor girl.

At Broad Street, she crossed the road to the Mitchell Arts Centre, named after Reginald Mitchell, the inventor of the Spitfire aeroplane who came from Stoke-on-Trent. She pulled on the door to the café and went inside. Bright green and white décor, dark tiled flooring. Everything was welcoming except for the forlorn figure sitting at a table in the window, nursing a cup.

Ray Morgan looked up as she walked over to him, nodded his head in greeting.

'Can I get you a fresh one?' she asked.

'Thanks.'

While she was at the counter giving her order, Allie glanced back at the man. He looked lost, bereft even, and the compassionate side of her felt sorry for him. But then the harder side, the side she needed to do her job, came into play and she knew she should feel nothing but anger towards him. He had turned his son into a monster.

A few minutes later, she set down two white cups, the tiny black emblem of a plane stamped on the side of each. She sat down, picked up her cup and blew on the liquid, finding the noise of a busy café compared to the noise of their office as refreshing as the tea. She gazed out of the window at the boarding across the way. Building work for the new civic centre seemed to be on target for completion later that year. Despite the millions the council would have had to borrow to create it, and the arguments for and against from the residents of the city about its location, she hoped it brought much-needed custom into Hanley.

'I suppose you think it was all my fault,' Ray said, after gazing out of the window for a moment too.

'He was spelling out the word *revenge*,' Allie told him. 'We guessed but there was no way of working out who the next victim would be. He left us clues, as if he wanted to be stopped. But I'm not one to judge, Mr Morgan.'

'I was an alcoholic back then.' Ray put his cup down. 'I suppose I'll always have the potential to be one again but for now, I've been sober for years. I got clean while I was inside. It's not something I'm proud of saying because I shouldn't have let the drink grab hold of me in the first instance, but I am proud of how long I've been off it. Patrick's mother left me when he was nine years old. She took my youngest two with her – Robert and Louisa.'

Allie nodded in recognition, realising they must have been the children in the photograph that was in Patrick's house. 'That was your wife?'

Ray nodded. 'I knew where she'd been staying for years. 'Course I never told Patrick – I was too selfish. I just used it to make him suffer, telling him all the time that his mother had left him behind because he was pathetic, weak, unlovable. That she couldn't bear to take Patrick with her because he was so like me. That she hated me, so she hated him too. That she was feeble and unable to cope with my ways. That it was his fault he'd been abandoned. Need I go on?'

Allie remained quiet.

'I hate myself for even saying that out loud.' Ray shook his head. 'But I was so fuelled by my own anger. I took it out on Patrick more and more. I never thought for a minute of what long-term damage it would do. All I cared about was where my next drink was coming from and how quickly I could get it down my neck and go back to the world I knew. Drink made me feel powerful. It is a demon.

'But, luckily, prison changed me.' He looked up, eyes pleading for Allie to believe him. 'When I was sent down, I soon realised there were much harder men in there than me and that I was a coward. I began to step away from the trouble.' He smiled half-heartedly. 'I got myself into more trouble because of it when I wouldn't fight back, but gradually I earned a little respect. That's what I wanted then from my son. I wanted his forgiveness too, I suppose. I knew I had ruined his life but I wanted to make amends when I came out. I wanted to start again, show him how much I had changed.'

The young girl who had served Allie began to wipe the tables around them. Allie wondered if she was being affected right now with anything that would change her life for the worse or for the better.

'Before I was due out, I wrote to Patrick,' Ray continued. 'For about two years. Lots of letters, telling him how much I had changed, hoping he'd come to see me. I never heard from him.

I sent him visiting orders too but he never showed up.' He glanced away for a moment as he composed himself. 'I suppose it was selfish of me to think that he would, but it did give me something to focus on. Somehow, I wanted to get through to him just how sorry I was. I had no idea he wasn't living there anymore, that his mail was being redirected.'

Allie knew some of this already. She'd read the letters Ray had sent to Patrick. Indeed, they might seem heartfelt if you were distanced from them. Add the real reason he was apologising all the time and she could just about grasp what Patrick had been going through. Ray Morgan had been a bully in every sense of the word. Emotional, physical, mental and monetary. Without help, Patrick never stood a chance.

She also couldn't help but take satisfaction from the fact they now knew that Patrick wasn't his son. If he had been, a partial match would have come up against Ray's DNA when they had run Patrick's through the system. Allie wondered if this was the reason that he'd been left behind by his mother – guilt perhaps, of an affair?

'Can you understand me better now?' Ray asked.

Allie shrugged. 'I don't have to understand you, Mr Morgan. That's not my job. But, yes, I can see why you would want to make amends. Shame you were into the demon juice for quite so long, though – and that it took a prison sentence before you realised that.'

Ray had the decency to hang his head in shame. A moment later, he caught her eye.

'I made a huge mistake.' Tears glistened in his eyes. 'One that I can never put right now, and I won't ever forget that Patrick died because of it.'

'I'm glad to hear that.' Allie's tone was harsh so she relented. 'When is the funeral?'

'At the end of next week. Friday afternoon, two p.m. Finally, he'll be at peace.'

It was on the tip of her tongue to mention all the families that would never have peace again because of loved ones that Patrick had killed, but she refrained.

Allie's phone rang and she smirked as Andy Williams burst into tune again. But the smile soon faded when she saw that the call was from Riverdale Residential Home.

She answered it quickly. 'Hello?'

'Hello. It's Dr Merchant.' A short pause. 'Allie, we've had to take Karen to the hospital.'

'What?' Allie gasped for breath for the second time that day. She stood up. 'Why? Is she okay?'

'She's become unresponsive in the last half hour. She's on her way now in an ambulance.'

'Miss, what's wrong?' Ray Morgan asked, looking up at her.

But Allie didn't answer; she was too busy running out the door.

Acknowledgements

Thanks to my amazing fella, Chris, who looks out for me so that I can do the writing. I wish I could take credit for all the twists in my books but he's actually more devious than I am when it comes down to it – in the nicest possible way. We're a great team – a perfect combination.

Thanks to the professionals – Emilie, Sana and Neil from Amazon Publishing in the UK, who are a joy to work with. Thanks to Victoria and Jennifer for adding the 'glitter' to my words. Also huge thanks to my agent, Maddy Milburn, who is always there for me – and Cara too, in the background! You ladies rock!

Thanks to Alison Niebieszczanski and Talli Roland, who give me far more friendship, support and encouragement than I deserve. Thanks to my early readers and friends Rebecca Bradley, Sharon Sant and Sharon and Chris Tatton – I love that you share the journey with me. Thanks to authors Elizabeth Haynes and Lisa Cutts, and also Juliet Prince from Staffordshire Police for help with research. Any errors are mine alone!

Finally, thanks to all my readers who keep in touch with me via Twitter and Facebook. Your kind words always make me smile – and get out my laptop. Long may it continue.

About the Author

Mel Sherratt has been a self-described "meddler of words" ever since she can remember. After winning her first writing competition at the age of eleven, she has rarely been without a pen in her hand or her nose in a book. Since successfully publishing *Taunting the Dead* and seeing it soar to the rank of #1 bestselling police procedural in the Amazon Kindle store in 2012, Mel has gone on to write three more books in the critically acclaimed The Estate Series.

Mel has written feature articles for *The Guardian*, the Writers and Artists website, and *Writers' Forum* magazine, to name just a few, and regularly speaks at conferences, events, and talks.

She lives in Stoke-on-Trent, Staffordshire, with her husband and her terrier, Dexter (named after the TV serial killer, with some help from her Twitter fans), and makes liberal use of her hometown as a backdrop for her writing.

Her website is www.melsherratt.co.uk and you can find her on Twitter at @writermels.

Printed in Great Britain
by Amazon